WITHDRAWN

Jane Brown

EMINENT GARDENERS

SOME PEOPLE OF INFLUENCE
AND THEIR GARDENS
1880–1980

VIKING

For Mac

VIKING

Published by the Penguin Group
27 Wrights Lane, London W8 5TZ, England
Viking Penguin, a division of Penguin Books USA Inc.,
375 Hudson Street, New York, New York 10014, USA
Penguin Books Australia Ltd, Ringwood, Victoria, Australia
Penguin Books Canada Ltd, 2801 John Street, Markham, Ontario, Canada L3R 1B4
Penguin Books (NZ) Ltd, 182–190 Wairau Road, Auckland 10, New Zealand

Penguin Books Ltd, Registered Offices: Harmondsworth, Middlesex, England

First published 1990
1 3 5 7 9 10 8 6 4 2

Typeset in 12/14pt Lasercomp Palatino
Printed in Great Britain by Butler & Tanner Ltd,
Frome and London

A CIP catalogue record for this book is available from the British Library
LCCCN 90–70922

ISBN 0–670–81964–6

Contents

AUTHOR'S NOTE   vi

LIST OF ILLUSTRATIONS   vii

ILLUSTRATION ACKNOWLEDGEMENTS   viii

Introduction   1

1. *Frances Wolseley*   20

2. *The Henry James Americans*   40

3. *Norah Lindsay*   60

4. *Academic Gardeners*   77

5. *The Lords Fairhaven*   95

6. *Christopher Tunnard*   115

7. *Gertrude Jekyll – At Home and Abroad* 139

8. *Endword*   161

NOTES   163

BIBLIOGRAPHY   173

INDEX   176

Author's Note

For particular help in writing *Eminent Gardeners* I would like to thank Primrose Arnander, David Astor, Janet Boulton, Sheila Browne, Anne Satterthwaite, Andrew Sclater, Caradoc King, Annie Lee, and my editor, Eleo Gordon.

List of Illustrations

1. Frances Wolseley's pupils from the Glynde College for Lady Gardeners, 1907.
2. King Edward VII's Sanatorium, Midhurst.
3. Viscountess Wolseley.
4. *Carnation Lily, Lily Rose* by John Singer Sargent.
5. 'The Result of the Test Match, 1890', cartoon by Bernard Partridge.
6. Court Farm, Broadway.
7. Alfred Parsons (1847–1920), a self-portrait in pencil.
8. The Old Garden at Hidcote Manor.
9. Hidcote Manor, Mrs Winthrop's Garden.
10. Hidcote Manor, the vista down the Red Borders.
11. Norah Lindsay at the Manor House, Sutton Courtenay, 1903.
12. The Manor House, Sutton Courtenay, the Long Garden, 1931.
13. The Manor House, Sutton Courtenay, 1930.
14. The Manor House, Sutton Courtenay.
15. Huttleston Broughton, 1st Lord Fairhaven, by A. Christie, 1941.
16. Anglesey Abbey, the garden in the making.
17. Anglesey Abbey, the house and the rose garden.
18. Planting Fields, Oyster Bay, Long Island, New York.
19. Anglesey Abbey, the Temple Lawn.
20. Anne Jemima Clough.
21. The Newnham staff in the garden in 1896.
22. The garden of Newnham College, as made in 1895 by James Backhouse of York.
23. Bentley Wood, Halland, Sussex.
24. St Ann's Hill, Chertsey, Surrey.
25. Gertrude Jekyll in old age.

List of Illustrations

26. Gertrude Jekyll's workshop.
27. The West Rosemary Garden for King Edward VII's Sanatorium, as planned and drawn by Gertrude Jekyll.

Illustration Acknowledgements

J. M. Barrie, *Allakbarries C.C.* (1899) (photo MCC), 5; *Country Life*, 2, 8, 9, 10, 11, 12, 13, 14, 23; Francis Frith Collection, 1; Francis Jekyll, *Gertrude Jekyll: A Memoir* (1934), 25; National Portrait Gallery, 7; The National Trust, 15 (photo James Austin), 16, 17; The Principal and Fellows of Newnham College, Cambridge, 20; Planting Fields Arboretum, 18; Reef Point Collection, Library of College of Environmental Design, University of Los Angeles, Berkeley, 26, 27; Ron Sidwell, 6; Tate Gallery, 4; Frances Wolseley, *In a College Garden* (1916), 3; the author, 19, 24.

Introduction

THERE are traditionally two kinds of garden books: those that are about plants, and those that are about gardening styles. This one is about people. Ten years of writing about gardening people – Gertrude Jekyll and Edwin Lutyens,[1] Vita Sackville-West[2] and Lanning Roper[3] – have left me firmly convinced that gardeners are the chief inspiration of other gardeners, and that the more personable and distinguished the gardener is, or was, the greater the fund of inspiration. The distinction is not necessarily in gardening terms, it is much more a matter of personality. Gardening tends to be a mature person's art; we come to it after doing other things, both for worldly and for psychological reasons. Making a garden tends to be part of that self-discovery that succeeds world discovery. Perhaps, as we become an ageing society, our gardening passions – and the industry that surrounds them – will inevitably grow? At the moment when we become one with Europe, will we become a nation of gardeners, a concept no European will ever understand?

In writing about Miss Jekyll, Vita Sackville-West and Lanning Roper, I have encountered my present subjects. My first, Frances Wolseley, was a shadowy figure in the Jekyll world. She is best known for one book, *Gardens, Their Form and Design*, and for her Glynde School for Lady Gardeners, of which Miss Jekyll was a patron. But her writing style is schoolmistressy and the schooling of ladies to garden is an idea that invites ribaldry. I confess to pursuing her at first from the purely literary vanity of her link with the last of Lytton Strachey's *Eminent Victorians*, but upon acquaintance she wins her own place. Her life makes an interesting parallel with Gertrude Jekyll's: they both came from military families,

1

but whereas Gertrude's upbringing was full of freedom, encouragement and the company of her brothers, Frances was a lonely child among grandiose adults. Gertrude Jekyll learned to love a place, Munstead Heath in south-west Surrey, which was the anchor to her life, but Frances was forever on the move and was never able to settle anywhere. Gertrude's artistic enthusiasms and talents flourished with the admiration of her family and friends, but Frances's interests were never taken seriously until her father realized she was good at growing flowers and told her so — when she was thirty years old. Miss Jekyll only had to settle down, make her own garden and write her books to become the gardening goddess of us all; she is the definitive eminent gardener. Frances finally broke out, and my first piece tells her story.

When writing about Vita Sackville-West I discovered her great admiration for the garden at Hidcote Manor in Gloucestershire, and for its maker, Major Lawrence Johnston. Vita's efforts as a member of the National Trust's Gardens Committee are chiefly responsible for the Trust taking Hidcote as its first garden, and for its continued conservation today. For a long time it has worried me that Major Johnston's creation leaves me cold; I see it as a great technical achievement, and as a triumph of scientific preservation, but I cannot muster any joy in, or affinity with, Hidcote Manor's garden, nor with the Major. I have been asked to write about him several times, but there was simply no book for me to write. Knowing, as we all do now from Victoria Glendinning's *Vita*[4] and from additional volumes of letters and diaries, of the gargantuan passions and despairs that Vita Sackville-West poured into the making of her half of the garden of Sissinghurst Castle (the other half being contributed by the wit and wizardry of her husband Harold Nicolson), how is it possible for Sissinghurst to be so frequently mentioned in the same breath as Hidcote? How could the birdlike, ineffectual little Major make a great garden by simply throwing money at it? I cannot accept that he did make a great garden, and I set out to discover why. 'The Henry James Americans', my second piece, is my trail of attrition. This is the trail that I believe leads to the revelation of Hidcote Manor's garden as the finest expression of a cult; perhaps it is more truly the finest *remaining* expression, for the trail passes through many more interesting gardens on the way, not all of which remain for us now.

Vita has a lot to answer for: she contrived to leave us Hidcote Manor and blithely ignored the true gardening talent, that of Norah Lindsay, which contributed most to Hidcote's exceptional virtues as a garden. Vita entered gardening as a private passion, along with her more human passions and the writing of poetry, and then – when she thought she was too old for passions of any kind – she woke up one morning to find herself a famous gardening personality. She could never take this wholly seriously; her innate good manners and her natural arrogance played a part in her gardening opinions, and, as ever, they displayed the two sides of her coin. When she discovered on opening what she thought was a bill, on the morning of Tuesday, 15 November 1954, that she had been awarded the Royal Horticultural Society's Veitch Memorial Medal, she grumbled to Harold that it must be for her 'beastly' little *Observer* pieces on gardening: '... Haven't I always said that one got rewarded for the things one least esteemed ...?' But she was too polite not to be grateful and pretend to be honoured. 'People' (she had tremendous *respect* for horticulturalists) told her that Hidcote was a marvellous garden, and she would not have dreamed of contradicting them. When she went there and found that the Major, wearing his English tweeds with a perfection only rich ex-Americans can manage, had achieved the kind of plantings (tapestried hedges, rivers of campanulas, fountains of tropaeolums and gigantic primulas) that she had scrimped and laboured for years to attempt, she must have been privately furious. What could she do but publicly praise him in an article written for the Royal Horticultural Society in 1949[5] (and much reprinted as part of the National Trust guide to Hidcote), in which she bows in inadequacy before the abundance, perfection, spilling cornucopia and worthy effort of it all. She was born to *noblesse oblige* and returned to it in her gardening prime; she felt that Hidcote *should* be saved (after all, it was being offered with astounding generosity in those mean post-war years) and it was her duty to save it. But she was by no means obliged to make sure that

Norah Lindsay, a lady of whom she did not entirely approve, was given any credit for her achievement. In the late forties they – Vita and the National Trust Gardens Committee – were really seeing the best of Norah's artistry in planting, for only she had the imagination to introduce the famous 'jungle of beauty' effect that was Hidcote's chief charm.

Norah Lindsay, my third subject, is the most elusive of twentieth-century gardeners – the one I would most like to be able to write a book about. She was a romantic and fey lady who reined in her passions and favoured safe gentlemen, and who flits in and out of the memoirs and gardens of the period from the end of the First World War until her death in 1948. She was truly a creature of Rex Whistler's painted world; a lady of great talents and flamboyant friends, she travelled far and fast – but alas, was too much a creature of her time, a butterfly. The architect Philip Tilden bemoaned her lack of staying power, for he felt she could have picked up Gertrude Jekyll's fallen mantle if only she had written anything down. Like so many of her kind, she danced through this world leaving little behind – there is a legend at Blickling Hall that her primrose scent lingered after her visits. But primrose scent is not enough material for a book.

Much of the truth about both Norah and Hidcote was obscured by the eccentricities of her daughter, Nancy Lindsay. Nancy's life is fairly shrouded in mystery too; she grew up to be a knowledgeable botanist and an avid plantswoman, with the not unusual acquisitive instincts. Her life and reputation were apparently marred on a plant-hunting trip to Persia, when she was delayed too long in a silken tent, and how could she cope with life in unforgiving English society after that? She became what we would nowadays call a drop-out, living in increasing decrepitude among her plants at the Manor House Cottage in Sutton Courtenay. In the crucial post-war years when Major Johnston was considering retiring to his home in the south of France, he intended to leave Hidcote in Norah Lindsay's care. But Norah died too soon, and Nancy continued to exert her habitual rights of familiarity over the garden at Hidcote, adding and subtracting plants as any gardener does. She clearly knew the garden better than anyone in England, but she did not take kindly to its ownership by the National Trust, and so her help was not available for Hidcote's benefit in its new role; arguments and bitterness and Nancy's scurrilous habits of plant hoarding muddied the memories of her last years. More than likely this meant that her doings, as well as those of her mother, were things seen as best forgotten.

The story of Americans gardening in England is a fascinating one; if only Major Johnston had wanted to remain an American perhaps I would have admired him more? When I was asked to write a book about Lanning Roper,[6] that charming, lovable, much-talented and well-connected American who found his vocation making gardens in England and inspired so many present-day English gardeners in the process, I discovered how this powerful transatlantic affinity worked. Lanning's American-ness, which was not far removed from the world of John Singer Sargent and Henry James, found him gardening with Ambassador 'Jock' Hay Whitney at Wentworth in the late 1950s, re-organizing Chartwell's garden in a way no Englishman would have dared a decade later, and spending over twenty years on regular gardening visits and plant-buying sprees with his Harvard classmate Henry P. McIlhenny, art collector and historian of note, at Glenveagh Castle in County Donegal. It was the fact that he was American, as well as his distinction as a *Country Life* contributor, that brought Lanning to the attention of Lord Fairhaven, for whom he wrote a majestic monograph, *The Gardens of Anglesey Abbey*, in 1965. I knew Anglesey as a garden-making undertaking of eighteenth-century scale which had been accomplished in the mid twentieth century and seemed remarkably unloved and unappreciated. Lanning's book took me back to Anglesey, to find out more, and I discovered the beginning and the ending of the Fairhaven gardening story which appears here. It is also an Anglo-American detective story; it illustrates, as does 'The Henry James Americans', why places like Hidcote Manor and Anglesey perhaps have a greater meaning for Americans in England, whether residing or just visiting, than they do for the natives.

By now my pursuit of these eminent gardeners was producing

some good stories, and more were to come. Because of Miss Jekyll's listed commission for work on the garden of Newnham College, Cambridge, I was asked to write a short history of the garden. Yet another stone turned, with endlessly interesting lives beneath it. Interest in the garden at Newnham arose from David Watkin's study of the buildings and their architect, Basil Champneys.[7] Newnham's garden is revealed as a remarkable Arts and Crafts period creation by a number of distinguished women, and one man, who believed strongly in the higher education of women, and thought that a garden, the right kind of garden, was an essential – almost rightful – background to a cultured life. In short, this means that Newnham has a garden that is all-of-a-piece with the buildings, in a way that has become traditional with the cloisters and quadrangles of the medieval colleges. But in the creation of its garden as part of the educational ideal of the women's movement it is unique, for it has been maintained in that way, and has never become an exclusive grove of privilege or the personal fief of a gardening don, as so many college gardens have. Newnham's is a garden well worth celebrating.

My sixth piece is about Christopher Tunnard, the lone representative of a renegade phase in twentieth-century gardening, that of allegiance to the Modern movement in architecture. Tunnard's name has intrigued almost everyone who has put a toe into the world of landscape or garden design, not least because he is such a mystery man. Among *aficionados* he is known for one angry book, written in the later 1930s, *Gardens in the Modern Landscape*. It was a diatribe against the evils of symmetry and formality in the Lutyens/Jekyll mode and contained a disastrous (for Miss Jekyll) comparison of her life with that of Claude Monet, with whom she was an almost exact contemporary. Tunnard's point of view was from the brave new world: he came from Canada into an English society of glittering hopefuls, the artists of the Constructivist movement and the architects who were Bauhaus-inspired to be Modern. He was the only theorist of garden and landscape design in the Modern movement in England. Being a colonial he was particularly susceptible to the historical English landscapes of the eighteenth century, and he even appreciated the large Victorian gardens which were an easy prey to the developers of the 30s. He worked out a philosophy that preserved these landscapes and allowed people to live in them in modern houses and flats, and he concentrated upon garden design theories that included gardens for fast-moving, Modern (the capital M is important) life-styles. He was before his time, a voice crying in the wilderness; his remarkable book still shocked in the sixties and still raises eyebrows among students today. What happened to him? That is what I have tried to find out.

Penultimately I have returned, as it seems we all must, to Gertrude Jekyll and to an aspect of her life – the appearance and atmosphere of the inside of her home – which it has only just become possible to imagine from the detailed sale catalogue for Munstead Wood which her great-niece, Primrose Arnander, sent me. Within the last few years we have become increasingly aware that the interior and exterior of a house do have a relationship with each other, particularly since fashionable interior designers such as John Fowler, David Hicks and John Stefanidis have begun designing both. What was the great Miss Jekyll's taste in interiors? That is what I have tried to describe.

Miss Jekyll was, as I have already said, the definitive eminent gardener; she was distinguished in other fields before she took up gardening, having lived her very full 'first' life of almost forty years both preparing to be and being a skilful artist and craftswoman. Those are the three words – artist, gardener, craftswoman – that are written on her tomb, and though there have been attempts at drafting her into the feminist cause, a *craftswoman* was what she believed herself to be. I suspect she was something of a Thatcherite as far as feminism was concerned; she was a spirited, practical and determined lady of 'independent means', who was impatiently scathing towards those less determined than herself – especially the men. Most of the men she encountered fell far short of her own capabilities or were beyond her moral pale, and consequently she made the best job she could of living her life alone. She had, when younger, militant friends in Barbara Bodichon,[8] Constance Lytton[9] and Emily Lawless,[10] but noticeably she did not join in their activities;

though she did design and embroider a large suffragette banner for Godalming, which is now in the town museum. Gertrude Jekyll was undoubtedly fortunate, and realized her good fortune; she was both sympathetic and generous to women's causes. But she felt that it was her duty to use her talents, and to devote her life to the things she did best. In that life she soared to the top of every tree she attempted (having learned so well to climb trees with her brothers in Bramley Park), perhaps in spite of being a woman, or perhaps it was being a woman that freed her to do it.

A modern Scheherazade would do well to have studied twentieth-century gardening, for there are probably as many interesting stories to tell as there are Arabian nights. The pursuit of eminent gardeners in love — for many of the best gardens have been made as offerings of love — could fill another volume. A short excursion is allowable here.

It is only very recently that people have begun to realize that making a garden can be as important an expression of personal creativity as writing a book or painting; gardens made by writers and painters, and most especially the latter, are an important part of their lives, but neither art nor academe have really taken them seriously. My gardening biography of Vita Sackville-West, *Vita's Other World*,[11] could have been written fairly only against the background of Nigel Nicolson's *Portrait of a Marriage*[12] and Victoria Glendinning's biography *Vita*.[13] *Portrait* was a paradoxical title, for the book consisted, in case anyone has forgotten, of Vita's diary of her passion for Violet Trefusis, which rocked her marriage to Harold Nicolson to its foundations. Victoria Glendinning's biography, a landmark even among the brilliant new galaxy of 'warts and all' biographies, mixed (even in Harold Acton's opinion) a huge and strong cocktail of Vita's literary and human passions.[14] But neither Vita's son nor her biographer gave much credence to the importance of her gardens as the background to the drama; Vita's home at Long Barn, the crooked timbered Wealden cottage near Sevenoaks where she made her first garden, was the anchor that held her to England, children and marriage, when all else pulled her to Violet and a romantic, bohemian life elsewhere. When, in 1930, she found the ruins of Sissinghurst Castle, the making of her garden became the constant factor and enduring means of creative expression; it did not fail her, even when she could no longer write poetry, and her lovers had lost their enchantment.

And it is for her garden at Sissinghurst, the real symbol of the strength of her relationship with Harold Nicolson, that Vita is mostly now remembered and loved. We do not see people in the round, as biographers do, we can know them in only a few aspects of their lives; those who knew Vita at Sissinghurst, in her garden, want to remember her thus. But the reverse is also true: let there be no doubt that the keenest of the 150,000 visitors who trample Sissinghurst, the most popular of the National Trust's gardens, nearly to death each summer do not come only for its flowers, but for something more – to see the setting, and the creation, of the passionate lives of both Vita and Harold Nicolson.

Even without Ronald Firbank's hilarious *The Flower Beneath the Foot*, and Virginia Woolf's derision, Bloomsbury had a talent for love in a garden setting. It was with the Bloomsbury acolytes that the garden, as a petalled prison, romantic refuge or fertile ground, assumed so much of the emotive aura of these essentially twentieth-century love affairs. William Morris's mawkish sentiment:

> *I know a little garden-close,*
> *Set thick with lily and red-rose,*
> *Where I would wander if I might*
> *From dewy morn to dewy night,*
> *And have one with me wandering . . .*[15]

happily translated from his earthly paradise, Kelmscott Manor, to the not far distant Garsington. Lady Ottoline Morrell, a non-gardener, was at one with her setting, which D. H. Lawrence found irresistible both in fiction – 'small figures on the green lawn, women in lavender and yellow moving to the shade of the enormous, beautifully balanced cedar tree'[16] – and in fact: 'The wet lawn drizzled with brown sodden leaves; the feathery heap of the ilex tree; the garden-seat all wet and reminiscent . . . the old manor lifting its fair, pure stone amid trees and foliage, rising from the lawn, we pass the pond where white ducks hastily launch upon the lustrous dark grey waters ...'[17] For Lawrence this was part of a vision – 'of all that I am, all I have become and ceased to be'[18] – a garden of the greatest emotion.

Another person to find this power and use it was the painter Carrington; her love affair with Lytton Strachey made her into a creative gardener. From 1917 until 1924 they rented the Mill House at Tidmarsh in the Thames Valley; what this meant to Carrington was expressed by her brother, Noel: 'For Carrington, Tidmarsh became an enchanted home, something beyond her dreams. There was Lytton to look after, cook for and generally spoil. She had time to paint and to garden. And there were week-ends with endless good talk amongst his friends ...'[19] The success of the Mill House was such that they bought Ham Spray House, with its large walled garden, set in the downland countryside Carrington had loved as a child on the borders of Hampshire, Berkshire and Wiltshire. Here she became a very knowledgeable and good gardener, and she also transferred her flowers into decorations in the house, and on to the doors and pieces of furniture of her friends. For Carrington, Ham Spray was the perfect place, and she must have poured all her inexpressible physical love for Lytton into its substance and soil; delicious home-made jams, daily fresh vegetable delights and bowls and bowls of flowers are the votive offerings in this and many another modern love story. Poor Carrington – unlike Vita Sackville-West, her garden and home could not hold her from the deepest depression and desolation, and after Lytton Strachey's death in 1932 she ended her life.

Meanwhile another Bloomsbury love nest had flowered. Vanessa Bell had found Charleston farmhouse in 1916 as a retreat for Duncan Grant and David Garnett, both pacifists and compelled to do farm labouring in order to stay out of prison. A Sussex farmer, Mr Hecks, had agreed to employ them. The farmhouse had a walled garden on one side and a pond with sloping green banks and willow trees on the other. It was here that Vanessa became 'earth mother'; the garden had to keep them in fruit and vegetables and she worked

happily all day among her ducks, chickens and children – her two
small sons by her marriage to Clive Bell.

After the privations of war, in the 1920s and 30s, Charleston's
garden became the setting for long summer idylls for the
Bloomsbury artists and their innumerable friends. It was remote (at
the end of a dusty track among the downland fields below Firle
Beacon), and was both a symbol of their united unconventionality
and a sounding board for their inspiration. Vanessa – as Queen Bee
in her hive – made her artist's garden; she chose her own bedroom
and studio to be on the ground floor so that she could walk out
into the garden in all weathers, when she liked, and also see all that
was going on out there. From her window she planned her paths
and borders, then set out to make them. She and Duncan Grant
made the small sitting 'piazza' inlaid with mosaic of china and glass –
both the idea and the left-over materials came from Roger Fry's
garden at Durbins in Guildford. In 1925 Duncan laid his claim to
some private outdoor space, making his court called 'Duncan's
Folly'.

Vanessa filled her borders with peonies, columbines, poppies,
pinks, irises, red hot pokers, michaelmas daisies, acanthus, lavender,
Jerusalem sage and old roses. The house and garden walls were
covered with more roses, figs, vines, clematis and Duncan's favourite
Hydrangea petiolaris. She had occasional garden flings: in 1933 she
filled the border with nothing but reds – zinnias, hollyhocks, sal-
piglossis and dahlias. But more importantly, she became expert at
keeping her garden in its place, as part of a whole – part of her
creation of an attractive life which kept her loved ones chained to
Charleston. Vanessa adored her garden and its daily bounty, which
she brought into the house for meals and put on to her canvases,
but it was for her balancing act of love that she was most admired,
especially by her sister, Virginia Woolf – who, blind to Vita
Sackville-West's passion for her gardening, was able objectively
to admire Vanessa's creation, her aura at Charleston, as 'sunlight
crystallized, of diamond durability'.[20]

This garden at Charleston absorbed and inspired many of the
great ideas of the first fifty years of this century, from the niggles

of Keynesian economics to the plot foibles of E. M. Forster's novels. (J. M. Keynes enjoyed weeding, and Forster loved musing there.) The spell lasted until Vanessa died in 1961; Duncan Grant existed on, immured at Charleston, until he was ninety-three, finally leaving in May 1978. House and garden had gone to sleep with him.

The most remarkable event of post-war conservation in England then happened. In April 1980 the Charleston Trust was founded; this was a gathering of Bloomsbury devotees and experts supported by the money of Lila Acheson Wallace, who had already funded the restoration of Monet's garden at Giverny. The house at Charleston, with almost every square inch covered in painted ornament of some kind, was handled with great care. The garden, under the supervision of Sir Peter Shepheard, was to be 'awakened'. In its crumbling, derelict state he found the place 'hauntingly beautiful', and willing to reveal its treasures to those who would work sensitively and listen. The matted grass was peeled away, and after careful weedkilling on paths and digging done with an archaeological attention to detail, the garden revealed a great deal of itself. Those who came to work at Charleston, both paid and as volunteers, were steeped in Bloomsbury legends and knew the people who had once walked the garden as well as if they were still present; on such devoted minds and hands the garden exerted its power. Peter Shepheard summed up the re-awakening process as aiming 'to please the ghosts when they re-visit the place, which I am sure they do'. This eminent garden was thus recalled to life because it had been captured in paintings, poems, novels, photographs, letters and memoirs down the years; as the garden had once given, it was now given in return, and its remarkable power can still be felt by every aware visitor.

Gardening has been important to so many twentieth-century painters that I feel we may have missed a great deal by not having more information about whether or not earlier artists gardened – Samuel Palmer, for instance. Carrington had shared an earlier love and a love of flowers and interesting plants with the painter John Nash; Nash had come to plants via winning the Botany Prize at Wellington School as a result of his method of avoiding cricket.

When he married Christine Kuhlenthal and bought a Chiltern cottage garden, his pursuit of interesting plants led him to Clarence Elliott. 'This was the beginning of a long friendship,' Nash wrote, 'with the Nurseryman, Plant Collector or, as he preferred it, "Gardener" ... and was an introduction to a vastly extended world of horticulture, where Elliott knew everyone.' Nash drew the plants that Clarence Elliott collected in the Andes or the Falkland Islands, or even in old English gardens, which he maintained were the best hunting grounds of all. He did the illustrations for the 1926 catalogue for Elliott's famous Six Hills Nursery at Stevenage, and for W. Dallimore's *Poisonous Plants: Deadly, Dangerous and Suspect*, which was published the following year.[21] Nash's two most famous flower books – *Flowers and Faces*, with H. E. Bates,[22] and *Plants with Personality*, with Patrick Synge[23] – appeared in 1935 and 1938 respectively. John Nash was in the forefront of a fine intellectual revival of eccentrically weedy and curious gardening that has the ring of true eminence: he later illustrated Robert Gathorne-Hardy's delightfully encouraging *The Tranquil Gardener* (1958) and *The Native Garden* (1961).[24]

After the war John and Christine Nash moved into Bottengoms, an old farmhouse at the end of a lane on the Essex–Suffolk border which became the centre for a large group of artistic gardening friends, all with a tendency towards 'naturalness'. Nash's painter's garden expressed an interesting alternative philosophy to that of his love of the strange and rare, as remembered by Ronald Blythe, then a youthful observer, now the inheritor: among the 'unspoken rules' were a certain weed tolerance ... 'the severe exclusion of some plants and the retaining of many seedheads for aesthetic reasons. A dead tree might also be thought a pleasure. Everywhere the garden was expected to merge imperceptibly with the wildwood. Tidiness must never get anywhere near suburban-ness, the ultimate damned state.'[25]

Ronald Blythe has described the Nashes' 'dear ones', their friends and a reachable circle of other artists and writers whom he knew in the 1950s, in a telling way – he discovered that they were kept together not so much by their painting and poetry as by their gardening. Crucial to this circle and not too far from Bottengoms was the ménage at Benton End, near Colchester in Essex, where eminent gardening flowered at its finest. In front of me as I write is a print of one of my favourite paintings: *Iris Seedlings* (1943) by Cedric Morris. The irises tumble from their golden vase, in shades of gold and blue, pink, amber and white, with velvety purple falls, with petals spotted, veined and frilled, some twenty-one beauties, lovingly reared and painted by the same artist-gardener. Irises were only part of the spectacular company kept at Cedric Morris's home at Benton End, but they were, especially during the late 1940s and early 50s, the celebrities. He produced the first pure pink iris, called 'Edward of Windsor' (he was fiercely patriotically Welsh and never ceased to admire the then Prince of Wales for his sympathy with the Welsh miners), a nearly black iris and some ice-blues – and apparently iris buffs went into raptures over the milky-mauve 'Benton Cordelia', which took the RHS Iris Show by storm in 1953.

Cedric Morris wrote about his irises in several issues of *The Iris Year Book;*[26] he firmly believed that plants needed to be happy, and 1,000 new seedlings burst into life each summer, hand-pollinated, seeming to prove his point. But the happy company extended to all kinds of plants, especially vegetables, which were both for eating, along with witty and wicked disputations around the 'well-scrubbed refectory table' in the kitchen at Benton End, and for painting. Perhaps the order should be reversed – painting first – for the vegetables in order to be interesting had to have certain paintable characteristics, to be phallically fierce and vigorous, facets which show in the energetic paintings of mushrooms and other fungi, lords and ladies, cabbages and carrots. There was a kind of vogue for this *double entrendre* – it was amusing to raise eyebrows or worse – and it owed much to the triumphantly sexual paintings of flowers and natural objects of the American Georgia O'Keeffe. Sir Cedric's softer sensitivities produced his irises, and his duality was the key to his art and to his gardening. His moods, whether of clown or truculent genius, and those of his lifelong companion Arthur Lett-Haines, as raconteur and *bon vivant*, ruled the explosive atmosphere of Benton End, which inspired a whole generation of writers, painters and gardeners, including Ronald Blythe, Maggi Hambling and Beth Chatto.[27]

There are eminent gardeners down musical byways too: Ralph Vaughan Williams, a large man of prodigious energy, confined to the country at White Gates, his home in Dorking, during the war, with an ailing wife and sadnesses all around – and little prospect of music-making – took to gardening 'with zeal and fury'. He devoured books on vegetable growing, he trenched, bastard trenched, weeded and hoed, and he spent a fortune on seeds and bottles of liquid manure to supplement the natural product, which he rushed out to collect from the lane when the cows passed.[28] He vented his frustration on his vegetables and survived because of them; and then his music came back, and when he wrote his *Oxford Elegy*, which was first performed at Queen's College on 19 July 1952, it was the following lines from *Thyrsis* that moved everyone so:

> *Soon will the swift midsummer pomps come on,*
> *Soon will the musk carnations break and swell,*
> *Soon shall we have gold-dusted snapdragon,*
> *Sweet william with his homely cottage smell*
> *And stocks in fragrant blow.*[29]

It was a special thought shared with his new wife Ursula, who wrote: 'We had them all, for we drove back with the Finzis to Ashmansworth to the evening scents of their garden, with jasmine fully out over the welcoming door.'[30]

Gerald Finzi and his artist wife Joy lived in a lovingly crafted house designed for them by Peter Harland and built immediately before the war. It was high on the Berkshire Downs and supplied the isolation and solitude which Finzi needed for writing music. As well as composing, he cultivated his garden, especially the orchard full of old-fashioned varieties of apples and pears. Gardening was an equal element of his life, along with music, food and love. In a third musical relationship the garden had a different role: the fiery Lady Walton, Susana Gil Passo, who had accepted life on the island of Ischia with William Walton, twenty-five years her senior, took out the difficult moments of 'being William's wife' – a demanding role fending off the world and allowing him to work – on the making of their beautiful garden. She knew well how to deal with her difficult genius: 'I sometimes used to say to him "When you leave me I shall be ecstatically happy in the garden"' – and the fact that she was, and that with Russell Page's help she created a garden that all their friends admired, made certain that he never did leave her!³¹

Eminent gardens undoubtedly lurk down many more painted pathways and in musical paradises and many other places – the hidden valleys and south-facing slopes of Wales, for instance. The Aberconways' Bodnant terraces are so lavish and grand that they seem to belong to another age, but they were actually started by Henry and Laura McLaren in the 1890s, and have been continued by the family to make a truly twentieth-century achievement. There must be something about the suntraps of north Wales that encourages the exotic, like Bodnant's rhododendrons, for tucked into another corner is the Italianate village in a garden, Portmeirion, conceived and built as a life's passion by the Welsh architect Clough Williams-Ellis; many of Clough's best gardens are hidden down the valleys of Wales, awaiting discovery and, in many cases, revival.

Clough ranks as one of three really eminent gardeners among twentieth-century architects: the others are Harold Peto and Frederick Gibberd. Harold Peto, once Lutyens's master when he was in partnership with Ernest George, gave up architectural practice shortly after his spell with the young Lutyens to concentrate on gardens. His passion for things Italian also played a great part in his gardens, particularly his own at Iford Manor in Wiltshire, which is a series of terraces adorned with fine statuary and columns, all collected in Italy. Sir Frederick Gibberd is loved far more for his own garden in Marsh Lane, Harlow, than for his surrounding New Town spaces. He made his garden in a dipping valley of six acres around 'a nondescript semi-bungalow built in 1905'; his idea, beautifully disseminated from landscape architectural theory, as befits an eminent architect and landscape architect who had first studied the law, is very interesting in this century of cinema and television. He has written that 'a garden is like making a series of pictures ... If you step into the picture it dissolves and other pictures appear; from two dimensions it becomes three, a flat plane becomes a space.' He continues: 'I regard garden design as the art of space. The space to be a recognizable design must be contained and the plants or walls then become part of adjacent spaces ... There are no doors in a garden, one space extends into another, there is a visual reaction between them ... the garden artist ensures that the colour and form of his composition will be sustained in the winter ... if someone tells me he is a keen gardener I ask to see his garden in February.'[32]

Sir Frederick's philosophy expresses perfectly my idea of an eminent garden. The gardener has to have a vision to see beyond the collecting of plants; garden-making is so much more than horticulture. And more than botanic knowledge, as so pertly expressed by Wilfrid Blunt (a *really* eminent gardener) on the subject of his friend Eric, 'who wants to grow what he can't and preferably where it won't', and to whom

> *Primroses by the river's brim*
> *Dicotyledons were to him,*
> *And they were nothing more.*[33]

These are the reasons why eminent gardening is rarely found within the bounds of the horticultural industry and seems to require the tension of an extra, outside purpose in life. Captains of industry have made wonderful gardens: the Hon. Robert 'Bobbie' James makes an all too brief appearance in 'The Henry James Americans' on page 40, and his great garden, St Nicholas at Richmond in Yorkshire, was an influence on Lawrence Johnston. During work hours Bobbie James was building battleships in Barrow-in-Furness. Eliot Hodgkin, who painted such delicious garden delights, was managing director of Shell UK Ltd, and the Hornbys, makers of one of the finest twentieth-century gardens at Pusey House near Faringdon in Oxfordshire, were at work bringing W. H. Smith & Son Ltd out of the panelled lending library era. We know well that in the eighteenth century the rough and tumble of finance and politics encouraged the transformation of the English landscape into a landscape garden; in this century Sir Winston Churchill has been the most eminent of gardeners in the political wilderness, making his garden walls and lakes at Chartwell in the years when he was out of office. At the present time Anne and Michael Heseltine, planting richly and generously, inspired by Lanning Roper, at Thenford in Northamptonshire, are perhaps doing likewise. Francis Pym and Lord Carrington are other notable political gardeners, and one of the best gardens made in England since the war, that of West Green Manor at Hartley Wintney in Hampshire, owes much to Tory grandee and Treasurer of the Party, Lord McAlpine of West Green; in this lovely garden he built, in true eighteenth-century fashion, an emblematic obelisk 'with money that might otherwise have fallen into the hands of the tax gatherer' to celebrate the 1979 Tory victory, and he commissioned the design of a triumphal arch dedicated to the first lady Prime Minister.[34]

Thus love, politics and money all contribute to the eminent garden, just as they do to the rest of life. And perhaps one of the nicest pleasures of the gardening world is just that the question of sexual discrimination does not have to rear its unwanted head. Those who like to think that this century has produced a number, a large number, of great women gardeners are right in a sense, and my chapter on Frances Wolseley goes a long way to explaining why this seems to be the case. But to make a political cause of this would not be wise; any list of these great women is easily compiled — Miss Jekyll, Ellen and Rose Willmott, Theresa Earle, Frances Wolseley, Eleanour Sinclair Rohde, Phyllis Reiss, Margery Fish, Eve Balfour, Beatrix Havergal, Daisy Warwick, Norah Lindsay and Vita Sackville-West — but the wisest of inner voices then speaks: 'But haven't there been just as many good homosexual gardeners?' And of course there have.

I hope in some ways that *Eminent Gardeners* does have more 'warts and all' than many other gardening books, though there are certainly not enough for present-day tastes. To be an eminent gardener demands great inspiration, energy, commitment and ability for love and friendship. Gardens are not a fantasy world of sunshine and flowers, though so many books may make them appear so; they are grounds for hard work and costly experiments. But above all, eminent gardens are an expression of the gardener's passage through this world, and they reflect for good or ill, accordingly. It is this expression, by a few interesting characters, that I have tried to track in the following pages.

1

Frances Wolseley

A TENTATIVE connection between this book and the volume of my quixotic predecessor is that Lytton Strachey's last subject was 'The End of General Gordon', and my first is the child of the man who had hoped to bring the siege of Khartoum to a very different end. My subject also offers a lesson in gentle revolution.

The soldier sent to rescue General Gordon, having begged in vain to be sent months earlier, was Garnet Joseph Wolseley, Baron Wolseley of Cairo, Adjutant-General to Her Majesty the Queen. He is a forgotten figure now, occupying one of the dustier niches in the halls of fame, but once he was a popular hero. In the late 1870s 'All Sir Garnet' became a catchphrase meaning all would be well; he was the model for the 'model of a modern Major-general' in Gilbert and Sullivan's *The Pirates of Penzance*, his caricature by George Grossmith bringing the house down nightly in the weeks after Wolseley's South African victory in the summer of 1875. Throughout his whole career, wherever there was trouble in the Empire, Wolseley went, or was sent. This was partly because both the Queen and her uncle, the Duke of Cambridge, her Commander-in-Chief, found him rather too pushingly energetic and keen on Army reform to have him long at home, but mainly because of his talent for victories. Wherever Wolseley went he always returned victorious – from the Ashanti wars, from Cyprus, from the Transvaal, and most gloriously from the Egyptian campaign of 1882 ('the tidiest little war' as he called it), after his victory at Tel-el-Kebir and the capture of Cairo. His Queen had to be gracious to him now, and she was, but that ingrained royal disapproval was the underlying reason for the ill-fated tardiness of the Gordon Relief Expedition and it made him too late to save his hero and friend. But that is another story.

Garnet Wolseley was a small, dapper, energetic and ambitious soldier. On an early posting to Dublin he managed to fall in love with a pretty and intelligent girl, Louisa Erskine, but managed equally well to put her out of his mind and go to North America. He eventually married Louisa on his thirty-fifth birthday in 1868; their only child, Frances Garnet, was born in Dublin on 15 September 1872, during a brief spell of domesticity. After that Louisa and Frances were to lead an Army life, for ever on the move and invariably alone. Louisa put her considerable energies into an interest in all the domestic arts and into a great deal of socializing; she was devoted to her husband, giving him all the admiration (often by letter) that he needed, and apparently only *once* complained of being left for six months of every year. Her love of home-making, decoration, old furniture and gardening was undaunted. In 1878 she took the four-year-old Frances, plus seeds of mignonette, sweet peas, wallflowers and heartsease, to Cyprus, where her husband wanted a garden, but they never saw the flowers grow, for he was recalled urgently and sent to South Africa. After that Frances spent her childhood on the move, from villas in Mortlake or Wimbledon to those in Versailles or Homberg or Deauville, from rented farm-houses and cottages, mostly in Surrey and Sussex, to smart Mayfair houses. She grew up as a loyal, sturdy soldier's daughter, who added the Soldier's Prayer to her own and followed her father's fortunes with pride. When he left for the Egyptian campaign he promised her the tip of Ahmed Arabi's nose, and when he failed to catch his adversary even after his great victory at Tel-el-Kebir, he sent Frances the visiting card found in his tent. She was ten years old.

As well as being a soldier's daughter, Frances became her mother's constant companion – and chaperone on occasion, for Louisa liked to go out and was very pretty. There is a story that such was the enthusiasm for the Egyptian campaign that even the Prince of Wales begged to be allowed to go, and tried to charm Louisa (or perhaps compromise her) into getting him his own way; Frances was strictly instructed never to leave her mother alone, not to leave the room, whatever the Prince said to her. So she sat through endless polite teas and soirées, a grown-up at an extremely early age, with neither a childhood nor friends of her own age. Understandably she grew up with a devotion to settled things, horses and dogs and gardens, and she became an energetic walker and rider to hounds.

In 1890, when Frances was nineteen, Louisa saw an opportunity to try her 'quiet life and gardening' at the Ranger's House in Greenwich Park, which was offered to Lord Wolseley as a grace-and-favour residence, but this idyll did not last long. Frances was presented at Court the following year and had a summer of endless balls, operas and country house parties. It was clear by now that she was no beauty; she was small, sturdy, good-humoured and wilful, and very different from the tall and willowy, rather fey and soulful beauties of that day, such as Lady Brownlow. It was at Lady Brownlow's Ashridge in Hertfordshire, that great Gothicized pile by Wyatville in all its chivalric high fig, that Frances spent her best weekend that summer, and perhaps then she realized that romanticism and soulfulness were not for her. Her treasure from her season was not a faded blossom from the Magnolia Garden or a crumpled glove, but a copy of the Reverend Augustus Hare's *Memorials of a Quiet Life*,[1] which her mother felt was a nice book for her to keep.

Louisa was understandably fearful for her daughter, being virtually a single parent, but she did not see herself clearly. Lord and Lady Wolseley were a completely devoted, mutually admiring couple, and if life had let them be together all the time, Frances would have been less possessively treated. In over forty years of published correspondence between Sir Garnet and his Louisa,[2] their daughter is featured as a kind of family pet; she is indulged, praised, and is amusing, she is at first a small personage, and then she becomes a child who is not allowed to grow up. They seem afraid that she will slip into artistic indulgences, yet they are proud of their friendships beyond the stiff military and court circles with such as Hallam Tennyson, Alfred Austin, Edmund Gosse, Henry James and the pianist Jacques Blumenthal. Louisa prattles endlessly (and rather knowledgeably) about exhibitions and painters, about books and furniture, yet seems petrified that Frances might sink to a Janey Morris kind of life. One wonders whether the Wolseleys' friendships with other notable military families, the Jekylls and the Earles, from which lady members fell from grace into arts and crafts and gardening, gave an awful warning or an encouragement! But what was Frances to do? She couldn't be a soldier. And clearly higher education did not appeal either, even though her father was most impressed by an encounter at a dinner with Lady Ulrica Duncombe, who had been to Newnham College in Cambridge for two years and 'thought out some of life's problems for herself'. Impressed he may have been, but he could never allow his daughter to do such a thing. She would be a Viscountess in her own right one day; wasn't that enough?

Fortunately, rescue for Frances was in sight, through an artistic association leavened with piety, of which Louisa could approve. This was with Charles Eamer Kempe, the maker of stained glass, who was to become a strong influence upon both Louisa and Frances and instrumental in their decision, eventually, to settle down in Sussex.

Kempe lived at Old Place in Lindfield and was in his early fifties when Louisa and Frances first visited him in October 1890. As a young man he had wanted to enter the Church, but through a mystical experience in Gloucester Cathedral he had been re-directed to serve God by making beautiful stained glass. He had trained with the fashionable architect G. F. Bodley, then worked for the famous firm of Clayton & Bell. In 1869 he had set up his own business, and his mysticism must have helped rather than hindered its prosperity. Stained glass by Kempe & Co. was made for several cathedrals, including St Paul's, and hundreds of churches and chapels: 'competent glass', it is now rather sniffily called by those who know, rather eclipsed for its quantity against the quality of the work of William Morris and Edward Burne-Jones. However, Kempe's work was very much to Louisa's taste.

Kempe had been educated at Rugby and Oxford, but his roots were in Sussex and he was an expert on the life and country lore of the old ironmasters; he found a willing listener in the ever-curious

Frances, who was to adopt Sussex for her own. At first, as always, however, it was Louisa and her interests that were in the van. She had decided, with Lord Wolseley's retirement and settling down in view, that she could indulge her own arts and crafts interests: she describes the 'Kempe Expedition' in a letter from the Ranger's House, dated 6 October 1890, to her husband, who was busy being Commander-in-Chief in Ireland. Louisa's letter is deliciously revealing and worth quoting at length:

... We got to Hayward's Heath at 1.25. Mr K. met us there himself, with his waggonette, pair, coachman and footman, very well turned out for an 'artistic' man. His house is in the village, a little way back from the road, date 1583, and close to it an old half-timber cottage which he bought also. The exterior of both *very* picturesque ... His garden is formal, and his yew hedges planted only fourteen years ago are magnificent. His receipt is *feed them*. The inside of his house is *ravishing*. Partly old, partly added to, but you could not tell the new from the old. His rooms are, as Bodley says, a 'series of Pictures'. All oak panelled, oak floors; *such* eastern rugs! Lovely little recessed windows partly of stained glass ... He took us all over the house, bedrooms and all. I *should* like you to see it. Except the 'great parlour' his rooms are all small. His dining-room small, long and narrow. The table *very* narrow; we all sat at one side and the servants handed things *across* the table. It was not in the middle but along the side of the room. Very quaint with its embroidered tablecloth. I felt I ought to have been an early Italian lady sitting at it. He is building a new wing, and asked me to lay the first corner-stone. I said Frances would. We had such a pretty little simple ceremony, all standing round the foundations in the garden – *all* being only we three and twenty workmen. We stood on lovely Indian rugs, the workmen bare-headed. Frances smoothed the mortar and tapped the stone and said *Floreat Domus*, putting a new coin under the stone. Mr Kempe made a little speech explaining *Floreat Domus*, and saying that, begun by good workmen, it must flourish. Then we all sang 'God Save the Queen'. Then we drank a loving cup, and the workmen after us. It was a nice brown crockery three-handled tankard and replenished from an old copper 'Black jack' shaped jug, with a bunch of borage in it. (I am sure he knew the blue of the borage would look well in the copper.) Then the workmen gave three cheers for me, F. and Mr K., and it was over. I very nearly asked them to give a cheer for 'Lord Wolseley' but was shy. It was quite the prettiest little ceremony ...[3]

Charles Kempe, Louisa and Frances became firm friends. He was Louisa's chief ally in her scheme to find an old house with a garden and to settle down. At the time of that first idyllic visit to Lindfield, Lord Wolseley was nearing sixty and she hoped he would retire. Five years later she was still hoping, and she reports from a September 1895 visit to the 'Kempe earthly paradise' with details of all the delectable houses and gardens that might be available to them. 'A nice old house in his village, with a *large* garden, to be sold, freehold, for a thousand pounds. I felt I could be quite happy there ...' and, on a visit to the Misses Saints at Groombridge Place, 'a wonderful bargain':

... untouched Charles II house ... old gardens with grass terraces, a fountain, peacocks, swans and ... flights of white pigeons against yew hedges ... The Duke of Orleans, taken at the battle of Agincourt, was imprisoned for seventeen years in the Castle which this house replaces. They were nice and homely and simple, and spoke of the *honour* it had been to meet you at Eridge when we were there fifteen years ago ...[4]

Three years later Louisa finally got Lord Wolseley to Sussex, and in late 1899 they moved into the Farm House (Trevor House), suitably old, which adjoined the gardens of Glynde Place. Louisa was to have twenty years to enjoy her antique furniture and china, her home and the countryside, just over twelve of them spent in continual everyday devotions to her 'dearest child' (not Frances but the Field-Marshal), who retired a sadly disillusioned and broken man. One of his few pleasures in his last years was to be taken by Frances to visit old castles and houses in Sussex. For Frances, however, this became a light and occasional duty; she was approaching her thirtieth birthday when they moved to Glynde and her life was about to begin.

IN March 1900 Lord Wolseley had written from London: 'If I have a moment I will write to Frances to thank her for the box of flowers; they are delightful. The violets scent my room. She is very successful in her gardening.'[5] During the late 1890s Frances had been busy: in Charles Kempe she had met a very good gardener of approved (by Louisa) artistic tastes, and she had learned from him and his gardening friends. As Louisa had reported, he had enlarged his late sixteenth-century house, timber-framed and brick-nogged, to make a 'spectacular' arrangement, even for one of the finest village streets in Sussex. He had made garden courts and yew-hedged rooms, added lovely ironwork and a large and fanciful pavilion, and planted masses of flowers in a careless and abundant style approved by his friend and not distant neighbour at Gravetye Manor, William Robinson. Kempe probably took Frances on her first visit to Gravetye – Robinson had been making his garden since 1885 and loved showing off his ideas and achievements – and she returned regularly afterwards. There were two of his gardening friends to whom Robinson would have undoubtedly led her, except that, as I have said, she would probably have found Miss Jekyll and Mrs Earle for herself, for they were both of Army families. Mrs Earle, sister of the Countess of Lytton, gardened at Woodlands, Cobham; her first book, *Pot Pourri from a Surrey Garden*, had been published in 1897, to be followed by *More Pot Pourri* two years later. During this time she acquired a nephew, through the marriage of her niece Emily Lytton to a young architect called Edwin Lutyens, who had an adopted 'Aunt Bumps' – Gertrude Jekyll. Miss Jekyll's first book, *Wood and Garden*, was published in 1899, but her garden at Munstead Wood was already well under way, as she had been working on it since 1883.

I feel Charles Kempe may have inspired Frances with one more meeting, by taking her to Compton near Guildford to see Mary Watts, the young wife of the hallowed and ageing painter, George Frederick Watts. Mary was a very talented artist-craftswoman and gardener, and at the time she was most interested in starting her Potter's Art Guild. In December 1900 she had written to a prospective manager for her pottery: 'I believe that neither man nor woman can do better than try to make a *delightful* village industry – beautiful things, beautifully made, by people in beautiful country.'[6] Frances would have found that this statement coincided with her own feelings: she might not have an art of her own but she could apply a similar intention to her gardening, and to celebrate her thirtieth birthday she founded her version of local enterprise, the Glynde School for Lady Gardeners.

Being Frances, she organized it with a military thoroughness. She chose her students herself, from applicants of spirit and intelligence (preferably the daughters of Army or Navy officers) who were prepared to put their heart and soul into two years' hard work and study that would equip them to 'earn a good living wage' as professional gardeners or growers. This was no half-hearted hobby for young ladies who liked flowers: she demanded real commitment. She began with about half a dozen students in the Wolseleys' own garden at Glynde, which she had made into a walled retreat full of roses on arbours and ropes, tumbling on to luxuriantly filled borders. One can imagine a rather nice glimpse of a frail little gentleman with a ramrod back, who had conquered half an empire in his time, gaining his morning amusement from the smart young ladies pruning his roses, dressed in their sensible gardening jackets, flap skirts and gaiters, with ties and hatbands in the school colours of red, white and blue.

After about two years the school had outgrown the garden and Frances bought some land on the southern slope of Mount Caburn (which sounds so un-English but is one mile west of Glynde village). It was a cornfield, one of the best fields for corn in the area, and it had an ancient name, Ragged Lands. It was of course chalky, and sloping, and faced southwards across the meanderings of the River Ouse towards the Channel; it was thus open to the sun but also to the Channel gales. Frances called her view 'the land of the glittering plain'.

She must have had to work very hard to keep the school going at Glynde and get the new land ready. The new teaching garden was terraced, and hedges were planted and pergolas erected to make sheltered growing spaces. A kind of gabled chalet called the Cottage was finished in the summer of 1906; it overlooked the whole garden, and provided accommodation for the 'Captain' of the school (now upped in status to the Glynde *College* for Lady Gardeners) and for teaching and offices. Frances appointed one of her first star pupils, Elsa More, as Captain of Ragged Lands when it opened for students, probably in the autumn of 1907. The garden at Glynde was returned to her parents as their private retreat.

The college was now firmly established as partly a centre for feminist ideals and partly a village industry. Frances proudly headed the prospectus[7] with the names of her patrons: Miss Jekyll, Mrs Earle and Miss Ellen Willmott were all there, as well as William Robinson. But despite the eminence of these great lady gardeners, Frances was under no illusions as to the difficulties her young ladies might encounter. She wanted to establish gardening as socially acceptable as a career for young women, but she also knew that she had to prove they could do it competently. She was extremely firm, with an undoubted resonance, in her statements – a soldier's daughter: 'The chief object of the course is to give sound practical training in gardening and in the management of the more hardy garden plants, to improve taste in the laying-out and arrangement of gardens, and to teach the routine of a private garden.' Along with this concern for her individual students was her inseparable but rather wider belief that the running of a productive garden made a great contribution to community life, and by multiplication to the greater welfare of rural England. I feel that Mary Watts was responsible for this extension of her thinking, which the college prospectus expressed thus: 'The College is run practically upon the lines of a Market Garden, so as to prove what an educated thinking Head can accomplish towards making land profitable, to show how much money can be made with a properly cultivated and well cropped garden.'

Frances expected the students to stay for two years; no recommendation was given for less. She even went as far as to say: 'Failure is the only result of a mere one year course.' Students were given medals for punctuality, good work and 'exemplary conduct'. They had to pay for their lodgings, as well as £20 a year for practical instruction and several pounds extra for lectures. They had a half day off each week and a month's holiday a year. Most importantly, they were expected to adopt a neat and professional appearance while remaining 'essentially becoming and feminine': Frances felt that this was achieved by a college uniform of a khaki-coloured coat and skirt, tweed for winter, linen for summer, the skirt at a rather exceptional mid-calf length for 'walking out', with a white blouse and a soft felt hat adorned with a twisted cord in red, white and blue. For work the students wore short skirts over breeches, with gaiters and boots, much better than the 'tiring drag' of an ordinary skirt for walking in and out of rows of wet cabbages, and much more conducive to keeping free from bad colds and running quickly up a ladder. Frances, a soldier's daughter, rather enjoyed the uniforms, but they were an innovation; photographs of Lady Warwick's Studley College students showed them to be still drifting around the borders in long skirts and picture hats tied with chiffon.

In return for the professional standards Frances exacted, she encouraged her students with confidence and responsibilities. They were taken garden visiting, mostly to Gravetye, which was certainly the best place they could see, and one imagines that the crusty, no-nonsense Mr Robinson enjoyed their company immensely. Second-year students were given first-years to direct, and took charge of special crops or a smallholding. The special crops were carnations, roses or chrysanthemums, which were sold by the college, and the smallholding produced vegetables for college meals, as well as for sale. The students in charge were paid 1s in the £1 commission on their produce. By the time they finished the course they had had the benefit of this experience, as well as hearing experts Montague Allwood on carnations, John Innes on fruit-growing, Frank Cant on roses and a representative from Pulhams on making rock gardens. They had learned everyday garden maintenance and plant care; all about glasshouses and stovehouses; forcing salads and violets; glazing, painting and carpentering; and how to prepare flowers, fruit and vegetables for market. On the lighter side, they had moonlight lectures, picnics and outings and off-duty theatricals and jolly japes. Frances may have made them work hard but she made sure they enjoyed life too, for what would this hard-won freedom be worth otherwise?

There are few indications of Frances's deeper concern for women's happiness – she took the practical approach – but it is well to remember that we are still in those Edwardian years before the *Daily Mail* coined the term 'suffragette'[8] and the fight for feminine freedoms really began. Frances was making her own stand for freedom from unhappiness and cruelty for women less fortunate than herself. All she was working for makes a rare appearance in a letter her mother wrote to her father in February 1903 when they had settled at Glynde and had advertised for gardening help: 'The applicant for the gardener's place slept here while I was away,' writes Louisa, perhaps with eyebrows raised.

F. was much struck with her. An *absolute* lady, *and* didn't flinch at manure stirring, or scullery drains, or anything! An unhappy marriage and failing in market gardening has brought her to this – Dean Hole [the famous rosarian Dean of Rochester] most strongly recommends her and has known her all his life. She says, I think I have forty years of work left in me – poor lady, digging her grave at eighty-two![9]

Frances founded her college to change this kind of situation: she saw her students into good jobs, so at least they had a choice. From a handful of students at Glynde at the start, by the end of 1907 the college was established at Ragged Lands with a dozen young women. Frances continued to teach garden design but felt she really had a wider role to play as publicist, campaigner and organizer for her wider cause, so she handed the day-to-day running of the college over to Elsa More (who eventually became Principal) and to her other staunch support and helper, Mary Campion, whose family lived at Danny, Hurstpierpoint. Now Frances had time to sit down and put everything into her first book, *Gardening for Women*, which was published by Cassell in 1908.

Here she explained in full the functions and purpose of the college, and at the same time tackled the logic of her philosophy. Why employ a woman? She gave her answer: well, would you not rather have a nice cheerful bright girl around the place if she really knew her job? She does not pursue the alternative, 'rather than what?' but head gardeners are a notoriously rebellious breed (think of that black-bearded tyrant who ruled the garden at Knole and terrified the high-spirited young Vita Sackville-West while thwarting her father Lord Sackville as well). In Frances's own childhood there were continually 'servant problems', according to Louisa's letters, and though history tells us that that was a universal cry, Louisa, timorous and girlish, spending half her time in the security of a military ménage and the other half cast out alone to manage in a rented house with recalcitrant retainers, was truly an innocent abroad. Many like her would answer yes to a woman gardener. As long as the woman was competent and capable, of course, and Frances expresses her belief that, being correctly trained, they were both. She emphasizes the importance of the right tools for the job, manageable by rather smaller hands; with the right tools a woman could accomplish almost any job that could be done by a man. She illustrates, proudly, the students ready for work, not only in white blouses and long aprons among the sweet peas, but getting on with sifting soil, gloveless, in sturdy skirts, leather gaiters and boots. These pictures of the students at work were sold as postcards.

Not put on to postcards, but still pictured in the book, were her friends who exemplified her ideas: she had them photographed in their gardens, with the emphasis on the *their*, and stressed that the management as well as some of the labour was theirs. Miss Douglas is shown in her greenhouse at Shedfield Grange, in Hampshire; Miss Hester Perrin works beside the gardener in her brother's garden near Dublin; and Alice Campion, sister of Mary, is at work in the family garden at Danny.

Gardening for Women also generously included mention of the other courses that were available at the time. The college run by Ellen Wilkinson at Swanley in Kent, and the Countess of Warwick's Studley College, with Miss Faithfull in charge, were the real equivalents of the Glynde College. There were horticultural courses for women at Reading University, at the Royal Botanic Society in Regent's Park, and at the Botanic Gardens in Edinburgh and Glasnevin. Frances particularly sought out private enterprises – there was the Thatcham Fruit and Flower Farm School near Newbury, and Miss Bateson's Market Garden at New Milton.[10] These enterprises were truly in the spirit of making, or growing, beautiful things in the countryside, as part of the useful, happy rural regiment of women Frances hoped her students would join.

THE college and her book made Frances a well-known champion of her cause. In 1913 she was elected to the Worshipful Company of Gardeners of the City of London; she always appreciated this as a great honour, perhaps because she had won it for herself. Her father, Field Marshal the Lord Wolseley, died in March 1913 at Menton. He was brought home and with due ceremony was buried close to Lord Nelson and the Duke of Wellington in the crypt of St Paul's. Frances was now the Viscountess, but felt she should spend more time with her mother. The college was thriving with Elsa More as Principal, so for the next six years she planned to maintain her interest, and teach garden design, but spend much time writing and gardening at home.

The beginning of the war in 1914 gave impetus to Frances's cause. She wrote articles for *Nineteenth Century* and the *Contemporary Review* on the part women should play in the revival of the economy of England's forgotten countryside. These articles became a second book, *Women and the Land*, first published by Chatto & Windus in 1916. Her philosophy may seem part of history to us now, but then it was new and sensible. She began with her own experience: she had come to know and love her Sussex countryside, but with her knowledge had come the realization that it needed pulling out of years of agricultural depression, that her people needed jobs on the land rather than rushing to city factories, and that now, in wartime, England needed every bushel of home-grown food that could be produced. This task, she wrote, was as important as fighting or making munitions in the war effort: 'Food alone will give vigour and warmth' to the soldiers, 'Food alone will keep up the spirits of those watchful sailors who guard our shores' — there speaks the voice of a good commander. The rural community needed to be given the confidence to be useful again, it needed leadership, and the daughters of Army and Navy officers were of the right calibre to lead in so many aspects of country life. If the Glynde College girls could head a garden staff of ten, they could also run village smallholdings, craft industries, local co-operatives and women's institutes, teach gardening in country schools, and organize the making of community gardens in towns and cities. They were capable of coping with sheep-rearing, poultry-keeping and dairy production, not to mention ploughing and hay-making. Frances invoked the war effort for her rallying cry, but she knew that the long-term revival of the countryside and the making of a place for women in its economy was her real aim. She bitterly decried 'the housewife's existence of our grandmothers'.

Frances's second wartime book, published by John Murray in 1916, was unfortunately titled *In a College Garden*. It sounds as though she is gently drifting around Oxford, when in fact she is, being Frances, giving a straightforward account of the making of the Glynde College. In the book's frontispiece her likeness comes into view for the first time: she is small and neat, in a plain linen suit. She has an oval face with a determined chin and very straight eyes that are, even in an old and faded photograph, obviously full of good humour and laughter. Her hair is piled up under a wide-brimmed hat, and I am reminded that she always told her girls of the old gardener's trick of filling one's hat with cabbage leaves as a protection while working out in the hot sun. She was now over forty, perhaps a little inclined to plumpness, but not in the slightest bit daunting or terrifying of demeanour. She had obviously inherited both her father's littleness and his energetic determination, a combination which made larger mortals defer, with affection: as Lord Wolseley was adored by his soldiers, so I imagine his daughter bustled her way into everyone's heart, and stuck to her ground, and her views, very firmly.

In a College Garden does its duty by the college, and is the source for much of what I have written already. But Frances fills the book up with diversions that are clearly now calling her onwards. She had founded a local co-operative, the Glynde District Federation of Growers, in 1914, and writes about this. She records her travels to Canada and South Africa; in Canada she was really interested in the women's institute movement, and was a keen advocate for the idea to be taken up here. She was fascinated by the game of stoolball, and presumably brought that idea home too, as the game still flourishes in the villages and small towns of Surrey and Sussex. She writes of ways of growing peaches and making pomanders, and at the end of all her ideas expresses her intention to write about 'gardencraft'. The outcome was to be the book that present-day gardeners know her for (if they know of her at all) – *Gardens: Their Form and Design*, published in 1919, with illustrations by Mary Campion.

I confess that I have known this book, at least by its title and illustrations, for some while, but until I came to write this chapter I did not know exactly what it was about – how brave, far-sighted and sensible Frances was, writing as a champion of that precious *rara avis* the garden artist, in 1919, when the 'formal versus natural' battle still raged. How brave and sensible and much-needed are her words now, seventy years on.

Frances took the middle road between arrogant architects and the closet leaf-tweakers of the fellowship of the Royal Horticultural Society. She wrote what Gertrude Jekyll could not have written, for it might have seemed immodest. There were so few of Miss Jekyll's kind of garden artist about that Frances had to mourn the lack of good examples to follow, and ask what the garden owner was supposed to do? They were obliged to choose, she writes, 'between the guidance of a nurseryman and their own intuition. It is but natural that they should find the latter preferable because in their travels ... they have acquired a knowledge of what they want.' The nurseryman's education, she added, fitted him for growing plants but he was hardly able to discuss design on a level educationally with an architect.[11]

But left to their own resources – 'all who possess an acre or more of ground think that they alone are fitted to plan out and arrange their gardens, just as they do their drawing rooms ... They do not bear in mind that garden design, as it is studied by the one nation that really understands it – the Japanese – takes many years of serious application to reach perfection. It is a very high art.'[12] Frances gives a few examples of resulting disasters; the formal flower beds laid askew on unlevelled ground, and an old walled garden, 'perfect in its simple restful lines', converted into a Japanese mountain scene.[13]

After her rallying introduction, Frances's book seeks to remedy the shortage of garden artists by guiding her readers to good garden-making. Allowing for her rather stately turn of phrase, the book is a good read, but its real strength is in her fresh and generous approach to a subject which had, in 1919, largely attracted polemic and single-mindedness. She draws her design examples from all aspects of the art: from the high priest of Victorian bedding-out, Edward Kemp, from the 'landscapist' Henry Milner, who loved serpentine paths and sinuous water courses 'expressing themselves', from Reginald Blomfield's favouring of architectural gardens, described in *The Formal Garden in England*, to William Robinson's love of plants. Carefully, from all these and more, she sifts out what the garden artist should approve.

She concentrates on ordinary-sized gardens and modest resources, both things she knows. From her hundreds of suggestions the following seem rather delightful. 'There is no profit other than historical association to be had from a clipped yew, but a gooseberry trained as a pyramid or parasol will yield more fruit than if it be left ... as a natural bush.'[14] On the subject of garden seats Frances is honest: 'For real comfort, perhaps, nothing is more luxurious than a chaise-longue with plenty of soft cushions',[15] a thought that may save needless expense on some architect's design fit only for perching. Poor architect, he is also rather too prone to overdo garden steps – and the humble tarred railway sleeper can often have just the right touch of ease, restraint and practicality.

Frances's sense of fun allows her to include many ideas for delight in the garden; she describes a shadow arbour – 'only twelve tall wooden uprights, cut square, supporting a latticed roof of wood'[16] – which the children call a bird-cage because the bluetits nest in it. Also for children is the tree balcony, a flight of ladder-like steps up to a railed gallery around the trunk of an old tree, making a retreat for reading or writing. Finally, from the vineyards of Lombardy, she brings back the dancing ring – roses and clematis grown around a central lilac or ilex and tied into it like the ribbons of a May pole.[17]

Frances is ever the pioneer. She writes about public gardens and roof gardens, and offers a chapter on drawing techniques; even more surprisingly, there is a section on contracts, with a specimen agreement between an artist-gardener and a contractor. Her book is a basic manual for a course on garden design in the terms of which we think of it these days, and have come to teach it within the last few years. *Gardens: Their Form and Design*, published in 1919, was, making allowances for changes in presentation and production, a forerunner for Rosemary Alexander and Anthony du Gard Pasley's *The English Gardening School*, published in 1987.[18] Where was Frances Wolseley when the ill-fated British Association of Garden Architects was being set up in 1928? Or when it was changing its name to the Institute of Landscape Architects in 1930? She should have been the first President, had they had any sense at all. Then perhaps her dreamed-of stream of English du Cerceaus and Le Nôtres, combined with the well-balanced judgements of a Humphry Repton, might have emerged.

WHAT happened to Lady Wolseley after the publication of *Gardens: Their Form and Design* in 1919? The Glynde College at Ragged Lands seems to have been closed soon after the war, after the tragically early death of Elsa More. Frances lived at Massetts Place, not far from Lindfield, and ran a smallholding for a time. Her mother died in 1920, and Frances dutifully wrote a memoir of her. Her final home was at Culpepers, Ardingly, where, perhaps because she did not have to prove anything any more, she relaxed into the life of a country lady with antiquarian interests, who liked walking, gardening and studying her countryside. She published her last book, *Some of the Smaller Manor Houses of Sussex* in 1925,[19] then faded from sight. She died in 1936, aged sixty-four.

FRANCES deserves our appreciation for her very enlightened views, and for the way in which she found a useful role for herself, despite the odds against her. She saw herself as having a lot in common with Henrietta Godolphin, Duchess of Marlborough. Henrietta inherited her title after the Great Duke's death, but little to go with it – certainly never Blenheim Palace. She was completely overshadowed by the all-conquering Sarah, and predeceased her. Frances, too, found it difficult to survive the honour and glory accorded to her father and the strength and spirit of Louisa Wolseley's personality: if she had been a boy it would have been so different. She probably possessed leadership qualities and skills of organization equal to those of her father, as she felt many other daughters of soldiers and sailors must do, though she and they were never encouraged to use them. So she encouraged herself, in a world which her parents would approve of but would not bother to enter, and to these ends she wielded her title as a weapon to her own advantage.

In this last respect she makes an interesting comparison with another lady, doing the same thing though from a subtly different vantage point. Daisy Warwick, wife of the Earl of Warwick, was rich, with two great gardens of her own at Ston Easton and Warwick Castle, a professional beauty and a favourite of the King when he was Prince of Wales; otherwise, she was motivated by the same love of flowers and the same concern for the economy of the countryside as Frances. Lady Warwick used her influence to win patronage and funds from everyone in her court circle, from the King downwards, and she was able to raise £25,000 to buy Studley Castle plus some 300 acres and install her college staff, with forty students, in 1903. Studley survived and prospered and produced many eminent gardeners: the Glynde College did not. Perhaps it shows what difference a different kind of title can make.

But one garden does remain a credit to the Glynde College of Lady Gardeners, especially the class of 1906–7, whoever they were. King Edward VII cared very deeply for beautiful ladies, but also for the welfare of his soldiers, and in 1906 he gave his name and patronage to a purpose-built sanatorium for the treatment of tuberculosis and consumptive diseases, which was built high on the Sussex downs above Midhurst. King Edward VII Sanatorium was designed by the most distinguished hospital architects of the day, H. Percy Adams and Charles Holden; they also planned the garden layout, which was rather special. The approach to the building is

from the north, through pines and rhododendrons, to a long entrance
wing, used mostly for administration and services, which runs from
east to west. Through the central corridor, with garden courts and
outdoor spaces to right and left, is the main patients' wing, a long,
angled building which looks out over its garden terraces to the
distant downs and the sea. The inner courts and south-facing terraces
were all laid out by means of sandstone retaining walls, 2,000 yards
of wall in all, and the beds and borders were filled with the sandy
spoil from building excavations. It was not a promising start. But
Gertrude Jekyll knew well how to cope with mean sandy soils and
she was commissioned to prepare the planting plans. The philosophy
was to provide as many scented and sheltered sitting places as
possible, along with easy plants that would give opportunities for
raised-bed gardening therapy on the patients' part. So scented herbs
and cottage garden flowers were the basis of her designs; she
attended to every detail of the borders and wall spaces in some
forty drawings. The Glynde College was to supply many of the
plants and do the planting; some plants also came from Miss Jekyll's
garden at Munstead Wood.

The garden was made in 1906. Three years later the *Country Life*
representative (probably the eminent gardening editor, H. Avray
Tipping) wrote lyrically of the wonderful result, and the illustrations
to his article prove his point.[20] Large beds show a grey, pink, lilac,
purple and white scheme with catmint, dwarf lavenders, purple
campanula and aubrieta, white cerastium, pink rock pinks and thrift,
purple and white iris, a taller lavender and *Geranium ibericum pla-
typhyllum*, Miss Jekyll's favourite. White foxgloves sprout from the
feet of low walls draped in stonecrops and Jerusalem sage; wall
borders abound with pinks, bergamot, iris, rosemary and roses. In
between the buildings were several enclosed gardens, in particular
the East and West Rosemary Gardens, with rosemary hedges surrounding plantings of *Galega officinalis, Cistus cyprius, Magnolia
conspicua*, fuchsias and 'Madame Plantier' roses.

Over the past eighty years King Edward VII's hospital has grown;
most of the 'inner' gardens have been built over, though there is a
glimpse of what might well be a mature *Magnolia conspicua* filling

a tiny inner court as one walks through the central corridor. The garden front is still magnificent; the terraces are in fine condition, sheltered within the spreading arms of the many-gabled, green-shuttered buildings. Every first-floor room has a balcony that looks over the terraces, and the lowest level shelters sitting alcoves. The flower beds are still filled with lupins and delphiniums, pinks and roses. There are two original magnolia trees on the second terrace, and Miss Jekyll's hedge of 'Madame Plantier' roses, with scented leaves and crowds of curly petalled flowers, survives. White foxgloves still sprout happily from every wall corner. Beyond the terraces and the roses and the foxgloves is the smooth green of the cricket field, then more layers of trees until green Sussex fades into the distant blue. It is unfortunately too rare, in this country, for a hospital for physical or mental ills to give proper recognition to the healing power of its garden. But King Edward VII's does. The rise in Miss Jekyll's reputation may be in part responsible for the careful restoration of the fabric of the walls and the rescue of the flower beds which has been recently undertaken, but when the simple, pretty, scented planting is covering the stones and earth once again, it will be well to remember the soldier's daughter and *her* good gardening in this place.

2

The Henry James Americans

T HOSE Americans who preferred to live and make gardens on this side of the Atlantic should really be called Mary Newbold Singer Sargent Americans, but that title would not fit into folklore half so well. Even so, it was Mary Sargent who perfected the art of not going home; as Stanley Olson so nicely puts it when exploring the personality of her eldest child in his essay 'On the Question of Sargent's Nationality': '... at no time in her campaign was she trying to deny she was an American; her only purpose was not to *live* in America.'[1] Mary Sargent was a pioneer in the cult which sprinkled Europe with like-minded romantics – Gertrude Stein, Edith Wharton, Bernard Berenson, William Waldorf Astor come immediately to mind – of whom the stories are legion. For my story it is pertinent that Mary Sargent infected her son, and though she, like many of her compatriots, preferred Italy or France, John Singer Sargent, like Henry James, found happiness and fame in England.

Sargent is a rewarding subject and much has been written about him; the rootlessness of his childhood, fraught with constant emergencies concerning the frail health of his younger siblings (his only brother and a sister, Mary Winthrop Sargent, died in childhood), gave him a sensitivity to the weaknesses of others that became an asset in his art. The splendour of Lord Ribblesdale's riding coat and Isabella Stewart Gardiner's long string of pearls, captured in their portraits, may have flattered their sitters, but they also betray a glimpse of their secret vanities. In such a way Sargent, even before he had left the welcoming company of other American artists in England and entered into the Edwardian *beau monde* to paint their

40

portraits, divined just how much English society loved its gardens, and painted a homage to that love.

That painting is *Carnation Lily, Lily Rose*, his impressionist vision of Polly and Dolly Barnard in a garden at dusk with their paper lanterns, standing among lilies taller than themselves and surrounded by roses and red carnations growing in the long grass. It is an unreal and improbable garden image, but all the more evocative of the powerful magic of a garden. Sargent apparently conceived the idea for the painting after he had suffered a harsh blow on the head in a swimming accident while boating on the River Thames; he saw white lilies growing under riverside trees, with the lanterns set out for a party. (These may have been *Cardiocrinum giganteum*, which it was an American East Coast and English fashion to grow in woodland at this period.) His companions, Frank and Lucia Millet, took him home to their rented house in the Cotswold village of Broadway to recover, and there he added the image of the Millets' garden.

The painting was put together during the late summer and early autumn of 1885. Sargent made endless studies of the patient children, the daughters of Charles Dickens's illustrator, Fred Barnard, who also spent their summers in Broadway. The paper lanterns were bought from Liberty's in Regent Street, and the Broadway village gardens were ransacked for late roses and carnations. The following year Sargent sent Lucia Millet lily bulbs so that she could bring them on in pots ready for the painting season; when, in high summer, he discovered a half acre of roses coming into bloom in a nursery at the nearby village of Willersey, he ordered, 'I'll take them all, dig them up and send them along this afternoon.'[2] But most difficult of all to catch was the particular light, which held only for fleeting moments in the fading summer afternoons. The Millets and their friends had to make up endless tennis matches to keep the artist amused; then, at the right moment, the game would be halted and Sargent would repair to his waiting easel, paint till the light declined, and then return to finish the game; it was almost as if he were going out to engage an Armada or Napoleon's army in a corner of the orchard.[3]

These prolonged agonies were all worth while. When *Carnation*

Lily, Lily Rose was exhibited at the Royal Academy in May of 1887 it 'went straight to the hearts of the British public' and – now in the Tate Gallery – it seems to stay there still. Sargent was to paint the Millets' garden at Russell House in Broadway many more times, in more naturalistic ways, but this painting is still his most famous garden image. It stands for all that was creative, bright and good about those apparently idyllic summers of the 1880s and 1890s in the Cotswolds, and created a mythology of the triple faiths: of being an artist, of being an American abroad and of being a gardener in the English countryside. Sargent bestowed the status of a legend on the Broadway community and its Anglicized version of the Americans' beloved summer place. For Americans in England, Broadway was their Martha's Vineyard or Oyster Bay, a fact which Edmund Gosse and Henry James were not slow to reveal; when James published an article on Broadway's charms in *Harper's Magazine* in 1889,[4] the good-natured Edwin Austin Abbey remarked that 'it did not do much for the privacy of the place'. But then it was Abbey and *Harper's* that had started it all.

EDWIN Austin Abbey was an American artist and illustrator who had come to England in 1878 with a commission from Harper & Row, the New York publishers and magazine proprietors, to capture Shakespeare's England. He came armed with an introduction to Fred Barnard, and through him had met the English artist Alfred Parsons. Abbey and Parsons became close friends; Parsons was thirty-two, the son of a Somerset doctor who was an amateur expert on rock plants and perennials and a friend of the gardening writer, William Robinson. Through his father's friendship, Alfred had provided many of the line drawings for Robinson's *The Wild Garden* when it was first published in 1870, and he was now well established as an illustrator and painter of gardens. He was also interested in gardening and garden design. Parsons and Abbey went on sketching and painting trips together, and during an expedition which took them to talk gardening and painting with William and Janey Morris at Kelmscott Manor in Gloucestershire, the Morrises told them of the delights of Broadway. (Morris had once rented the tower on Broadway Hill as a retreat.)

Venturing northwards, the two artists had found this large village, with its long street lined with a seemingly endless variety of fine buildings in a burnt yellow stone. In spring the whole village was wreathed in blossoms from hundreds of apple, plum and cherry trees, for it has the same fertile soil as the Vale of Evesham; in summer, it seemed overtaken by its gardens, with house and garden walls covered with roses, valerian and columbines. Once it had been a prosperous community, wool rich, and many of the sixteenth- and seventeenth-century houses were built well and elegantly for yeomen who lived contentedly side by side with happy cottagers. By the late 1880s this Merrie Englande was gone, sunk in years of agricultural depression, and the village presented an air of decay and romantic disrepair to the travelling artists' eyes. Many of the houses were empty, ripe for renting cheaply – Edwin Austin Abbey and his friend Frank Millet rented Russell House, then Farnham House, two of the grandest stone houses on Broadway Green, and Parsons soon installed himself nearby.

Much of the success of the Broadway coterie, and most likely much of the comradely indulgence that was given to Sargent over the painting of *Carnation Lily, Lily Rose*, was attributable to the personality of Edwin Austin Abbey. He was warm-hearted and generous, gregarious and yet a hard worker; he was quick to achieve fame on both sides of the Atlantic, with his dramatic set-piece illustrations for Shakespeare's plays and his murals for Boston Public Library. His heart was firmly enslaved to the Cotswolds, to English cricket and English music, and he drew a galaxy of interesting people to him. Despite his reservations about Broadway becoming too popular, his own personality was a great part of the attraction; he played host to endless visiting Americans, but also to Sir James Barrie's Allahakabarries cricket team, and to Sir Lawrence Alma-Tadema's and Sir Edward Elgar's musical evenings. In 1896 Abbey married 'a rich young American with influence in the art world' named Mary Gertrude Mead; she was a younger sister of the architect William Rutherford Mead, of the McKim, Mead & White partnership, the architects of Boston Public Library (finished in 1895) – and she had narrowly escaped the pursuit of George Frederic Watts.[5]

The Abbeys soon moved to Fairford, to a house called Morgan Hall, but Broadway's attractions were well established, and the village had gained an even more attractive personality. This was the American Shakespearean actress, Mary Anderson. In the midst of rave reviews and acclamations at Stratford-upon-Avon and on Broadway in New York, she had decided to retire, to 'become a real person', and to marry and settle down. She married a rich Spaniard of Basque origins and American upbringing, Antonio de Navarro, found Broadway, and fell in love with it. They bought Court Farm, beside the village street, in 1892, added the farm next door, and restored the buildings. Mary asked Alfred Parsons to help her with the garden.

Parsons's taste in gardens was traditional – a mix of a Robinsonian love for freely-blowing, hardy flowers and the straight lines, clipped hedges and good stonework of the old seventeenth-century garden pleasaunces of England. Mary's Court Farm garden shows Parsons at work in a garden for the first time. The farm is on the south side of Broadway's street, and the land slopes down to a little stream and then rises towards the hill on which the tower stands. Behind the farm buildings, where she felt her garden should be, Mary had found a huge elm, a shapely yew and a few bright pink roses, but otherwise nothing but nettles, pigsties and disorder. Parsons organized the removal of the rubbish, terraced the lawns with small stone retaining walls, turned one lawn over to the necessary tennis, made a pond into a swimming-pool, and gave Mary a rose garden among clipped box hedges. There was also a pool garden, a walk between long herbaceous borders, and beyond the stream a coppice of lilacs, hollies, cherries and aspen underplanted with anemones, lilies and autumn crocus. Mary wrote that Parsons loved his straight, well-laid paths, wide flower borders, topiaried box, seats round big trees, rose-covered pergolas and larkspur. He made all these for her, and also, as he became a fervent fan and probably an acquaintance of Gertrude Jekyll, he planted her a nut walk. Mary Anderson de Navarro became a passionate gardener, and gardening under her tutelage became one of the absorbing interests of the Broadway community.[6]

With the help of the architect Charles Bateman, Alfred Parsons built himself a house called Luggershill, in Springfield Lane, off China Square and the Green. In his own garden some of the sedate Englishness of his taste survives: his smooth lawn ('delicious to one's sentient boot-sole' in Henry James's irresistible phrase[7]), walls of rose-covered brick or dark yew, generous flower beds and a frolic of corkscrew topiary. When Henry James found his English retreat, Lamb House at Rye in Sussex, he was reliant on the help of his friends, the architect Edward Prioleau Warren[8] for the necessary alterations to the house, and 'the best of men as well as the best of landscape painters and gardeners'[9] – Alfred Parsons. James remained characteristically sentimental about his garden, and Parsons was gentle and wise enough not to disturb his conservatism. Lamb House garden was written into eternity as Mr Longden's garden in *The Awkward Age*; full of charming features, its 'greatest wonder' the pinky-purply old brick wall, 'the air of the place, in the August time, thrilled all the while with the bliss of birds, the hum of little lives unseen and the flicker of white butterflies ... [with] sitting places, just there, out of the full light, cushioned benches in the thick wide spread of old mulberry boughs'.[10]

James's non-gardener's affection for bullfinches and cabbage whites was perfectly understood by Parsons, an easy fellow who would not have minded if the garden had become a tangle. Perhaps James's fragility was in part intentional, in the face of the overwhelming energy of his other gardening friends and visitors – Mrs Wharton herself, who criticized his unkempt borders, her niece whom he nicknamed 'the earthshaker', Beatrix Cadwalader Jones,[11] and Susan Muir-Mackenzie, a friend of Gertrude Jekyll's sent to assist him.

For gentlemen of a sensitive disposition, Alfred Parsons was undoubtedly the perfect gentle gardener, perhaps uniquely so in a world that was at the time rather dominated by women and some absent-minded clerics. Parsons's long border within yew walls, topiary and rose garden survive at Wightwick Manor, near

Wolverhampton, where he worked for Samuel Theodore Mander of Mander brothers, paint and varnish manufacturers, in the late 1890s. In 1904 he designed a garden for his cousin by marriage, Dr Daniel, the Provost of Worcester College, Oxford. Mavis Batey describes it in *Oxford Gardens*: 'There was a sundial in the centre of the garden and round it beds of roses, pinks and snapdragons. All the beloved "old-fashioned" flowers, the delphiniums, tiger lilies, peonies, sweet peas, wallflowers, larkspur and irises grew happily in the shelter of the stone wall that separated the Provost's lodgings from the main quadrangle.' This garden had exactly the elements of Parsons's gardening which Henry James referred to as the 'nook quality'.[12]

The key to Parsons's garden taste is in his real work, his paintings. In the year that *Carnation Lily, Lily Rose* was begun, 1885, he had had a one-man show at the Fine Art Society in London. His landscape and garden paintings were well known in England, and because of his visits to America with Edwin Abbey, he found an American following as well. He painted the old gardens of England as Americans loved to see them – with long moss-covered balustrades, pretty peaked roof pavilions, elegant wrought-iron gates leading to vistas of long flower borders, with cheerful topiary peacocks gazing at the roses and clove carnations. The botanical accuracy of his flowers was of a very high standard, and he also paid careful attention to the colour arrangements of the borders. He painted gardens much more grandly than he made them; he lived on cottage scale and painted on seventeenth-century manor house scale, and many of the gardens he painted found the accolade of taste for the revival of Arts and Crafts gardening in Reginald Blomfield's *The Formal Garden in England*, published first in 1892.

During the late 1890s and early 1900s much of Parsons's time was taken up by his most famous commission, the plates for Ellen Willmott's *The Genus Rosa*. He painted 132 watercolours of roses at their optimum of blooming, and he travelled to Warley Place, Miss Willmott's Essex home, and to her gardens in France and Italy to capture them. He also went to less conventional places, for 'Janet's Pride', *Rosa eglanteria*, illustrated by Wilfrid Blunt in *The Art of Botanical Illustration*,[13] was found growing wild in remotest Cheshire, far from habitation. Because of difficulties with Miss Willmott, *The Genus Rosa*, which appeared in 1910, was never the great success Parsons deserved, but fortunately the plates have recently been republished and have been acclaimed by a wider audience.[14]

By the turn of the century, dilapidated little Broadway had become a star. As Alan Crawford has so nicely put it: 'Artists came to Broadway because of Abbey, architects because of Dawber; later, all the world came because of Mary Anderson.'[15] Guy Dawber was a well-connected architect who drew and wrote about the Morrisian delights of the village's buildings, making it, during the 1890s, a place of architectural pilgrimage which has lasted to the present day. The railway came to Broadway in 1904. The Lygon Arms, already famous, needed to be extended, and the work was done by Charles Bateman, a Birmingham architect who was a friend of Parsons. The Lygon was loved by Americans even then: a guide, *Over the Hills to Broadway*, had been published in Philadelphia in the mid 1890s, in the aftermath of Henry James's *Harper's* piece, 'Our Artists in England',[16] (meaning Broadway), published in 1889. The touch of the master was repeated with *English Hours*, published in New York in 1905; has there ever been a better travel copy writer? The chapter 'In Warwickshire' begins: 'I have been interviewing the genius of pastoral Britain.' The Jamesian vision of that genius takes the form of Kenilworth Castle — 'a sombre, soft, romantic mass, whose outline was blurred by mantling ivy'[17] — as he weaves Shakespeare's England (which Edwin Abbey painted) into the cobwebby aristocracy (which Sargent portrayed), mixed with mists and mossy greens, all melded into an irresistible posset for the American soul. Stratford-upon-Avon and the Lygon Arms were irresistible too: 'We were a merry little colony,' wrote Mary Anderson, 'all friends – fencing, gardening, riding together. Everyone who had visited wanted to live there but no houses were to be had.'[18] Such was the effect of *Carnation Lily, Lily Rose* on a tumbledown corner of England in twenty short years.

*

THIS irresistible world, enshrining the faiths of being artistic, being American and being a gardener, not unmixed with a strong Roman Catholicism, which was very important to many of the Broadway coterie, came to the notice of a particular lady in distress. It was inevitable, for Broadway was her natural home from home, but her distress needs some explanation.

Gertrude Cleveland Waterbury was born in 1845 and belonged to the truly Jamesian world of the élite 'Four Hundred' families. She was brought up in her father's town house in New York and summer place on Long Island. She married first Elliott Johnston, the forty-four-year-old son of Baltimore bankers, in 1870, and their first son was born in Paris the following year, on what was probably their wedding sojourn in Europe. But Gertrude Johnston had more than a touch of Mary Sargent about her, and rather avoided going home; sadly, their lives were comparable in other aspects too, and Gertrude Johnston's ensuing years in France were haunted by the deaths of a second son, a baby daughter, and eventually her husband. She naturally turned her energy and devotion to her surviving boy. In 1887 she married again, this time a New York barrister, Charles Winthrop, who fortunately also liked living away from America. He died in 1898. By that time, Mrs Winthrop's focus had moved to England, for the sake of the education of her son, Lawrence, a small, delicate, fair and sensitive young man, bright enough though of no particular genius (at least not enough to deflect him from doing exactly as he was told), but with a disarming shyness which masked a private thoroughness and perfectionism.

Mrs Winthrop took a house at Great Shelford, outside Cambridge, where her son could be 'crammed' for entrance to the university; he went up to Trinity College in 1894 and came down in the summer of 1897 with a tolerable history degree. Trinity was his first experience of the friendships and idealism of his fellows and he was determined to hang on to both. He took British citizenship in order to fight in the Boer War, and when he returned he persuaded his mother to buy a farm in Northumberland, to be near a particular friend and comrade, Savile Clayton. The farm was at Crookham, in the remote countryside near Flodden field. Coldstream was the nearest community, and the very name must have made Mrs Winthrop shudder – it was remote and wintry all the year round, dull and grey, and so very different from the salons of Paris and the sunshine of southern France. She despaired. Was her precious only son to moulder here among Walter Scott legends and hunting squires? How could these neighbours possibly understand the kind of life she was used to, how could they properly appreciate her appearance in svelte grey satin and pearls – her most customary attire? Mrs Winthrop was bred to look like a Sargent portrait, not a border baronial matron. Lawrence Johnston would probably have been perfectly content farming these remote hills, but his mother had other ideas. One of the major reasons that Americans liked living in Europe was that they were noticed; Gertrude Winthrop liked to be noticed, among her own kind, and it was only natural that Henry James's 'midmost England' should attract her. She found a small estate – 300 acres, a farmhouse and a hamlet of seven cottages – for sale by auction in Chipping Campden on 2 July 1907, and she bought it. It was called Hidcote Bartrim, just five miles from Broadway, nine from Stratford-upon-Avon; it was good farming country, with plenty of society – perhaps there would even be, with a little encouragement, every American mother's heart's desire, a titled English bride for her son, perhaps even a Lygon, a Charteris, or a Berkeley?

When mother and son moved to Hidcote the following year, Lawrence was thirty-seven; he was still shy and reserved, with a birdlike energy. He set himself high standards of perfection in all that he did, whether it was painting or playing tennis, both of which he enjoyed. As rich American newcomers the Johnstons would not have been ignored; Charles Bateman and Alfred Parsons were on hand to advise on the restoration of the rambling old manor house and its outbuildings, and no doubt Mary Anderson de Navarro soon followed, discovering Johnston's interests and introducing him to her merry little colony of like minds. Who would he have met? Certainly Captain Simpson Hayward of Icomb, a great cricketer and gardener and founder member of the Alpine Garden Society, whose rock garden was a local legend: '... the flowers look as if they have been rained down from heaven,' wrote Mary Anderson in her tribute to his skills.[19] There was also George Lees-Milne, with his elegant topiary garden down the Vale at Wickhamford, and, a little farther on, the other Willmott sister, Rose, married to Robert Berkeley at Spetchley Park. Rose had come to Spetchley in 1891, and between then and her death in 1922 she made a garden with one of the finest collections of plants in the country. She had an equal share of the gardening gifts showered on her sister, an inspiration demonstrated year after year in the breathtaking drifts of Spetchley's daffodils and spring flowers, in the long borders dressed in an abundant array of carefully chosen colour sequences, and in the pattern of box-edged beds filled with ferns, mulleins, hostas and iris swords in fine and restrained taste. Rose Berkeley, rather overshadowed by her sister's reputation, was accomplished in every aspect of gardening taste; she could handle everything with equal assurance, from the huge cedars that fringed her hedged allées to the tiniest drifts of violas and arabis; hers was that kind of gardening *style* that was unmistakably inspiring to the interested observer.

There seems little doubt that the powerful aptness of Broadway society chose Lawrence Johnston's course for him, and promised that he would find it enjoyable. The old Hidcote Bartrim manor house was restored and made comfortable in the best traditions both of Broadway and of William Morris's Society for the Protection of Ancient Buildings. In these early years of the century the spirit of genuine craft conservation was pervading the Cotswolds, emanating from architects like Guy Dawber, Charles Bateman, and Frederick Landseer Griggs, who was reviving old Chipping Campden. In this stronghold of the Arts and Crafts revival there was no way of doing things other than with the picturesque integrity that glows from the very stones of these places. Inevitably, Lawrence Johnston was prevailed upon to restore the Old Garden around his house in Parsons's best nook tradition, with old hedges and newer box plantings coaxed into the 'smug broody hens, bumpy doves and coy peacocks' that Vita Sackville-West was to delight in, with masses of roses everywhere. Johnston began to study gardening with his characteristic thoroughness while he set about bringing the farm into order and organizing the work yards and greenhouses. He catered for his love of tennis by levelling what is now the Theatre Lawn, retaining the original ground level around the 200-year-old beech tree, so making the 'stage', with thick wind-resistant hedges. The rest of his would-be garden was fields, with a general slope away to the south, and a dip then rise, parallel to the Theatre Lawn enclosure, up to the western sky. Lawrence Johnston spent the years from 1907 to 1914 settling in to the Broadway world, and slowly his shyness was warmed away by the like-mindedness of his new friends.

To have the advice of Alfred Parsons, who was the friend and adviser of Henry James, must have made Johnston's ever-present mother, Mrs Winthrop, preen with pride. But Johnston himself, the intelligent perfectionist, with an acute awareness of good taste as a result of his French and English upbringing, doubted that 'nook quality' cottageyness that marked Parsons's gardens. There were many in his new Cotswold world who asked for a greater elegance of style, who were too travelled and fastidious to accept that often criticized, humble, rather bucolic traditionalism of the Arts and Crafts ideals. The charming and gregarious Mary Anderson de Navarro smoothed Johnston's pathway into her world, with a mixture of tennis, cricket and gardening which he could not resist. Cricket connected Captain Simpson Hayward, the alpinist making his famous rock garden at Icomb Place, to the Edwin Abbeys, keen gardeners, and their cricket festivals at Morgan Hall, Fairford. Walter James (undoubtedly some distant English cousin of Henry), later Lord Northbourne, was a devoted attendant at Morgan Hall; eventually he succumbed to gardening, at Betteshanger Manor in Kent. But there also appeared his more famous gardening brother, Robert 'Bobbie' James, who started his garden at St Nicholas at Richmond in Yorkshire at the same time as Johnston began at Hidcote. Robert James had a fine, fastidious taste that allowed nothing cottagey at all; the garden he was making around his Tudor manor house had large and elegant garden 'rooms' and eighteen-foot-wide double borders in a hornbeam-hedged allée 130 yards long. He was a close friend of Mark Fenwick of Abbotswood, Stow-on-the-Wold;

Fenwick had commissioned Edwin Lutyens, outgrown his youthful cottageyness, to enlarge Abbotswood and design the formal garden in 1904. Lutyens's Abbotswood is a dramatization of Cotswold traditions, with swooping roofs and peaked gables, a severe canal garden and an elegant rectangular lawn, terraced, with a cone-shaped garden house in the corner. Meanwhile Fenwick too indulged his passion for rock gardening, on an expansive slope on the other side of the house.

Among these gentlemen of taste and style, Johnston found his milieu; but it would be a mistake to suggest that he had completely forgotten his American ancestry. Paris may have rid him of any hint of New World vulgarity (such as an American accent), and he may have been technically British, but as a gardener, his American blood gave him a distinct advantage, a spirit of adventure, that was completely un-English. While in appearance he was undoubtedly one of those transatlantic cousins who can don tweeds and Clydella shirts and look more English than any Englishman, there was a European piquancy in his make-up that rarely pierced the English phlegm. He may not have encountered, nor wished to, Henry James's friend, the imperious Mrs Wharton, but he would certainly have read her book, *Italian Villas and Their Gardens*, which had appeared in 1904. This book, with Mrs Wharton's remarkable perception and the wonderful Maxfield Parrish illustrations, high-lighted an American sympathy for Italian gardens that somehow eludes the insular English.

It is American gardeners who have proved most susceptible to the charms of the Villas Gamberaia and Lante and the tumbling waters of the Villa d'Este. While 'Italian' gardens in England, however charming, had a tendency to become sculpture galleries, such as Harold Peto's Iford Manor and Lord Astor's Hever (even though he was American), the Americans in the wake of Edith Wharton passionately embraced the Italianate revival and made a great number of such gardens in the first two decades of this century. Their New World bravura found a distant echo in the confidence of the Renaissance for sweeping wide swathes of vigorous vistas across a hillside, connecting the house with a distant view, and fussing about the spaces in between at a later stage. The English, as garden-makers, pace out furtively into the rainy gloom, consolidating each patch of newly-won territory but never gaining any far-flung sense of space at all. This was a very basic characteristic difference; the Rockefellers, Vanderbilts, Ryersons and Fahnestocks were easily the new counterparts of the Medici princelings and the cardinals.

These connections, then, were the genesis of Lawrence Johnston's garden-making. He had the space, he had the resources (not only the money but his farming machinery and know-how), to fling his vistas out from the cosy enclave of the Old Garden around the manor house. The set of the landscape determined how far his east–west vista, which halts on the brim of that breathtaking view out over the Vale of Evesham, could go; how far he got with the actual work by the summer of 1914 is uncertain, but his garden-making was interrupted because, again, England went to war. Johnston, still gazetted as a Major in the Northumberland Fusiliers, was well over forty; he may not have wished to marry one of the daughters of the neighbouring Souls, but he went off to fight with their sons, and with the sons of their gardeners too. Fortunately, unlike Ivo Charteris from Stanway and Edward Horner from Mells Manor, Johnston did return. He had been wounded twice in battle and left for dead. According to Alvilde Lees-Milne, it was then that fate, Broadway fate, intervened in the person of the officer in charge of the burial party, Colonel Henry Sidney. Colonel Sidney not only recognized Johnston, but saw him move; he was saved and was invalided home in early 1915.

Later in the year he was well enough to return to his garden-making, now more than ever determined, as those who have close encounters with death so often are, to work with certainty and enthusiasm. During the following fifteen years he made Hidcote into the garden that we recognize. The long vistas to the sky enchanted Mary Anderson de Navarro; she took her Italian friends to visit and recorded their approval of 'how Italian' it felt. The feeling is enhanced in the rooms leading off from the vista to the south, especially the Bathing Pool Garden; this brimful circular raised pool, like a Roman emperor's bath, fills the whole of its yew-hedged room. The clipped English yews ranked together in the Pillar Garden mimic the sentinel cypresses of Italian gardens; they border the plain grass floor of the room, in which the flowers about the yews' bases are an additional grace, a delicious embroidery of *Romneya coulteri* (the Californian tree poppy), peonies, pinks, lavenders (the blue 'Hidcote' variety) and philadelphus. From the Bathing Pool Garden a stream takes off down the southern slope, escorted by a sequence of varied plantings: ferns, herbaceous plants and roses, and an area of pernettyas and rhododendrons in a patch of made-up lime-free soil. The joy of Hidcote is how all this mixture of vistas and spaces was built up, with living walls, hedges of yew, hornbeam and box, and mixes of yew with holly, yew with box. And the skill was in Lawrence Johnston's vision, when he planted his young hedgerows, of how it would all be one day.

Though his American blood and Mrs Wharton's prose may have done much to inspire Johnston, there was little practical sympathy available to him in England, except from his friend Robert James. The many similarities between St Nicholas and Hidcote come from shared American-inspired tastes and from the fact that the best tangible sources of expansive, stylish, Beaux Arts design were also American. In particular, Johnston at any rate seems to have made a garden in the style of Charles Platt's ideal for straight vistas with attenuated rooms of differing character; there is a Platt painting of the Quirinal Garden of 1893 which echoes the Hidcote feeling exactly, with a high hedged vista to a distant gate balanced by a massing of flowers.

Platt was almost certainly a friend of Parsons, and his book, called simply *Italian Gardens*, had been published in 1894;[20] for guidance in plan form, from the eye of a professional designer, it was a unique volume, of much greater appeal to the enthusiastic Johnston than the endlessly glutinous volumes of pretty photographs that English publishers were turning out. Johnston would have found a great sympathy for Platt; the latter had already been a well-established landscape painter when he took his younger brother, whom he felt to be inadequately instructed in the art of garden design, to Italy to see the gardens. This younger Platt was drowned in a swimming accident and the elder felt it his filial loyalty more or less to abandon painting and design gardens in his brother's place. Charles Platt, along with Edith Wharton's niece, Beatrix Farrand, became the designers by appointment to the gilded age of American East Coast gardens during the years 1900–1920. They had the space, and their clients had the money, to make the Beaux-Arts-inspired gardens for which the English, in the middle of their own Arts and Crafts revival of the seventeenth-century bowers, were too timorous a breed.

Johnston would have had a further Beaux Arts shunt from the Henry James Americans. A frequent visitor to Fairford was Mrs Abbey's brother, William Rutherford Mead, a partner in the most prominent firm of Renaissance revival architects, McKim, Mead & White, who worked with Platt. (McKim's Johnston Gate into Harvard Yard, 1889–90, bears a strong resemblance to the design later used at the end of Hidcote's Long Walk.) Two prominent clients for American houses and gardens – William Choate, then Ambassador at the Court of St James, and the great, legendary J. Pierpont Morgan – were visitors both to Fairford and to Mrs de Navarro, and thus the feeling of what was right in American eyes was ever present.

The American influences on Johnston were inescapable, but after he had dealt with the design, his main interest settled into planting. He must have learned much from his clever gardening friends, Captain Simpson Hayward, Mark Fenwick and Rose Berkeley, and their nurseryman by appointment, Clarence Elliott the plant collector and nurseryman, at Moreton-in-Marsh, who became Johnston's friend. Another opportunity for planting came in the early 1920s, when he began making winter trips to the South of France for the sake of his mother's health. He bought La Serre de la Madrone, in a sheltered valley behind Menton, almost on the Italian border. Here he encountered the English gardening community abroad, and widened his interest in plants, which had been sparked off by his brief look at South Africa during the Boer War. Having this wonderful Mediterranean habitat in France, and with the bones of Hidcote put together at home, he could now study, in his usual perfectionist way, a luxurious range of planting, and this soon became his prime gardening interest. At home he took on a new head gardener, Frank Adams, who was to have a great impact on the garden. Presumably Johnston stayed in England as long as he could every year for autumn plantings, and – according to well-established legend – he planted and planted with an energy, flamboyance and expenditure that only a born American could display. Johnston kept up a fascinating plantsmen's dialogue with Clarence Elliott, and the Stream Garden must have received many Elliott plants. Perhaps the lime-free selection came from Mark Fenwick at Abbotswood? One definite source and inspiration was Sir George Holford's Westonbirt, for in 1926 Johnston planted his Ridge Garden, named 'Westonbirt' for its collection of acers, sorbus, unusual birches and other rarities.

Lawrence Johnston's mother, Mrs Gertrude Winthrop, died in 1926. He was now free to indulge his new love, with plant-hunting expeditions first with Cherry Collingwood Ingram to South Africa and then with George Forrest to Yunnan. By now his knowledge of plants had grown to equal the company he was keeping, but it is such a pity that he never wrote a word of it down, or even talked to someone who would understand![21]

Vita Sackville-West encountered Johnston in his garden, probably on one of her gardening jaunts around England in the later 1930s. When she returned to Hidcote after the war, to write her famous 1949 article for the RHS *Journal*,[22] he was absent and ill, and she bitterly regretted that she could not ask him all her questions about how the garden was made. Will we ever know the answers? But Vita did, of course, appreciate his plants; her article, for years the best guide to Hidcote, is filled with her admiration and enthusiasm:

I remember in particular a narrow path running along a dry-wall; I think the gardener called it a rock garden, but it resembled nothing that I had ever seen described by that name. At the foot of the wall grew a solid mauve ribbon of some dwarf Campanula. It is *C. portenschlagiana bavarica* and this, of course, after the Hidcote principle, had been allowed to spread itself also in brilliant patches wherever it did not rightly belong. Out of the dry-wall poured, not the expected rock plants, but a profusion of

1. Frances Wolseley's pupils from the Glynde College for Lady Gardeners, in the garden beside the chapel of King Edward VII's Sanatorium, Midhurst, in 1907.

2. King Edward VII's Sanatorium, Midhurst: the garden was designed by the hospital architects, Adams and Holden, in consultation with Gertrude Jekyll, who prepared the planting plans. The making of the garden was carried out by the Glynde College for Lady Gardeners.

3. Viscountess Wolseley, pioneer of gardening as a career for women, from the frontispiece of her book *In a College Garden*, published in 1916.

4. *Carnation Lily, Lily Rose*, John Singer Sargent's romantic interpretation of a Cotswold garden, exhibited at the Royal Academy in 1887.

5. Mary Anderson de Navarro's dictatorship of enchantment over the social, gardening and cricketing community of Broadway is highlighted in this cartoon by Bernard Partridge from J. M. Barrie's *Allahakbarries C.C.* (1889).

6. Court Farm, Broadway, the home of Antonio and Mary de Navarro. The garden was designed for them by Alfred Parsons, their Broadway neighbour.

7. Alfred Parsons (1847–1920), a self-portrait in pencil. Parsons, a painter, botanical artist and garden designer, was the doyen of Cotswold gardening.

8. The Old Garden at Hidcote Manor, the first garden to be made around the house, which illustrates what Henry James called 'the nook quality' of Alfred Parsons's garden tastes.

9. Hidcote Manor, Mrs Winthrop's Garden, named for Lawrence Johnston's mother, who found the Anglo-American society based on Broadway much to her liking and so bought the Hidcote estate in 1907. This photograph of the 1920s shows a repetitive arrangement of plants, called 'mingling' by the late Victorians, and the standard achievement of a competent head gardener of that time.

10. Hidcote Manor, the vista down the Red Borders: after the First World War Lawrence Johnston and Mrs Norah Lindsay became great gardening friends and her talent for planting design influenced Hidcote's garden.

11. Norah Lindsay, photographed in her garden at the Manor House, Sutton Courtenay, in 1903 for *Country Life*.

12. The Manor House, Sutton Courtenay: the Long Garden, photographed for a *Country Life* article written by Mrs Lindsay which was published on 16 May 1931.

13. The Manor House, Sutton Courtenay: a hedge of York and Lancaster roses by the gate from the Persian garden into the Long Garden, 1930.

14. The Manor House, Sutton Courtenay: the Long Garden and the house — Mrs Lindsay wrote, 'Where the dwelling is old and sleepy the garden, too, must lie under the spell of the ages.'

Lavender ... and wands of Indigofera ... *Choisya ternata* also, and some Cistus ...[23]

In the kitchen garden she found

many things more worthy of contemplation than Cabbages. Major Johnston was no orthodox gardener: he spilled his cornucopia everywhere. There is ... a raised circular bed round a Scotch pine, foaming with rock Roses of every shade, a lovely surprise, as light as spindrift, shot with many colours the rainbow does not provide.[24]

When she wrote that piece, in 1949, Vita was playing her part in an honourable campaign, to save Hidcote for the nation. Was she rather overly effusive in her praise? Her charming lapses of memory and wide-eyed gasps at all she saw were perhaps, in part, her way of persuading as many influential people as she could reach that this garden should be taken into the care of the National Trust, to rank equally with treasured houses like Montacute or Blickling, unmistakably noble piles. She succeeded, and Hidcote today has a place of honour as the first garden to be taken by the National Trust, as the result of the campaign for the conservation of gardens that was started after the Second World War.

But had we followed Vita and Major Johnston around on her earlier visit, I think the overheard conversation would have been rather different. Imagine them, absolute opposites: a tall, dark, distinguished lady striding out, in a large hat, a soft silk shirt with a rope of enormous pearls, a crumpled linen skirt, mid-calf, and stout shoes, and the dapper little Major in immaculate tweeds, bareheaded, fair, with a bemused smile on his pleasant round face, and his pack of dachshunds trotting at his heels. (Vita adored big dogs loping at her side, and probably kicked the dachshund that nipped her ankles.) Vita and Major Johnston epitomize the truth that gardens, like portraits, betray our secret fears and vanities. For this famous and aristocratic English lady's garden at home, at Sissinghurst Castle, was a refuge of enchanting rooms in which she could escape to her beloved past; and here was the Major, looking as if he could not say boo to a goose, bravely flinging out vistas to meet the sky and the unknown future. Vita would have admired, but also rather envied, his new world bravura; she had visited America and become enthusiastic about all things American, at least for a while. And she would have good-naturedly envied, without admiration, Johnston's wealth, for that was the secret of his garden; he could, after all, have everything that money could buy. For her, every mark made in Colonel Hoare Grey's catalogue or Clarence Elliott's list meant another boring article to be written to pay for it, or the monthly debate with her husband Harold Nicolson about how many of the treasures he found at the RHS shows they could afford. Sissinghurst's garden was made in spite of everything, against every difficulty: Hidcote Manor's had all the advantages of being the adored, indulged and only child.

Major Johnston left England after the war, having handed his garden over to the National Trust. He died in France in the spring of 1958. His 'English' garden, which has more in common with the American gardens of Charles Platt and Beatrix Farrand than with any of its English fellows (other than perhaps St Nicholas) is a nice tribute to the Henry James Americans, now that they are all gone. In Broadway Mary Anderson de Navarro's garden at Court Farm has been carefully tended into the late twentieth century by her son and daughter-in-law, but now they have left the scene too. But the garden that really evokes Lawrence Johnston's Hidcote Manor in its prime is, ironically – perhaps happily – in the village of Monkton in Maryland, just outside Baltimore. It was made, almost certainly from Hidcote's inspiration, by a wealthy, witty and cultivated man named Harvey Ladew, whose life was devoted to twin passions for gardening and hunting. He entertained his artistic and hunting friends in a white weatherboarded eighteenth-century house on his estate, filled with more relics of the chase than John Peel could have dreamed of: horses and hounds, and the occasional fox, in pictures, prints, books, on china, embroideries, table linen – a flamboyant and yet elegant expression of his life's loves. Horse and hounds in box chase across the drive too, but after that the garden is a beautifully sophisticated reiteration of Hidcote Manor's, with hedged vistas and flower-filled rooms, tropaeoleums clambering through green walls, a great yew-hedged 'theatre' lawn, stilted hornbeams, cottagey box-edged parterres, a rocky water rill, and endless amusements and ornamental tricks. Harvey Ladew's Topiary Garden is carefully preserved and well known as an American landmark, but it deserves to be more so; it also deserves to be a place of pilgrimage for English garden lovers, for there they would see an illuminating reflection of Hidcote Manor's garden.

3

Norah Lindsay

NORAH Lindsay was born in 1876 and died in 1948. She was, by so many accounts, a naturally brilliant gardener, but elusive in many ways: brilliance in gardening is the most intangible aspect of an ephemeral art, but she also had a will-o'-the-wisp personality and left little but her memory behind.

The trouble was that Norah really had too much social life, as the names that glitter through this chapter will show. It was more important for her to be seen at the dining tables of Emerald Cunard, Sibyl Colefax or Nancy Astor, or week-ending at Blickling, Faringdon or Godmersham, than to be sitting quietly noting down what she had just planted in the borders and why. Philip Tilden, architect by appointment to a glittering group of personalities of the 1920s and 30s for whom Norah also worked, makes the point in his *True Remembrances*[1] that she could have written half a dozen books if socializing hadn't taken so much of her energy. It is a common disease. He also says that she was 'one of the most instinctive gardeners' of her generation, and pays her the ultimate compliment of thinking her of the 'same calibre' as Miss Jekyll and fit to carry on her work.

Norah Lindsay's own garden, at the Manor House, Sutton Courtenay, is remembered as the most magical of illusions. Lady Diana Manners, her niece, remembered it in the 1900s, with flowers literally overflowing everything and drifting off into a wilderness. She recalled her aunt, 'dressed mostly in tinsel and leopard-skins and baroque pearls and emeralds', and her fluttering white hands, which played the piano divinely or served, equally divinely, chicken kedgeree and raspberries and cream for garden lunch.[2]

One day in the 1930s when she was struggling with the beginning of her own garden at Sissinghurst Castle, Vita Sackville-West rushed back from Godmersham Park and the 'too beastly-rich Trittons', reporting enviously *yet another* wonderful Norah Lindsay flower border being planted. In February 1943, as recorded in his diary, James Lees-Milne found Norah standing in as hostess for an indisposed Lady Colefax, dressed in black and white with red cherry buttons and a flat hat 'like a pancake' down over one eye. 'She is kittenish, stupid-clever and an amusing talker,' he wrote[3] – quite a remarkable judgement on a lady nearing seventy. At that time she was ruling the garden at Hidcote Manor, or certainly acting as though she was; Lawrence Johnston had long intended that she should inherit Hidcote. She must have had considerable charm then, as well as determination, for she ruled many great gardens in her time. She was clearly colourful and eccentric. Is it possible to get any further? For years I have been collecting scraps of information, and now it is time to put them together and add a little imagination.

THE best place to encounter a gardener is at home. Norah's home, the Manor House, Sutton Courtenay, is beside a stream called the Mill Brook which joins the River Thames just downstream from Abingdon. The house occupies an ancient site, a dry standing in a complex waterland of cuts, channels and pools. There was a Norman manor here before it became a monastic rest house, and in Jacobean times it reverted to being the manor house of the Courtenays. For Christopher Hussey, writing in *Country Life*, certain houses caught the spirit of their places and crystallized 'a scene and a season': he chose Sutton Courtenay 'for golden marshes, flickering silver of poplar and willow, old red roofs and lilac ... in a word ... May in the Thames Valley'.[4]

So, let it be May, a May morning in the late 1920s, for then the garden must have been at its best. The approach from the village is along a short gravel drive that curves, with a ribbon of daisies down the centre of the wheel-tracks, between borders with cherry trees underplanted with spring flowers. Round the curve of the drive are two impressive gate piers, but no gates, and through them one really arrives, to a gravel sweep around a circle of grass with more daisies. In the centre of the circle is a tall sundial, set in a planted pavement sprouting santolinas, thymes and cottage flax. Beyond the sundial is the door of the mellow, gabled and timbered house; it is guarded by clumps of rosemary buzzing with bees. Wisteria droops along the lines of the old timbers. It all looks as though it has been there for ever.

Inside, with flagged floors and panellings of dark oak, a screens passage gives into a large room, used as a dining hall. The furniture is all old, of highly polished wood – wheel-back chairs, a refectory table, two Jacobean dressers, small gate-legged side tables, all dotted with small pewter jars and large china bowls of flowers. The house is low-ceilinged, its dun-coloured walls supporting heads of strange beasts – markhor, ibex, shapoo and oorial bear from the Himalayas; it is full of polished oak, heavy curtains of broccatello in crimson and dark greens, and flowers. The exception is the small sitting-room that leads to the garden – it is light and airy and comfortably furnished with chintzes, a painted piano and more flowers.

How did Mrs Lindsay come here? Well, in short, by her marriage. She was born Norah Mary Madeleine Bourke; she was a grand-daughter of the 5th Earl of Mayo (the murdered Viceroy of India), and the daughter of Emma Hatch (the daughter of an Indian judge advocate) and Edward Roden Bourke, a cousin of Wilfrid Scawen Blunt. The Bourkes had a wonderfully swashbuckling descent from a Norman conqueror, William Fitzaldelm de Burgo (who wrested Ireland from Strongbow for William I in 1177), via another piratical type (who sounds as if he should have owned a cat in boots), given the title Marquis of Mayo by Philip II of Spain. Norah's blood would seem to make her the equal of Gertrude Jekyll and Vita Sackville-West combined.

Her childhood is lost (to me at any rate) in Irish mists. She emerged, on 27 April 1895, to marry Harry Edith Lindsay, grandson of the 25th Earl of Crawford and the younger brother of Violet Lindsay, who was to become the Duchess of Rutland (she had married Lord Granby in 1882), the angel of the 'Souls'. Harry Lindsay, the inevitable soldier and big game hunter, also shared the artistic tastes of his sister, and he was very knowledgeable about old furniture and pictures, acting as adviser to many friends of good taste, such as Colonel Reginald Cooper.

The Lindsays were given the Manor House as a wedding present by a Lindsay family friend, Lord Wantage VC. This hero, worshipped for years by Violet Lindsay, had eventually married an heiress and did not require it for himself.

Norah was only nineteen or twenty when she was married; her husband was ten years older. There is a photograph of her which makes her look very like a candidate for the coterie of Souls, along with her sister-in-law: she leans on the sundial in the front court of the Manor House, wearing a georgette blouse trimmed with lace and long ropes of pearls (the 'baroque pearls'?), the pearls gathered into a corsage of rose buds with the black silky ties coming down from a large hat. Her waist is drawn in tightly, and a long taffeta skirt drapes to, one suspects, velvet-slippered feet. Her face is pale and fine, with a long nose and pensive eyes. She presents a very romantic picture, and must be a romantic gardener, for she has the whitest, long, slender hands.

The Lindsays' marriage produced a son, Peter, and a daughter, Nancy, but after that it did not turn out well. Colonel Harry, like the gentleman he was, simply slipped quietly out of the scene, leaving Norah in peace in her garden.

The Manor House in summer is a garden house: the doors are left open till midnight and the garden offers itself at every door and open window. On the long south-facing façade of the old house are two large rectangular garden enclosures, which Norah calls the Long Garden and the Persian Garden.

The Long Garden is spectacular. Its plan is simple – from the garden door there leads a straight gravel path, which is not in the centre of the space and thus unequally divides the garden into 'halves'. The smaller 'half' is completely filled with plants, but the larger space is partly made up of round lawns with generous borders. The walk down the path, edged with thick, knee-high box hedges, is a perambulation between gardens as fantastic as any in Wonderland. It is like being on a highly decorated games board, with large as life clipped yews in pillars and domes and great humps of box that one almost expects to rise and walk away on hedgehog legs. Between these creatures crowd the flowers.

Norah's own gardening philosophy was one of *laissez-faire*. This came partly from her own nature, but perhaps she had also read the good Canon Ellacombe on the subject: when Forbes Robertson remarked that the wallflowers should not have come up in the box edging, the Canon replied: 'Never mind, we must manage to get on without hurting the wallflowers.'[5] Norah's way of putting it comes (as do all her words that follow) from her article in *Country Life* about her garden, published in 1931.

In a garden where labour is scarce and the soil beneficent, all manner of tiny seedlings get overlooked till, lo and behold! a handsome clump has established itself in the most unlikely position, claiming squatter's rights and in nine cases out of ten succeeding in establishing its claim.[6]

Her philosophy explains the apparent cunning of the garden: how lupins and anchusas ('easy English flowers') seed and succeed with mallows, thalictrums, hollyhocks, campanulas and 'tropical rods of eremuri' so that not a spare inch of bare earth shows. Behind this apparently 'thoughtless abundance' there is an artistry of careful colouring: rich blues, deep purples, various pinks and lemon yellows are allowed together but well away from the hot scarlets of poppies and the metallic golds of sunflowers and rudbeckias. These 'flaming yellows' are planted with silvery grasses and thistles, and the 'fascinating bloodless candelabra' of *Salvia turkestanica*, the Vatican sage.

Among all these herbaceous residents are roses on poles, on trellis and on rustic arches over the path. Not much money is spent on fancy architecture in this garden, and the plants cover a variety of gardener's structures. Everywhere inside the box edging are clumps of lilies, Turks' caps, 'their gold or tawny reversed bells crowned with a valiant tuft of leaves', to be followed by Madonnas – 'their alabaster chalices drenching the air with honey-sweetness'. Norah is a total romantic, which gives her the understanding of this old place; she accepts and revels in its ancient sleepiness. Of the house and solemn trees she says: ' ... these were before you, these will live after you, so listen to their message and humbly follow in their sedate and simple footsteps'. She likes the look of the garden to be easy and spontaneous, as if 'the flowers and trees had chosen their own positions, and like the house, been overlooked by the rushing tide of men'.

To her garden she brought her love of things Italian: 'I would have been a much lesser gardener had I not worshipped at the crumbling shrines of the ancient garden gods of Florence and Rome.' From there she brought water into her garden: the crossing path of the Long Garden is marked with a circular, brimming pool, with a raised rim for sitting on. Further on is a square pool with 'in the centre a fat and foolish lead baby hugging a lead fish with such intensity that from its throat pours a rapid, feverish gurgle of water, not very high, but making a continuous cool plop into the pool below'; the edges of this pool tumble with valerian and graceful *Diervilla pulcherrima*, 'called so charmingly in Ireland "the faerie fishing rods"', and clumps of yucca swords. Norah likes the candy pink of the valerian with the intense violet of *Iris laevigata* and the lilac bunches of a successful 'squatter', *Campanula centidifolia*.

An old brick wall is the division between the Long Garden and its parallel enclosure, which began life as The Pleasaunce but was re-named the Jewel or Persian Garden, because of the success of its flowers. This was the sunniest side of the wall, clothed in *Piptanthus laburnifolius* (the Nepalese laburnum), *Abutilon vitifolium*, *Akebia quinata*, with raspberry-coloured flowers in April and, a rarity in England, *Fendlera rupicola*, a relative of the philadelphus. Further denizens of the wall were a deep purple but unnamed clematis, with *C. armandii* as a gentle neighbour to a 'lolloping' *Phlomis fruticosa* (Jerusalem sage) of gigantic proportions — its 'gaudy golden cockades' tumbled from the top of the wall to lie heaped on the path below. *Feijoa sellowiana*, a shy-flowering myrtle with crimson and white petals and long crimson stamens among felty grey leaves, also grew here.

The path from the Long Garden through into the Persian Garden ran beside a hedge of mixed *Rosa damascena*, York and Lancaster roses: 'It is about four feet high and flowers so profusely that for six weeks there is hardly any foliage to be seen. The colour and diversity of the petals, now all crimson, now all white, now carefully striped, and now delicately feathered as if with a fine brush, the eager buds of close bright rose held well aloft as if waiting to be picked, and carrying their scent with them into the house' – Norah not surprisingly had a great fondness for this feature.

The Persian Garden is planted mostly with roses of all kinds, surrounded by clove pinks. Norah does not like roses of uniform height, or the sight of thirty bushes of the same colour: she has planted mixes, keeping pinks, reds and burgundies together and away from tangerines, lemons and creams. On the right of the beds, presumably nearest the lemons and creams, is another mixed hedge, a tall screen of 'Penzance' roses and sweetbriar. (Norah just calls them 'Penzance'. Both 'Lord Penzance' and 'Lady Penzance' were introduced in 1894; 'Lord Penzance' is fawny-yellow, 'Lady Penzance' a coppery pink. I think 'Lord Penzance' is more likely here.) The Persian Garden ends in an arched alcove of blue-painted wooden pillars supporting a lattice wreathed in vines, which bear enough fruit for a house vintage. Beneath the arbour, in the shade, squatting ferns and ivies have taken over among mosses and tumbling water from a wall fountain.

The right-hand wall of the Persian Garden is a long and high hornbeam hedge, which forms an alley to the kitchen garden, fully productive of flowers, fruit and vegetables, and to the riverside, fully redolent of romance in all its forms. Norah has made a remarkable alley of climbing roses, with a brick paved strip down the centre of the path which breaks into alternating rectangular and twin circular pools holding bog and water plants, plantains, marsh marigold, bogbean and iris. This was already in her garden as early as 1904, immediately after Miss Jekyll had planted the iris rill across the lawn at Deanery Garden, Sonning. Had Norah seen that, or read Miss Jekyll on the subject of bringing water plants into the garden? I rather think she may have made the circles and squares (which appear *later* in the Lutyens design for Hestercombe's garden) for herself, and thus may claim to have got there first. As a way of introducing the mind to the subject of water after leaving the garden, en route to the river bank with its kingcup meadows, and clumps of sedges and water iris, it is a lovely idea.

As much as Norah loved her garden, she loved the river too. The garden gave on to fields where the Mill Brook entered the Thames channel which meanders well away from the navigation channel at this point. The pleasure boats processed through Culham Cut, leaving these sidestreams to a few intrepid punters and rowing boats. Norah loved the 'cool green savannahs' of the watermeadows as a rest from the colour and labour of her garden, and she happily romanticized about this land of water vole and willow wren, just along the river from the haunts of Ratty and Toad.

In spite of her long white fluttering hands, there is no doubt that she worked to make this garden herself. Most of it must have been made well before the First World War, and she refined the planting through the 1920s. As she said, her philosophy allowed for a good deal of *laissez-faire* in lieu of a large garden staff. She did have garden help, almost certainly a head gardener who lived in the Manor Cottage and whose wife helped in the house. He was helped by village boys; he did not have to do a lot of mowing, as, interestingly, Norah did not go in for bowling-green lawns, merely grass walks that sprouted wild flowers and were surely cut late and infrequently, but he did have the fruit and vegetables to see to. The flower garden, therefore, was really Norah's territory, where she clipped and pruned, plucked and prinked at her plants.

She must have worked in the garden daily when she was younger; she complains of 'an arduous hour of tying up the heavy and contrary heads of the regal poppies' on a hot June day, as though she has been doing it for years. She certainly paid daily attention to the courtyard which was enclosed by the arms of the house. She 'lived' out there as much as possible in summer, taking all her meals on the loggia terrace outside the kitchen. This court resembles one of those inn yards where Shakespeare's players set up their performances; it has an overhang edged with carved Jacobean oak and wreathed in wisteria tassels. The house walls are washed a salmony pink which fades to a delicious colour; the faded pink, the wisteria mauve and the red tiles, with the distinctive patinated carved wood, give the setting a theatrical charm. The floor, of course, completes the picture – a planted pavement of thymes, sages, arabis, tiny iris, clumps of candytuft and rosemary and larger clumps of laurustinus.

This was where the romantic Mrs Linsday was to be found at home, at least during the years before the First World War when her children were growing up. When her friends came to look at her garden, she couldn't help giving them suggestions for theirs. And as her friends were the Astors, Emerald Cunard and Sibyl Colefax, her exquisite garden taste caught on like wildfire. It was Nancy Astor who suggested that Norah should not be afraid to, indeed must, charge for her services, and she commissioned Norah to 'dress' Cliveden for the Ascot house parties. The flowers inside the house were known for their unbelievable lavishness: from the Italianate and scented rooms one would gasp for fresh air on a fresh June evening, as the blue faded from the sky. From the terrace the view was of the sky come to earth, with carpets of blue forget-me-nots spread across the parterre beds. This creative leap, from the traditional grandeur of the Victorian bedding style of begonias, salvias, tagetes and their battle colours to the simple heavenly blue of forget-me-not, was typical of Norah's wit and taste.

Another of her early professional forays was to Port Lympne, for Philip Sassoon: it was there, in the early twenties, that the young Kenneth Clark observed her as one of a breed of grand ladies whose opinions on gardens could never be flouted or questioned. Perhaps Norah, in one of her imperious, umbrella-pointing moods, embodied or commanded an enthusiasm for garden arts that Kenneth Clark felt should be applied to more serious art?

At Port Lympne the garden was taken very seriously. The modest house in pretty, curly-gabled, Dutch colonial style by Herbert Baker had been built before the war. When Baker went off to New Delhi with Edwin Lutyens, he was replaced by Philip Tilden, who enlarged the house and made the grandest garden features. The 135-step Great Stair in Cumberland stone did not daunt Norah, nor did each of the special terraces below, devoted to dahlias and asters (one terrace for each flower), and the two small enclosed gardens to be viewed from the house, to be planted in flowered chequers and stripes. There was also a mammoth herbaceous border, rather inelegantly running down the slope below the terraces, but magnificently stuffed with flowers. The real point of the garden was that it was required for one month in the year only — August — when Sassoon, the MP for Hythe, was at home in his constituency for summer house parties. Norah dressed this garden too: the Aster Terrace was planted with rich purples and mauves, blues and pale pinks, the Chequers Garden was squared in grass and late-seeded forget-me-nots, and its companion, the Striped Garden, was decked with stripes of dahlias in yellows, flames and scarlet.

Norah undoubtedly enjoyed the company of rich, rather eccentric and lively people, like Sassoon and her neighbour, Lord Berners, at Faringdon. There she found musical company, and she would have delighted in the famous rainbow-hued doves, dyed to suit the decor. Both at Faringdon and at Lady Ottoline Morrell's Garsington Manor, both lovely gardens, she may well have dispensed her ideas, but there is little chance of ever really knowing for certain. A lovely garden is the last thing most people are willing to share the credit for!

In 1925 Nancy Astor's friend, Philip Kerr, was appointed Secretary to the Rhodes Trust, which was based in South Parks Road, Oxford, at Rhodes House, designed by Herbert Baker. It is tempting to think that Norah inspired the long herbaceous border that survives in this garden. When Kerr became Lord Lothian and inherited Blickling Hall in Norfolk among his estates, he chose to retain it as a week-end retreat and asked Norah to help him with the garden. Her chief job was to convert the parterre on the garden front from a jumble of topiary pimples and points and a chaos of small flower beds into the sanity that reigns today. Two of the beds follow Norah's colour scheme of metallic golds, burnt yellows, rusts, flames and silvers (with heleniums, golden rods, golden roses, crocosmia, achilleas and silvery erigeron, *Stachys olympica* and *Verbascum chaixii*). The second scheme, for the other two beds, has delphiniums, mallows, geraniums, aconites and phlox in blues, purples, pinks and mauves. Norah also made a long, softly coloured border in the shelter of the southern wall of the parterre.

One of the most tangible pieces of evidence about Norah's life-style that survives is the Blickling Hall visitors' book, which Lord Lothian kept during the 1930s.[7] Her name appears often, frequently among the same group of familiar friends – the Astors, Geoffrey Dawson, Paul Phipps the architect, Nancy Lancaster – and once for a musical gathering with the Vaughan Williamses. She always slept in the Chinese bedroom, overlooking the entrance court, with its golden landscape wallpaper, little ivory pagodas and japanned and painted wardrobe; she is remembered as leaving a primrose scent behind her.

Vita Sackville-West's mention of Norah working at Godmersham Park in Kent for the Trittons has already been noted. Norah also planted a small parterre, acknowledged as hers today, for Mrs Gilbert Russell at Mottisfont Abbey in Hampshire. These commissions, along with Port Lympne and Trent Park for Philip Sassoon, invite the tempting conclusion that wherever Rex Whistler worked, Norah followed, and in some ways her garden style was the equivalent of his decorative taste. Norah was also very friendly with Sir Edwin Lutyens's daughter, Barbie Agar, another of Rex Whistler's friends and patronesses, and advised on the Agars' garden at Beechwood, Lavington, in Sussex, during the Second World War. It is agreeable to think of Norah's work in terms of the highly decorative effect of Rex Whistler's work indoors. She could have managed his flower-draped arches and urns for real, in garden settings, and their arts would have exactly complemented each other. There is no doubt (though little hard evidence) that Norah brought the ephemeral art of dressing gardens to such extremes of delight that all who saw her gardens at their best were inspired to greater things. In this way her legacy was perhaps more for those good gardeners who were also artists in other ways, including Nancy Lancaster, Cecil Beaton, Constance Spry and John Fowler.

Norah also achieved another remarkable feat in bringing up her daughter to share her own interest. During the 1920s Nancy Lindsay became, when she was only in her twenties, a knowledgeable and enthusiastic plantswoman. She ended up by knowing a lot more about plants than her mother. In 1933 she went plant-hunting in Persia; she and a friend, Alice Fullerton, persuaded the Keeper of Botany at the Natural History Museum to support their expedition (which surprisingly he did), and they set off in the spring of 1935. In her book, *To Persia for Flowers*,[8] Alice Fullerton is not very forthcoming on the subject of the actual flowers, but she does mention a few things that thrilled Nancy.

Their chief hunting ground was the southern foothills of the Elburz. They found a lovely lupin, *Sophora alopecuroides*, with 'faint elusive scent', massed in vine fields by a stream; an 'ugly' dianthus, cut and torn-looking, but with a strong delicious smell; erigerons and eryngiums of infinite variety with 'wicked' spikes and 'flaunting heads of blue, brown and purple' – all of which were eaten by the donkeys; hollyhocks of soft pale yellow, white, mauve and bright pink; and a 'best find', a particularly fine blue hyssop which Alice Fullerton grew well at home in Surrey. 'One of the greatest treasures we brought back ... [were] some bulbs bought in a bazaar. These turned out to be, to us, a new Sternbergia with a head of several flowers, not the usual single bloom. No one knew from whence it came and we only managed to get a few bulbs. Those sent to Menton have flourished ...'[9]

Alice Fullerton's mention of Menton refers to Lawrence Johnston's garden, La Serre de la Madrone, and establishes the last and greatest gardening friendship of Norah's life, which had started some time after the death of Major Johnston's mother, Mrs Winthrop, in 1926 and was well formed by 1933, when Nancy brought her treasures back from Persia. Was Nancy and Alice's trip partly supported by Major Johnston, because he could no longer go plant-hunting himself? It seems very likely that he would have wanted to encourage them, and Norah too would have supported their claim. But why did the trip produce only Alice's charming but inadequate book, which is almost totally concerned with the domestic arrangements? Why didn't Nancy produce her own account of the excitement of plant-hunting? That she could have done so with all the spirit of the best of the Farrers and Wilsons is proved by the following extract from a letter she wrote to Vita Sackville-West years later, probably in the early 1950s, after her mother's death, on the common passion of Norah, Nancy and Vita, old roses:

Another rare and distinct rose is the Persian I found at over 9,000 feet in the boulder-strewn wastes of the Elburz beyond the Sharastanek Valley towards Quilan. There was one tiny, lonely thicket over a trickle of water; the only patch of green for miles, where no garden has been for 2,000 years. Tradition ascribed the vast, tumbled boulders to the ruins of one of 'Alexander's Castles' i.e. of one of Alexander's generals who settled there on his return from India. I call it the 'Sharastanek Rose'. It is very distinct, very elegant, not at all a wild rose, perhaps it is the last survivor of Alexander's general's mountain Paradise? It is a graceful, three-foot bush with lacquered cinnamon bark and small, frosted celadon-green leaves. It has small clusters of medium-sized, very double, brilliant chemise-pink satin-petalled flowers. The pointed buds are lovely, with long, ferny sepals. It is the most deliciously and strongly fragrant rose I know.[10]

From this sample of Nancy's writing on flowers it seems we have missed a great treat. This passage allows a glimpse into the picturesque way of looking at life that mother and daughter shared; it is perhaps tinged with a touch of lost romance, for (though I write in hushed tones) fairly persistent gossip has it that Nancy was distracted from her flowers and lingered in some Persian tent too long. This explains the absence of any memoir and her later apparent eccentricities; maybe it suggests why, back in the social whirl of the 1930s, Norah came to prefer more quiet times at Menton and Hidcote with the kind Major Johnston.

Whatever the reason, there is no doubt that it was Norah's almost constant presence during the 30s and early 40s that refined and glorified Hidcote's plantings into the great achievement that Vita Sackville-West acknowledged in her article published in the RHS *Journal* in 1949.[11] Vita would not have acknowledged Norah's contribution. But her talents emerge from so many of Vita's praises: 'This place is a jungle of beauty ... what I should like to impress ... is the luxuriance everywhere; a kind of haphazard luxuriance, which of course comes neither hap nor hazard at all.'[12] Vita could have been describing the Long Garden at Sutton Courtenay just as well, but to return to Hidcote: she noted that the flowers were not in bold massings, as Miss Jekyll had decreed, but in scatters of small clumps – the 'spottiness' that Miss Jekyll disparaged was turned to brilliance by Norah. Her conventional wit also provided for Vita's notice 'a patch of humble annuals nestling under one of the choicest shrubs, or a tall metallic *Onopordon acanthium* towering above a carpet of Primroses'.

Norah's Hidcote was captured in a series of photographs taken during the summer of 1947; they were published in *House and Garden* the following spring[13] and show glimpses of the 'jungle of beauty' and its immaculate hedges. Campanulas, tall and stately squatters, spring round the Bathing Pool: in Norah's words, 'Wherever the flowers themselves have planned the garden, I gracefully retire, for they are the guiding intelligences and strike where we fumble.' Creeping linaria and spraying cotoneaster embroider the steps up to the Stilt Garden, enhancing its immaculate symmetry: the 'young' pillars, resembling in their youth their cousins in the Long Garden at Sutton Courtenay, rise from a cloud of *Philadelphus* 'Belle Etoile'; in the courtyard the clipped buttresses of yew stand firm against masses of *Hydrangea paniculata*; and roses are planted in the same mixture as at Sutton Courtenay – the rich, butter-coloured 'Hidcote Yellow' and a neighbour of rich flames and oranges, 'Reveil Dijonnais'.

Much of the final glory of Hidcote's garden took shape in those years of the late 30s and during the war, when Norah and the Major were happily gardening together. A 'wizard' he may have been, but it probably needed Norah's flamboyant taste to egg him on to the richness of contrasts that made the garden so wonderful in *their* time. When the war ended and he came to the decision not to face another English winter but to retire to the South of France, it was by then so much Norah's garden that he wished her to live there for the rest of her life. She had actually come to the painful decision that she could no longer afford the Manor House, which had been let for several summers, so this was a most generous act of friendship. But Norah died suddenly in the spring of 1948, at the age of what had seemed a sprightly seventy-two.

A last glimpse of Hidcote as Norah and Major Johnston made it comes from Nancy Lindsay, who more or less took command of the garden and of its treasures after her mother's death. She offered some to Vita Sackville-West: the double golden briar rose from Persia, *Rosa haemispherica*, the rare mauve *R. centifolia* 'Tour de Malakoff' and the precious maroon 'Nuits de Young'; also a tall blue iris, *I. spurea*, old double primroses and clove pinks. Major Johnston left for France, leaving his garden to the National Trust and to Nancy's proprietorial feelings.

Hidcote managed to retain its elegance through the war largely because of Major Johnston's and Norah Lindsay's own hard work. Norah's grand 'garden dressing' for great occasions or seasons was now a thing of the past, and her highly individual laissez-faire style at Sutton Courtenay was no longer quite so smart. The Hidcote combinations, as they appeared in the pages of pictures in that 1948 *House and Garden*, were the sign of things to come. Norah's friend Sibyl Colefax had been professionally involved in decorating houses since the mid 1930s; gardens had remained really rather private fields of operation, their geometry occasionally measured out by architects who included Trenwith Wills, Geoffrey Jellicoe, Claude Phillimore and H. S. Goodhart-Rendel, but planting was still a matter for the owners themselves. Post-war privations brought the memories of Norah's Hidcote to the professional attention of the interior decorators and smart garden designers. As John Cornforth writes,[14] it was in late 1946 or early 1947 that Nancy Tree bought Sibyl Colefax Ltd and turned it, with the young decorator John Fowler, into Colefax & Fowler. Fowler had also seen Hidcote, and when he found his own little hunting lodge at Odiham the same year, he immediately planned outdoor rooms with aerial hedges of hornbeam on stilts, and box furnishings filled with flowers. His garden took time to grow, but it is true to say that through him, a great deal of Norah's taste was translated as suitable for smart present-day gardens.

And what of the Manor House at Sutton Courtenay? A name

frequently found in the Blickling visitors' book at the same time that Norah was there was that of Nancy Astor's son, christened Francis but always known as David. During those Blickling years he was in his early twenties and up at Balliol. David was developing very un-Astor-like liberal tendencies, which would send him to work in a Glasgow factory and for the *Yorkshire Post* before taking up his inheritance at the *Observer*. He also loved gardening, and came out from Oxford at week-ends to help Norah at Sutton Courtenay. He served in the Royal Marines during the war, and when he came home in 1945 to find that Norah needed to sell her house, he bought it. He knew the garden as well as anyone, he knew it could not live without Norah, and he could not devote enough time to it himself – especially once he became Foreign Editor of the *Observer* in 1946. It would be interesting to know whether Norah ever knew that he asked Brenda Colvin, then a rising star of landscape architecture with a fine sense of design, to alter the garden. I imagine not; Brenda Colvin's design was featured in *Modern Gardens* by Peter Shepheard in 1953,[15] five years after Norah's death. The front drive was closed up; a semi-circular curved paved terrace kept the memory of the gravel sweep and gave vistas out into the woodland, which was decorated with sculpture by Siegfried Charoux. The Long Garden was laid to lawn, and the Persian Garden was given a restrained parterre of box-hedged beds filled with 'Hidcote' lavender, *Senecio cineraria*, roses and lilies. A nice touch of the changing times was that Brenda Colvin neatly listed the pots and vases she found around the garden: forty-two in all, some still with their plants – a copper holding lavender, stone and terracotta pots with agapanthus and tradescantia, wooden tubs with plumbago. Norah's sundial was re-sited in the new side entrance court, where it stands today.

Norah's daughter Nancy remained in the Manor House Cottage until her death. A Nancy Lindsay Memorial Fund at Oxford, 'to assist women in the study of botany and in particular in the collection of plants and seeds of possible horticultural value', commemorates both her talents and her misfortune. She was eventually ousted from any say in the management of Hidcote's garden, for she did not see eye to eye with the new regime; she retired, like a miser with her treasures, to her cottage, where she became increasingly strange. A last tribute was paid to her by Graham Stuart Thomas in *The Old Shrub Roses*, his classic book which reinstated these flowers in the forefront of modern gardening.[16] Nancy's garden at The Cottage, Sutton Courtenay, was one of those he visited, and he 'was delighted to find several ancient roses which she had collected in Persia, together with some most beautiful French kinds'; he credits her with 'Gloire de Guilan', a sprawling shrub rose with clear pink cupped flowers which open flat — this is the rose used for attar of roses in Persia.

GARDENING is so much a matter of the moment and the inspiration is hard to catch; Norah Lindsay seems the perfect illustration of this inescapable fact. After concentrating so much on her, I feel I could and should make a 'Norah Lindsay garden' with all her favourite features, for they are also mine: wide planted pavements, hedges of roses and honeysuckle, large plain beds hedged in thigh-high box, passed by gravel paths so that one rubs shoulders with haphazard verbascums and tumbling damask roses, with clumps of santolina and gypsophila and more and more spires — lupins in creams and pinks, thalictrums, mallows, Canterbury bells — all guarded by sentinel Irish yews. A second garden would have deep beds of roses of all kinds and heights and colours of leaves, edged with old clove pinks; the garden would be dotted with pots and tubs, garden structures simply made from old poles or painted wooden struts in sombre blue. There would be no lawn (what a relief), just grass paths through meadows of wild flowers which melt into the wood. Unfortunately I have no River Thames at the bottom of the garden, but I feel that can be overcome! Norah's best ideas have been taken over by the smart garden-dressing world for which she worked; at Hidcote Manor her contribution was never acknowledged and has now been lost. It would be good to distil her ideas out of the past into a garden again. I think that she, and her garden, inspire me more than any other gardener of our time. But, as Philip Tilden said, it is a great pity she did not write half a dozen books.

4

Academic Gardeners

THE gardens and groves of academic institutions have not
been noted for their beauty. English nineteenth- and early
twentieth-century schools had playgrounds that were little
improvement on prison exercise yards, and only very recently –
with the discovery that making a pond can serve as part of the
biology syllabus – has the notion of nature in the school landscape
been given a chance. I have raged against the damage that this has
done, and the missed opportunities, elsewhere[1] (though it is a subject
that needs much more attention); I have also time and again felt my
heart sink into my boots at the prospect of a historic or once
beautiful garden coming into academic ownership. Most schools
and colleges come second only to religious foundations in the
insensitivity they inflict on their gardens. There seems to be a
tyranny in the education of the young that sacrifices everything
to the erection of huts, the trampling of studded boots and the
convenience of daily invasions of parental cars. Private and public
education are equally culpable, and the more precious the garden
or landscape the higher the expectations, and the harder they fall.
Stowe School in Buckinghamshire, the tenant of the most sublime
English landscape garden in the world, could launch its pupils into
the world equipped with an environmental sensitivity and integrity
that counts for rather more than the current fashion for turning true
blues, or bright reds, to deep green.

For all these reasons it has been a joy to research and discover,
recently, that one Cambridge college has a garden that was regarded
as an essential part of its educational role. This is the story of the
making of that garden.[2] Newnham College, Cambridge, was founded
as a women's college in the early 1870s; it was unusual from the

start in that it grew out of the efforts of a group of brilliant young men, led by Henry Sidgwick (later Knightbridge Professor of Moral Philosophy), to organize lectures for women in Cambridge. Another unusual aspect was that when the buildings were started, in 1874, they were to designs by Sidgwick's friend, the architect Basil Champneys, a man of great charm and candid goodness, who was to give Newnham's buildings a delightful country house character. The interiors of Newnham, unlike the narrow dark stairs of tradition, were filled with light and airy corridors, pretty woodwork and William Morris wallpapers; each student's room overlooked the garden, and was furnished with a Morris chair and gateleg table, a desk and an open fireplace. The inspiration for the domestic charm of Newnham – the idea that it need not be sacrificed to Spartan suffering in the cause of learning – reflected the college's enlightened attitude to women's opportunities and came to a great extent from the first Principal, Anne Jemima Clough.

Anne Jemima was born in 1820, the daughter of a Liverpool cotton merchant, and she spent part of her childhood in South Carolina. Her education was 'adequate'; her parents realized that in her and her younger brother, Arthur Hugh Clough, they had two extremely intelligent children, even though it was accepted that Anne Jemima's education could lead nowhere in particular. When her brother was at Oxford in the early 1840s their father died; it was understood that Anne Jemima would remain in Lancashire as companion to her mother, awaiting eagerly Arthur Hugh's vacations, when he would tell her of his Oxford talk, of the philosophies of Carlyle and Ruskin that were to shape their lives. He was her ambassador to a world she could not enter, and he was her devoted champion, too; with his encouragement Anne Jemima took teaching posts in Sunday schools and day schools. When he died in Florence in 1861, aged forty-two, deeply mourned by his friends ('But Thyrsis never more we swains shall see ...' wrote Matthew Arnold), his loss was an especially bitter blow for Anne Jemima.[3] But she would have been a tower of strength in the circumstances, a support to her sister-in-law, Blanche Clough, and her two young children. Blanche, who was the cousin of both Florence Nightingale and Barbara Bodichon, repaid Anne Jemima's devotion by encouraging her to go to Cambridge and work for the women's cause.

Barbara Bodichon and Emily Davies had founded Girton College, at Hitchin in Hertfordshire, in 1869.[4] There was a considerable atmosphere of resistance to women being allowed to study in Cambridge, but this was being tackled by Henry Sidgwick's General Committee for Ladies' Lectures, which became the Association for Promoting the Higher Education of Women in Cambridge. He took a house in Regents Street to provide lodgings for the students, and invited Anne Jemima Clough to come and run the fledgeling college in 1871. Anne Jemima, with real work to do at last, was in seventh heaven; she later recalled that she had found happiness for the first time in her life, just after her fiftieth birthday.[5]

Almost upon arrival, she found another home for the students in an old house called Merton Hall, which met her Ruskinian ideals for sympathetic surroundings: '. . . the fairy college with its rambling rooms, its doors and windows leading to the garden, the old orchard covered with blossoms in spring, the long shady walks and arbours, the medlar tree under whose shade the students held their debates.'[6] She was convinced, by seeing the students' evident happiness both in their occupation and in their surroundings, that this serenity of contact with natural things was important; it was in part a bower, secure from the scowls and other unpleasant attentions of a Cambridge that by no means welcomed their presence – at least, not for the right reasons. How much more brave perhaps than the new Girton, set apart 'the thousand odd yards of green fields' along the Huntingdon Road, considered by Emily Davies and anxious mothers 'as sufficient precaution against the wiles and sinfulness of a University Town'.[7]

In the autumn of 1873 Henry Sidgwick and Anne Jemima launched an appeal for building a new college, which attracted the attention of a second remarkable lady. She was Eleanor Mildred Balfour, a young lady of family and consequence. Nora, as she was known, was born in 1845, the daughter of James Balfour and Blanche Cecil; she was thus the granddaughter of the 2nd Marquess of Salisbury and the niece of Queen Victoria's Prime Minister. Her younger brother, Arthur, was also to be Prime Minister. Sister and brother had very similar calm, oval faces, with serious eyes and a melancholy uplift to their mouths. A good deal of their childhood was spent in the mellow splendour of Hatfield House, but the place all Balfours loved most was the 'kingdom', Whittinghame in East Lothian. Here Nora was happy, gardening, riding and walking in the hills; it was later written of her that natural beauty had much more power to move her than the painted kind.

James Balfour died when Nora was eleven years old. Arthur would, when he came of age, inherit everything, and in the meantime had to be educated, first at Eton, then at Trinity College, Cambridge. Nora, equally inevitably, stayed at home to become the constant companion of her widowed mother. Fortunately, though Blanche Balfour apparently spent a great deal of her time in bed, she was of a lively intelligence and was interested in liberal happenings, especially the movement for the higher education of women and the work of Emily Davies. Nora was a naturally brilliant mathematician, and she worked and studied hard; her other interest, sparked off by her brother Arthur and his undergraduate friends, was in psychical research. But by the time she was in her early twenties her full-time occupation was running Whittinghame, managing the house and garden and entertaining Arthur Balfour's Cambridge friends as well as the select army of cousins and guests who were allowed to invade the 'kingdom' and share the clan secrets during long holidays: '... such guests had to be initiated into Balfour customs and pastimes ... the family newspaper in holiday time ... they must be shown the sacred spots or conducted about the more precipitous parts of the grounds by night.'[8]

Arthur Balfour came into his inheritance in 1869, the same year that Emily Davies and Barbara Bodichon set up their college at Hitchin; Nora expressed great interest but was firmly tied to home. She had, though, met Arthur's brilliant Cambridge colleague, Henry Sidgwick, and discovered her interests were shared by him. In May 1872 Blanche Balfour died. Almost two years later, Nora sent £500 to Henry Sidgwick's Newnham College appeal fund, and on

4 April 1876 she married Henry Sidgwick at St James's, Piccadilly, in London.

For some time before her marriage Nora had been helping Anne Jemima Clough in Cambridge. The appeal from the Newnham Foundation was successful enough to allow Henry Sidgwick to appoint Basil Champneys (another Trinity man and his fellow member of the Savile Club) to design the first building. Miss Clough and the students had grown out of their beloved Merton Hall, and she was glad to have Newnham Hall to move into in the summer of 1875. The new college was built on two and a half acres of flat fields west of the River Cam and Queens' College, across what is now Queens' Road. At first Newnham Hall was on its own, but it soon had Ridley Hall and Selwyn College as neighbours. Nothing symbolizes the differing outlooks on education more than the architectural styles of Ridley and Newnham (or for that matter Girton and Newnham) – Ridley is severe, angular, ecclesiastical Gothic; Newnham has the prettiest buildings in Cambridge, of warm red bricks with curly gables, carved swags and white-painted windows. Champneys had adapted his Board School traditions (they were to be 'beacons of enlightened learning into city suburbs'[9]) and mixed them with curly gables adapted from Blickling Hall in Norfolk, to produce Queen Anne-style buildings of 'sweetness and light'.[10]

As a personality, Champneys fits perfectly into the Newnham circle. He thought of himself as a literary man; he was a close friend of Coventry Patmore, as well as an artist, which gained him his friendship with Sidney Colvin, Director of the Fitzwilliam Museum at that time. Champneys had adopted the Queen Anne style, which was to become the high-point of the country houses of the Arts and Crafts movement in the hands of Ernest Newton and Edwin Lutyens within the following thirty years. That he did so for Newnham was especially appropriate, for he established exactly the atmosphere of an English country house of liberal persuasion, where the female half of the population could be allowed the time and the tolerance to escape from under the black bombazine skirts of the Widow of Windsor. Inside, Newnham was light, airy and comfortable. Outside, Anne Jemima made the garden in the rather Victorian way that was familiar to her, with serpentine paths among shrubs, a croquet lawn, blossoming trees and a young medlar in memory of Merton Hall. It was this remarkable lady, who in her happiness was forever exhorting her charges to 'beautify their home places', who caught the first air of William Robinson's garden revolution and established the idea of a garden as essential to a women's college.

Anne Jemima reigned happily at Newnham through the 1880s decade; from her window she watched the building of Champneys's second hall, now Sidgwick Hall, which was finished in 1880, and saw Mr Gladstone plant an oak tree in front of it seven years later. By that time Champneys's third building, to be named Clough Hall in her honour, was well under way. This was, and still is, a place to enchant everyone who sees it: it is a long building, two-thirds of it being the residential hall with a façade strongly reminiscent of both Blickling and Hatfield (both the work of Robert Lyminge), and the remaining part being the dining hall where, as David Watkin points out, Champneys has played somewhat irreverently with the 'high table oriels' of medieval colleges by using full-height, white-painted oriels to light the tables of both the fellows and the students.[11]

Newnham College, as illustrated in *The Builder* of 8 June 1889, now possessed an imposing L-shaped group of buildings, facing on to a parklike green, dotted with trees and drifts of wild and garden flowers. But it was not quite so idyllic as the artist's impression makes out, for this 'garden' was crossed by a public road, with the first building, now Old Hall, on the opposite side to the rest. Henry and Nora Sidgwick had to put in considerable effort in terms of persuasion and financial support (for there is nothing that touches the nerve of English democracy quite as provocatively as denying the public a right of way) to rid the garden of Newnham Lane and construct, to the north of the Newnham land, Sidgwick Avenue, complete with lime trees, which they paid for and saw opened in 1893. To celebrate, Champneys built the Pfeiffer Arch as the main entrance to the college on the site of the old lane, with wrought-iron gates wreathed in flowers and fruit and dedicated to the memory of Anne Jemima, who had died in February 1892.

The enchanting Clough Hall and the memorial gates wreathed in her favourite sunflowers are Anne Jemima's tangible memorials. But she left behind also the steadying influence of her philosophy of unselfishness and good-humoured devotion; she was one of the greatest of the unsung heroines of women's rights. She had exerted benevolent control on the college from the start; for present purposes, she had exercised her keen interest in gardening (behind the laboratory she kept pigs, as garden essentials) and enthused all her students about the value of a garden of their own – or just a window box if they were confined to city life. The only likeness of her in old age shows a strong, square face with a generous mouth and a gaze steady enough to sink a battleship; all topped with a frippery of lace over severe white hair.

Anne Jemima had brought her nephew and niece, Arthur Hugh Clough's children, to Cambridge: Arthur junior had taken a Double First in Classics and Moral Philosophy at Trinity, and Blanche Athena was on the staff of Newnham. She was a young lady of action, and after her aunt's death it was she who took the garden in hand. She consulted the landscape gardening firm James Backhouse of York and set them to work gravelling entrances and planting hedges along the college's Sidgwick Avenue frontage, while she sought the Garden Committee's approval of Backhouse's plan for the main garden and persuaded the committee to vote her £750 to spend on the project. Less than three years later, for the February Commemoration of 1895, and for under £1,000 all told, Newnham had a fine neat garden. The buildings were all trimmed with beds of briar roses, irises, jasmines and pinks, and connected by straight gravel paths. When the path left the end of Clough Hall it changed its character and snaked around a large area of western lawn to end at a mound, on which sat a telescope in a small observatory, a gift to the college. Around this mound were amoebic beds of purest landscapery, dotted with young plants. The serpentine and amoebas came directly out of the landscapists' bible of the day, Henry Milner's *The Art and Practice of Landscape Gardening*, which had been published in 1891; nothing was said, but it was clear that Blanche Athena had got it right around the buildings but wrong when she let the landscape gardeners have their head – the amoebic beds did not stay long.

Even if not quite in harmony with the Queen Anne buildings, at least Newnham's garden was organized and everyone could walk dry-shod. It would soon mature, and in the meantime, the college got on with its proper business. Nora Sidgwick had succeeded Anne Jemima as Principal; her husband was Professor of Moral Philosophy at the University, and they took up residence in small, white-painted Morris-type rooms over the Pfeiffer Arch. Mrs Sidgwick, now nearing her fiftieth birthday, had matured into a distinguished, even awesome figure, at least the equal of her Balfour brothers, Arthur and Gerald, who were her frequent visitors. The Sidgwick marriage was a partnership of perfect devotion and compatibility; Henry and Nora shared the twin causes of women's education and (perilously) psychic research (they were joint founders of the Society for Psychical Research). It was risky to admit it in Cambridge circles, but Nora did have an other-worldliness about her, which formed a remarkable duality with her solid academic achievements and scientific abilities. Her anti-philistinism, and this spirituality – Balfour characteristics which made Arthur the darling of the Souls – were forceful aspects in the development of Newnham, strongly favouring the right atmosphere for a place of study which is reflected in the garden.

The Balfours as a clan were strongly supportive of many of the artist craftsmen who followed William Morris; with Basil Champneys's delightful buildings, Morris interiors and furnishings, an attractive avant-garde mood was established. It was happily adopted by the young: Gwen Raverat, in her famous Cambridge book *Period Piece*, recalls the 'drab' Newnham girls,[12] but they were of course actually all dressed in dark flowing gowns in imitation of Lizzie Siddall and Janey Morris.

As *Period Piece* also so delightfully recalls, the proper business of Cambridge in summer, after Tripos, was tennis, river picnics and garden parties. Gwen Raverat, who was born Gwen Darwin and spent her childhood at Newnham Grange, was taken to Newnham garden parties in the late 1890s. Her father, George Darwin, was on the Council of the college, and her uncle, Frank Darwin, was married to Ellen Wordsworth Crofts, who lectured in English there in the 1880s. The Darwins, of course, did not care about Art and Fashion but were much interested in what was 'right and highbrow'[13] – and in this childhood perception of the battle of the Titans lay the unfortunate outcome of the story of Newnham's garden.

In the meantime, though, more artistic influences are gathering around the ladies of Newnham as they wait in their garden for their guests. Mrs Sidgwick is accompanied by Helen Gladstone, the daughter of William Ewart Gladstone, and Katharine Stephen, a cousin of Virginia Woolf. Miss Mary Ann Ewart, an early bene-factress of the college, has come to Cambridge from her home in Surrey, Coneyhurst on the hills at Ewhurst, which has been finished to the designs of Philip Webb. It is one of Webb's most interesting houses, much admired by the young architect Edwin Lutyens and his patroness and friend Gertrude Jekyll. Miss Jekyll's own house, one of Lutyens's first major country houses, has just been finished at Munstead Wood, a short pony trap jaunt from Ewhurst. She is a distinguished artist and craftswoman, a friend of Sir Edward Burne-Jones and of several pre-Raphaelite artists, and now her writings on gardening are well known. Sir Michael Foster, the Cambridge physiologist and expert on irises, is also her friend. And Nora Sidgwick is now almost her relation – for, with much encouragement from his 'Aunt Bumps', Edwin Lutyens has married Emily Lytton, the younger sister of Nora's sister-in-law, Betty Balfour. Lutyens, ever mindful of the usefulness of family commissions, is already designing a house for Gerald and Betty Balfour, Fisher's Hill on Hook Heath near Woking, which will be finished in 1900, with its Jekyll garden, and will become the headquarters of the Balfour clan. Finally, even Blanche Athena is becoming prey to this web of garden intrigue; her brother Arthur has bought some land at Burley in the New Forest and has built two houses, one for himself and his wife, Eleanor, and one for his mother and Blanche Athena when she is down from Cambridge. He is a clever amateur architect, faithful to Arts and Crafts inspirations, and will continue to build in Burley village, large and small houses of warm red brick or roughcast, with hipped roofs and dormer windows, and white board overhangs – pretty houses, which will attract just the kind of independent, talented ladies of private means who will choose Miss Jekyll to design their gardens. (This one small village acquired four Jekyll gardens, entirely because of the Clough connection.)

Blanche Athena clearly took a great interest in Gertrude Jekyll's garden theories. For one thing, the straightforward and practical style in which they were written was far more attractive to a busy intelligence than the flowery vapid prose of so many gardening books of the period. Gertrude Jekyll *was* the intelligent woman's gardener. In 1900 she published her second book, *Home and Garden*, which is full of encouragement for a would-be gardener with a new house, who needs guidance as to 'Things Worth Doing'.[14]

The desire to rid their garden of its landscaping tendencies and replace them with mixed borders of cottage flowers and old roses, with arbours and pergolas for sitting and strolling beneath, may have infiltrated to the ladies of Newnham, but it was a sad event that encouraged them to start. Professor Sidgwick died in 1900 at the age of only sixty-two; the small, rather dapper figure of this immensely distinguished philosopher who had carried their cause into the corridors of power was to be greatly missed in the garden he had loved so much. It was agreed that some sort of garden memorial should be devoted to him, and that the whole garden needed a fresh look. Miss Mary Ann Ewart knew just the architect: a young man of perfect Arts and Crafts integrity, a pupil of John Dando Sedding (who had written *Garden Craft Old and New*, published in 1891, the first book referring Arts and Crafts gardens back to seventeenth-century origins), Alfred Powell, who was building a cottage called Long Copse next door to Miss Ewart's house at Ewhurst – and she asked him to have a look at Newnham's garden.

Part of the Arts and Crafts way of doing things was to draw a splendid and attractive plan of one's intentions. Alfred Powell's plan for Newnham's garden is still in the college archives – it is a delightful water-coloured layout which shows how he intended a complete conversion to Arts and Crafts principles. He has straightened every path and made every one into a vista, duly closed with some kind of ornament or feature. Then he has taken the halls of residence and given each a distinctive garden connection: Old Hall's sacred garden, designed by Anne Jemima Clough, was allowed to keep its curving paths but was given a square pool surrounded by wisteria trellis and a rondel of poles, iron hoops and chains for roses in pure Jekyll fashion; in front of Sidgwick he made a sunken rose garden with four beds around a circular pool; a pergola covered the entire length of the path in front of Clough Hall, and in front of the latest of Champneys's buildings, Kennedy Hall, finished in 1905, he put a parterre of flower beds around a sundial. When it was decided that a last building, Peile Hall, would 'close' the rectangular garden at its western end, he realigned the path from the 'front' door to the Observatory Mound, which was now in a hedged square.

It was a thoroughly organized design – but it contained two rather shocking signs of disrespect, the straightening of Anne Jemima's sacred paths, and the screening of the whole frontage of Champneys's finest building, Clough Hall, to allow its acceptance by the Garden Committee. They agreed to the parterres in front of Kennedy, in a slightly simplified version, and allowed the sunken rose garden in front of Sidgwick Hall to be built as it was designed. The circular pool still bears the inscription that Nora Sidgwick chose to be carved around its rim: 'The daughters of this house to those that shall come after them commend the filial remembrance of Henry Sidgwick.' I think it is not one of the least of Newnham's attributes that it was a women's college founded by a man.

In 1906 Blanche Athena had double borders laid out beside the path from Clough Hall's garden door, and she supervised their planting according to her Jekyll studies: she chose blue, yellow, cream and silver as colours to harmonize with the rich warm brick of the building, Jekyll mixes from *Home and Garden*, including Jerusalem sage and verbascum, gypsophila and globe thistle (this is a treasured giant of the border still), lyme-grass (*Elymus arenarius*), santolina and catmint, with dwarf lavenders and sisyrinchium, peonies (the yellow *P. mlokosewitschii*), creamy lupins, blue delphiniums, yellow achilleas and heleniums – a perfect Jekyll planting plan, like those she was doing at the time for Lutyens's gardens.

Blanche Athena was now a thoroughly converted gardener and we may imagine how her knowledge was growing. In 1910 at Christmas, Nora Sidgwick decided to retire as Principal; significant commemoration of her services to the college was obviously in order and a committee was formed to launch an appeal. The appeal letter sent out to all Newnhamites suggested either endowing a research fellowship in psychology or physics or carrying out garden improvements, and it is interesting that the replies voted 3:1 for the garden. £1,000 was collected. Mrs Sidgwick agreed that the memorial should be in the garden, and on this auspicious occasion there was only one person to ask – Gertrude Jekyll.

Her plans for Newnham, lovely blue and beige-washed water-colours, show a thoroughly sensible layout. The brief was that the college intended to move the Observatory from its Mound where the trees now obscured the sky; the Mound would remain and would need to be included in a design for the whole western end of the garden now that Peile Hall was finished. Miss Jekyll suggested a garden pavilion on the Mound, with its twin placed farther south; the path between the two would be hedged in yew scallops, making sitting carrels for studying and reading. Though by now her travels were quite a rare occurrence, she must have come to Newnham, for she has tied her planning neatly into the rest of the garden with hedges and shrub planting – nothing complicated, nothing demanding constant labour. It is a design of masterly balance.

Her friends at Newnham were undoubtedly delighted, and Blanche Athena's Garden Committee agreed to spend most of Mrs Sidgwick's Commemoration Fund on this scheme – in the vote, everyone but George Darwin agreed. Never overly hasty, this December 1911 meeting thus gave 'general approval' but asked for further details of the proposed pavilions.

The timing is very important. In Miss Jekyll's papers there is a sheet of faint sketches for the pavilions, drawn by Edwin Lutyens. She, most emphatically, would not have attempted such architectural design, and the pair of hexagonal pavilions with domed roofs sound very much like his suggestion. He knew Mrs Sidgwick well, he was related to her by marriage, and he would have thought it in character to give her suitably elegant memorials. It seems likely that the decision of the December meeting at Newnham was not relayed to Munstead Wood until after Christmas, and by early January Lutyens was frantically making ready for his first trip to Delhi. Did he then disappear for three months so that there was no hope of getting an exact drawing? Did Mr Darwin grumble that Lutyens was much too famous now and they couldn't afford him? Did 'Aunt Bumps' say apologetically that she couldn't worry him about such little things for a good while now? I doubt that the last is true, for Lutyens always found time to do little things for his friends in the midst of his greatest schemes. There is a further complication, in that the pavilions do have a look of Delhi about them – he was immersed in the study of vernacular Indian architecture as the preliminary to his plan for Viceroy's House, and they do resemble the *chattris* that decorate this building. But all my surmises go unanswered. There is no clue in the minutes of the Garden Committee, nor in the archives in general, on the subject of the scheme during the summer of 1912; at the end of the year the Roll, the annual report of the College, announces that 'after much consideration of plans' a design by Mr Watson of Edinburgh had been accepted. Mr Watson? Who was he?

Walter Crum Watson of 50 Queen Street, Edinburgh, was an Oxford MA (in this web of Trinity connections) and sometime pupil of the architect Alfred Waterhouse, who was working at Cambridge at the time. He was of indeterminate age, and though seemingly the possessor of considerable talents and qualities, these were not related to the garden arts. The certain fact about him is that he wrote a comprehensive study, *Portuguese Architecture*, which was published in 1908.[15] He spent three springs in Portugal, making an exhaustive tour of the remotest hillside monasteries and palaces, but never a mention of a garden. He does pay detailed regard to the importance of the use of glazed tiles, but there is not one illustration of the wonderful tiled courts and fountains he must have found at Queluz and Fronteira. He must have spoken the language like a native to make these thorough researches, and his interests are noted as languages, architecture and flowers. But did this qualify him to design a garden in Cambridge?

Unfortunately it did not, for his plan was an amateur affair which borrowed Miss Jekyll's ideas but destroyed all her intended balance and harmony. The Mound was now to be contained within a wall of seven unequal sides, with four paths radiating from a central plinth in a rather hit-or-miss relationship with other paths. At some off-alignment to the south a small hexagonal pavilion was set among lilac-hedged squares, and the rest of the western garden was lined out with fruit trees. The nicest idea, one which was stolen from Miss Jekyll anyway, was a nut walk parallel with the southern boundary of the garden. The last aberration was a hideous, crazy-pattern rose bed opposite Peile's front door.

Fortunately, few of these ideas were carried out exactly as Mr Watson drew them, and Newnham's garden as it is now combines features from both Mr Watson and Miss Jekyll. Some of the orchard trees were planted and so was the nut walk. The hedged squares exist, rather in Miss Jekyll's style, and made, luckily, with yew and not lilac; Mr Watson designed a four-sided summerhouse which has mellowed into a pleasant feature of the garden (but hardly has the glamour of a Lutyens pavilion), and there is a path connecting it to the Mound, now contained within a wall and surmounted by a columnar sundial which is surrounded by a garden seat in marble. This is Mrs Sidgwick's memorial – memorial indeed, and a little funereal in materials and appearance, considering it was erected in 1914 and she had twenty-two more years to live. And perhaps *Portuguese Architecture* accounts for its somewhat baroque appearance, which is not in harmony with the personality of its subject. Does this not sound like Darwin rightness triumphing over art and sensitivity? At the foot of the column, on a stone plaque set into the east face of the plinth, carved in beautiful Gill Perpetua lettering, is an inscription 'In proud and grateful remembrance' of Mrs Sidgwick's years as Principal, 1892–1911. This is one of Eric Gill's rare Cambridge works and at least of a quality to match its subject.

The letter to subscribers announcing how their money had been spent was sent on 10 September 1914; Newnham's garden became one of so many completed in the nick of time, just before the war. It was a triumphant statement for the value of a garden as a cultural influence upon life, a correct balance for things of the intellect, exactly as Anne Jemima Clough and Nora Sidgwick believed. It was also, at the time, a very definite statement about the right of women to be in Cambridge, at the University, taking their proper place. Of course, the war was to be the winning of their cause in many respects; in 1921 the University of Cambridge passed a 'grace' giving authority for degrees to be granted to women.

Nora Sidgwick lived in a house in Grange Road, beside Newnham's garden, until she finally retired to the Balfour redoubt, Fisher's Hill at Woking. On her eightieth birthday the college sent her a bouquet of 'the finest flowers Cambridge could invent' from their garden; she died at Fisher's Hill in 1936. Blanche Athena Clough remained at Newnham until 1939, when she too retired to her own home and garden in the New Forest.

THE remarkable thing about Newnham College's garden, which has been faithfully maintained until this day, is that the philosophy behind its making was so completely in tune with the philosophy of the place and time that it is a perfect expression of Arts and Crafts gardening ideals. The collective college mind, the Fellows, the Council and the Garden Committee, seem to have been comfortably inspired by the Misses Clough and Eleanor Sidgwick; without this harmony no garden could have been created.

Oxford and Cambridge are, of course, full of lovely and interesting gardens, but Newnham is unique in its expression of the mood of its founding years. There are other college gardens that are exquisitely serene or fascinating because of the famous figures they have sheltered,[16] but the fiercely guarded groves of academe rarely allow outside influences to penetrate the thick stone walls – and when they do, they treat them with a cavalier disdain. At Emmanuel College, Cambridge, John Codrington has achieved a large part of his clever design for the box-edged triangles in the Kitchen Court, carefully fitted in between the desire-line paths of undergraduate feet, but the Fellows will not allow his coloured gravels and glossy anthracite chippings as the (correct) foils for the herbs – presumably for fear of a coal chip in the mint sauce. But he does better than Dame Sylvia Crowe, whose designs for Downing College, called for twenty years ago, are still being 'considered'.

Occasionally, despite certain collegiate reserve, gardeners do emerge from within college life. Professor Nevill Willmer, a Fellow at Clare College, was absorbed in the psychology of colour perception and applied his interest to the borders of the college's Fellows' Garden, where his spectacular red border and blue and yellow beds are still carefully tended. John Raven, Senior Fellow at King's College, made a smaller impact (now difficult to see) on his college garden, but his own garden at Docwra's Manor, Shepreth, just outside Cambridge, is an eloquent tribute to the interests of an ultra-civilized mind. John Raven was a classical philosopher and a botanist, though he regarded himself as an amateur in the latter status. He was a passionate collector of hawkweeds, a botanical artist (an interest inherited from his father, Canon Charles Raven), and is best known for the *Mountain Flowers* volume of Collins's inspired New Naturalist Series (1965).[17] The 'professional' half of the partnership for the book was his co-author, Dr Max Walter, Curator of the University's Herbarium; but John Raven's introduction is a good insight into his passionate interests – especially in the mountains of Scotland. But then this philosopher-plantsman had such a wide range; from 1974 until his death in 1979 he was Honorary Curator of the Broughton Collection of botanical prints and drawings at the Fitzwilliam Museum (see pages 109–10). In his very 'lowland' garden at Docwra's Manor, still looked after by his wife Faith, there is a very definite impression of peace, an awareness that a philosophical strength has prevailed. The garden produces consoling pictures – sprays of white rock roses, the white looking severe against an interesting grey stone paving; a willow-leaved pear which has been allowed to layer itself into the stones and drape around a stone sink, where pink saxifrages have been joined by a pink columbine. Docwra's Manor garden is full of rare and mysterious plants too, and a predominance of many kinds of euphorbia and peony – it is a discretionary treasure house in which the mind of its most interesting maker is revealed.

Oxford has a wonderful Jekyll figure in Miss Annie Rogers,

educational pioneer and feminist of St Hugh's College, whose story is described beautifully by Mavis Batey in *Oxford Gardens*.[18] Miss Rogers won an exhibition to Worcester College in 1873 by not revealing her sex, and was, of course, not allowed to take up the place. Quite understandably she came out fighting and, rather on a par with Henry Sidgwick at Cambridge, was a moving force in getting women accepted at Oxford; her gardening enthusiasm, however, was a more private recreation, and she took St Hugh's garden in hand as her personal fief (to which no one objected), making it into the finest of 1930s gardens in all of Oxford.

Apart from St Hugh's, the chief gardening college at Oxford seems to be St John's, which in successive Keepers of the Groves has produced some very eminent gardeners. The famous Bidder Rock Garden was made by Dr Henry Jardine Bidder (1847–1923), Vicar of St Giles and college bursar among many other roles. The rock plants were brought back by travelling Fellows at Dr Bidder's instigation; Mavis Batey recalls a delightful picture of the rock garden as a haven for 'lovers of the minutiae of Nature in Pre-Raphaelite art':

The dainty flowers nestling in the local coral ragstone had a bejewelled effect ... 'the outline of whorl-leaf of the tiny, delicate, filigree-like plants that cling to the grey stone, and the thousand points of colour, white and grey, mauve and heliotrope, orange and brown, with which it is spangled' was seen as a new garden art.[19]

Professor Geoffrey Blackman was a subsequent Keeper of the Groves who typifies a much more modern, scientific approach to gardening. His subject was what was known between the wars as 'rural economy', and which we call ecology. Professor Blackman symbolizes the 'triumph of nurture over nature',[20] a scientist's domination through understanding. He refused to live in Oxford because he could not grow his beloved rhododendrons, and made his woodland garden at West Wood House, on the edge of Bagley Wood (owned conveniently by St John's), where he worked hard rearing eastern treasures. Professor Blackman's view was that gardening should reflect man's adventurous spirit. He was a great admirer of Frank Kingdon-Ward, and – with the help of massive injections of leaf-mould from Bagley Wood – it was the Kingdom-Ward rhododendrons, primulas and Himalayan poppies which he grew. In 1976 the Blackmans moved into their own house, Wood Croft, again at Bagley Wood, and their plants went with them. The Professor's second garden was a triumph more of understanding than of science; he had accomplished so much for the world (he pioneered the use of sunflowers as oil-seed crop, researched selective weed-killers and went to the United States to advise on the revival of the Vietnamese landscape after the war), and all this experience was poured into his beloved new woodland garden in a remarkable way. 'The Professor set it going ... he put the plants in their rightful places, where they wanted to be,' explains Mr McDermott, the week-end gardener at Wood Croft, 'and it's now so relaxed that I am quickly led towards any plant that is unhappy. The Professor set the clock ... what he's done is going to last for ever.'[21]

Professor Blackman died in 1980; the present Keeper of the Groves at St John's, restorer of Dr Bidder's rock garden, biographer of Alexander the Great, gardening correspondent of *The Financial Times*, author of *Variations on a Garden* and *Better Gardening*, is, of course, Robin Lane Fox.

The academic groves, the villages around Cambridge, the leafy roads of donnish North Oxford, must conceal any number of eminent gardeners. Even in these days of rather less leisured academic lives, there are many who pour their arts, philosophies and sciences into their gardens. Perhaps this is one of the truest fascinations of gardening – that a garden can be all things to all disciplines and no matter how many gardens are made, they will all be different. But these personal gardens are just a particularly rich strand of everyone's secret gardening; Newnham College's garden remains unique, as the socially apt expression of a collective philosophy in tune with the arts and sciences of that distant day.

5

The Lords Fairhaven

IN 1931, at the height of his fame, Sir Edwin Lutyens returned to his youthful occupation of designing little lodges in Surrey. Between finishing off Imperial New Delhi and starting the Roman Catholic Cathedral of Christ the King in Liverpool, he designed two pairs of pavilions that mark the boundaries of the Magna Carta meadow at Runnymede. These pavilions guard the public road through the meadow and they are fittingly monumental: little masterpieces in soft red brick and finely finished Portland stone. All the passer-by needs to know is cut on to the faces of the stone gate piers (with no gates) which stand beside the lodges:

'In Perpetual Memory of Urban Hanlon Broughton 1857–1929 of Park Close Englefield Green in the County of Surrey sometime Member of Parliament These Meadows of Historic Interest on 18 December 1929 were gladly offered to the Nation by his widow Cara Lady Fairhaven and his sons Huttleston Lord Fairhaven and Henry Broughton.'

In this story Urban Broughton's memory is necessarily only brief. He was a bright young English civil engineer who sought his fortune in America and found it. He married Cara Leland Rogers in 1895, and they had two sons, Huttleston, born on 31 August 1896, and Henry, born on 1 January 1900. Broughton was a staunch supporter of the Conservative Party; after he returned to England he was MP for Preston during the First World War, and he bought Lord Brownlow's mighty Ashridge estate in Hertfordshire and gave it to the Party. He was awaiting the conferment of his barony when he died suddenly, aged seventy-two. As the title had been gazetted, his widow became a baroness and his elder son, Huttleston, became the 1st Lord Fairhaven.

Lady Fairhaven and her sons were all to be great gardeners. Anglesey Abbey near Cambridge, where Lady Fairhaven lived until her death in 1939, has the grandest garden made in England this century, and it became a further bequest to the nation upon Huttleston Fairhaven's death in 1966. Henry Broughton, the 2nd Lord Fairhaven, was quite a different kind of gardener: he loved all flowers, real and painted, and has left us an enchanting, almost secret water garden in Norfolk, and his outstanding collection of paintings, prints and drawings of flowers, which he bequeathed to the Fitz-william Museum in Cambridge. These brotherly paradoxes express different sides of the strong personality of Cara Fairhaven. Who, then, was she?

THE Fairhaven title acknowledges a small town in Massachusetts, one of a nest of old whaling settlements on Buzzard's Bay, sheltering behind Cape Cod and Martha's Vineyard, watching the ferries ply to Nantucket. Once upon a time, in the 1840s, a Fairhaven boy named Henry Huttleston Rogers set out to make his fortune in the way boys do, by delivering newspapers. When he left school he worked on the railway, saved hard, and at twenty-one, with 600 dollars in his pocket, left for the Pennsylvania oilfields. There he invented and patented a vital piece of machinery for separating naphtha from crude, and by the time he was thirty-four years old he and his invention had been taken over by the Rockefellers' Standard Oil. At the age of fifty Henry Huttleston Rogers was vice-president of Standard Oil, driving the twenty oil, gas, steel, coal, transport and investment companies towards vast profits and titanic anti-trust battles with the US Government. He was known, to his enemies and victims, as 'Hell-Hound' Rogers, when he wasn't being called 'a fiend of money-hunger' or a rattlesnake.[1]

To his family and friends his image was equally vivid. In 1862 he had married a Fairhaven girl with a kind, round face, named Abbie Palmer Gifford. They had four daughters, one of whom died very young, and a son; Rogers was a generous and kind father. The family kept a lovely house in Fairhaven, with others on Long Island[2] and in Manhattan; they spent summer holidays in Europe and winter ones in the Bahamas, even though Rogers himself was most usually found at his desk at 26 Broadway. He was a charming, considerate host, a wonderful storyteller and a loyal friend; he had a benevolent interest in both homoeopathy and psychiatry as cures for the ills of those he loved. His indulgence to his native town was fatherly: he gave Fairhaven paving and street lighting as well as the more usual memorial buildings. In 1936 Cara Fairhaven gave Fort Phoenix, a civil war fort, to the town as a park, in final memory of her father. But Rogers finds his most comfortable niche in history for quite another reason; he was the man who saved Mark Twain.

In August 1893 there was a Wall Street crash. One of the 1,000 businesses to go was Twain's publishing company, upon which his never very sound financial security depended. Twain hated money matters; he was profoundly depressed, having struggled to finish *Pudd'nhead Wilson*, and had little faith in his future. His friend Clarence Rice suggested that there was someone who might help, an admirer who read his books because they reminded him of his own childhood. So Twain told his troubles to Rogers at a meeting in a Manhattan hotel one evening in September 1893; the next morning Rogers sent him 8,000 dollars. This was the beginning of a mutually warm friendship which lasted to the end of Rogers's life.

Rogers managed Mark Twain's business affairs as a kind of private hobby; the tact and gentleness with which he handled the feelings of the protective Livy Clemens, Twain's wife, were to his even greater credit. In return Twain graced and entertained parties aboard the *Kanawha*, the fastest steam yacht in American waters, which Rogers bought in 1901 both for commuting from Fairhaven and for taking parties of friends around the Bay shore and the Caribbean islands. Twain was to say of Rogers that he was 'the only man I care for in the world; the only man I would give a *damn* for'.[3] And in 1909, when Rogers died suddenly from a stroke, Andrew Carnegie wrote to Mark Twain: 'Well, his memory will be kept green in your heart and I doubt not history will do him justice because you will take care to record him as your friend in need, showing the real man.'[4]

But Henry Huttleston Rogers's memory is greener than Mr

Carnegie could have known. Like many ruthless businessmen he had another soft spot, for flowers and gardens. He had little time himself, but the interest was passed on to his daughters. The youngest Rogers, Mary, known as Mai, married an Englishman, William Robertson Coe, in 1900 when she was twenty-five. Coe was a successful insurance broker, a naturalized American with a passion for horse racing. The Coes' dream house, with a racing stable for him and a large garden (almost a park) for her, was Planting Fields, overlooking Oyster Bay on Long Island's north shore. The house, in a brain-teasing mix of Gothic/Elizabethan, packed with English oak, Genoa velvets, Spanish brocades and Van Dycks, was completed in 1920. The large garden had been laid out with the help of Andrew Robeson Sargent, son of the great Charles Sprague Sargent of the Arnold Arboretum; it now sports a collection of trees which accords it the status of an arboretum, as well as a fine formal garden alongside the glasshouses where Mai Coe indulged her particular passion for growing camellias.[5] She was the inspiration for Planting Fields, but sadly she did not have long to enjoy her gardening, for she died in 1924, aged only forty-nine.

So it was largely up to her sister Cara. Cara was first married to a man named Bradford Duff in 1890 when she was twenty-three, but her husband died three years later. Two years after that she married the young English engineer who worked for her father in Fairhaven, and with their two young sons the Broughtons returned to England to live in 1912. Their home was Park Close, on the edge of Windsor Great Park, a Gothic pile built at the beginning of the twentieth century and surrounded with rhododendrons and azaleas.

THE Broughtons bought Anglesey Abbey, genuinely medieval and a former Augustinian priory, in 1926. They restored the buildings and planned to plant shelter belts around what was to be the garden, for shelter was much needed in this flat countryside on the edge of the Cambridgeshire fen. Anglesey offered, besides its genuine antiquity, acres of good partridge shooting, nearness to Newmarket and the stud the Broughtons owned, fertile farmland, and a 100-acre canvas on which to make a garden. But it is impossible not to surmise that for Cara Broughton (as she was then) Anglesey presented a memory to compensate for the loss of her younger sister, Mai. For to see Planting Fields and Anglesey today is to see two places, separated by an ocean and 700 years, which have been brought very close in mood, atmosphere and visual appearance, and have an undoubted sisterly inspiration. When her husband died in 1929, Lady Fairhaven was perhaps even more bound to pass her filial duty to her sons.

The three of them began working on Anglesey's garden; in 1932 Henry Broughton married and went to live in Surrey, so it was to be largely Lord Fairhaven who carried out his mother's wishes. He was in his early thirties, ex-Harrow and the Guards, dark, handsome and distant – his portraits leave the impression that being painted was merely another duty in a strictly regulated life. His vigorous personality dominates his creation, so if little can be discerned from his likeness, perhaps more can be discovered from his belongings.

At first glance the Abbey's rooms have the well-known National Trust air of highly polished perfection which eradicates the past so effectively. They seem to offer a fairly standard procession of Bruges tapestries and stone flags, carved and polished oak, well-padded dining chairs and comfortable chintzy sofas, Samarkand rugs, giltwood commodes, Ming vases and expensively tooled leather bindings. But second time around, the amazingly un-English eclecticism of it all exudes from this gathering of *objets d'art et de vertu*, revealing a mind that must have trawled the cellars and sale-rooms of old Europe with a New World energy; the polish is rather more Long Island than National Trust.

Clearly Lord Fairhaven yearned to be an ideal Englishman, with a combination of the virtues of the landed gentleman and his civilized urban counterpart such as never actually existed in eighteenth-century reality. He seemed to pursue this dream life-style with a studious intelligence, and the pursuit shows: the house reverberates with his coats of arms, in Bavarian giltwood with supporting cherubs, in tapestry, on firebacks – and his motto: *Si je puis.*

He courted saints and warriors. St Florian, St Anthony,

St Nicholas, St Christopher, the Baptist and assorted popes, bishops and monks re-populate the Abbey. Along with Prince Rupert's rapier, a sword from Malplaquet field presented to the Duke of Marlborough and a mortar turned into an inkstand, there are further grave discomforts – the Horse Guards in cork, a sabretache turned into a blotter, and a gilt pendulum clock set to swing unnervingly in the window light of the Gallery, precious time turned to a bauble in darkness and light.

Lord Fairhaven liked royalty. He lived with Tudor portraits, Tsar Paul I's bureau, Ch'ien Ling phoenixes from the summer palace in Peking, François I's bronze salamander in flames and the Emperor Napoleon's side table; a place of pride in the living-room is accorded to the Emperor Maximilian's Garter, which rather has the air of being rescued from the soiled linen box by the *valet de chambre*. He clearly liked animals, too: a 2,000-year-old Egyptian cat, a terracotta goat, a silver stag with a collar of precious stones, a sleeping fox, lions, an elephant or two – and, most appealing of all, Queen Victoria's spaniel Dash, painted by Landseer. And here is the nexus of Lord Fairhaven's passions, for so many of the virtues he admired were enshrined for him within the Royal House of Windsor. In a house where the Windsor corridor leads to the Windsor bedroom, Queen Victoria and her connections are much in evidence. To be precise, perhaps more than the people it was their place – or to be very precise, their castle – that won his allegiance. It is hardly surprising that a little boy brought up in America should be so singularly struck by his first views of the real England, when they were of Great Cumberland's statue on Snow Hill and the Long Walk leading to the distant castle, so lately vacated by the Widow herself. What may be surprising is that he carried this Hentyesque vision through life. Anglesey Abbey is crowded with images of Windsor Castle – a collection of 100 paintings, 150 water-colours and drawings and some 500 prints. It is among them, in a gallery especially designed by Professor Sir Albert Richardson in 1955, that you are most likely to find the soul of Huttleston Urban Rogers Broughton.

*

AND what of Huttleston's garden? The faint echoes of the Great Park are perhaps implicit in his impressive statues gazing down long vistas, but in Cambridgeshire the vistas are very flat. Anglesey Abbey is dominated by the atmosphere of the Fens, that countryside of direct dykes and enormous skies, and seemingly of few people but many ghosts. Combine harvesters and tractors roam gigantic fields in convoy, and there is also a feeling that the shades of long-disinherited monks from many ruined abbeys are still calling their Hail Marys. (Or perhaps I have been reading too many novels – Dorothy L. Sayers's *The Nine Tailors* and V. Sackville-West's *Dragon in Shallow Waters*?)

Lord Fairhaven's garden is grand, but it is not a landscape garden in eighteenth-century terms. On his 100 virtually flat acres he raised no Brownian mounds and dug no lake: he has made a very large formal garden, rather French, made up of direct vistas and enclosed spaces. He planted for effect – his appreciation of scale was in total harmony with the landscape and its great, open sky: his trees march in avenues, daffodils sprawl in sheets, hyacinths and roses mass and dahlias sweep like a Grand Duchess's train. Lord Fairhaven thought of grass as one of the greatest assets of the English garden, and his dispositions of grass smooth, grass rough, grass with shrubs, grass with spring flowers, grass sweeping under browsing lines or up to leafy skirts, are one of the definite delights of his garden.

To begin at the beginning. The entrance to the Abbey needs to command attention in this nondescript landscape, and it does this with lions on rusticated gate piers that once marked the entrance to the Port of London Authority. The drive is allowed one fairly purposeful curve through parkland; large chestnuts, beeches and limes stand around like dowagers in crinolines, chased in spring by ribbons of snowdrops, golden aconites or cowslips. Near the house the curve of the drive tightens and the trees are in close company, underplanted with ivy to great effect. At this period (though the trees are older) and in this place, this ground covering is likely to have had its origins in modern landscape planting culled from America. Ivy dappled with light under dark trees is a lovely thing.

The drive bursts into the sunlight of a clean gravelled court;

Anglesey Abbey

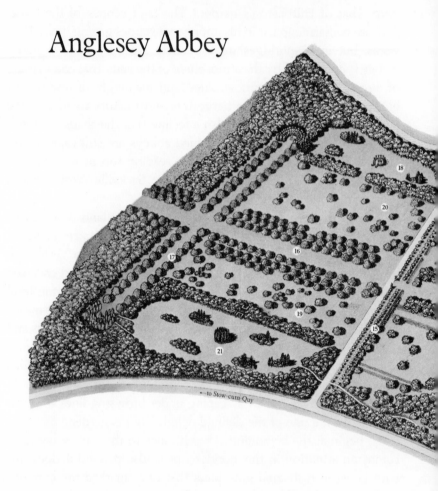

←to Stow-cum-Quy

Key

1 South Front	11 Entrance Front	21 Pilgrim's Lawn
2 South Glade	12 Temple	22 Narcissus Garden
3 Hyacinth Garden	13 Emperors' Walk	23 East Lawn
4 Dahlia Garden	14 Pinetum	24 Wrestlers' Lawn
5 Herbaceous Garden	15 Jubilee Walk	25 Rose Garden
6 River	16 Coronation Avenue	26 Monk's Garden
7 Quarry Pool	17 Cross vista	27 Lode Watermill
8 Arboretum	18 Temple Lawn	28 Visitor's Centre
9 Lime Avenue	19 Specimen trees	including
10 Spring Garden	20 Specimen trees	Information Room

Areas **24**, **25** and **26** are p

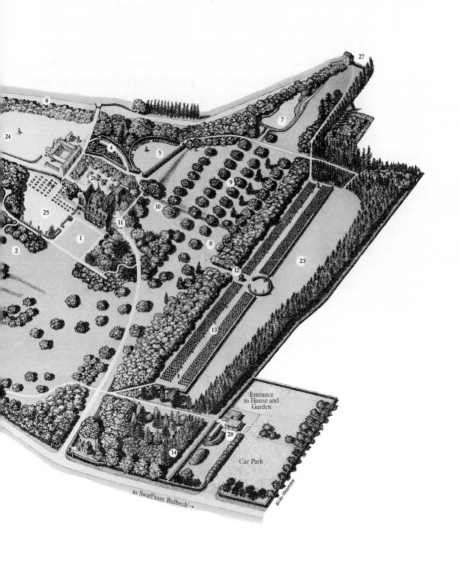

Entrance
to House and
Garden

Car Park

to Swaffham Bulbeck

Eric Thomas

the only decorative planting to catch the eye is an immaculately espaliered pear on the gable end of the former Chapter House. The Chapter House and Monks' Common Room remain from the old Abbey and sit at right angles to one another, with the new entrance porch in between: these old stones do have a mottling of age, but they have been so beautifully manicured as to give an impression of supreme good health. Beyond them the Abbey rambles away, partly Jacobean manor house, but now mainly Lord Fairhaven's re-modelling of the 1920s and 30s. The way to the garden runs through the house to a small door in the corner of the living-room, which looks out invitingly on to an expanse of billiard-green lawn to the South Glade. The living-room is comfortably Jacobethan, the garden front of the house is sympathetic in age; perhaps it is pardonable to have certain expectations – a vista to a lake, with a classical boat-house? Anglesey does not have this. But this *is* a twentieth-century garden and the neo-Romantics have put flagged and flowered terraces, yew-walled parterres and summerhouses around every manor house. But no, Anglesey presents none of these either. At this point I would like to stand up and repeat that this is a twentieth-century garden, and everyone knows that in our time the old rules have been renewed by re-interpretation; but then I remember Lord Fairhaven's allegiance to the past, and I begin to feel uncomfortable.

The plan of Anglesey is important; it lies on land virtually as flat as paper, so clearly it was conceived on paper. The plan[6] (see pages 102–3) reveals the South Lawn to be almost in the centre of the 100 acres. The enclosed gardens are concentrated around the house. To my immediate right is the Rose Garden, from which the exit leads through the Monk's Garden (planted with spring flowers and cherry trees) to the Dahlia and Herbaceous Gardens and a long walk via the Quarry Pool and the Emperor's Walk taking in the eastern half of the garden. Alternatively, one can cross the South Lawn and turn right to the Hyacinth Garden, an enclosure from which there is no escape except by retracing one's steps back through the trees into the South Glade and taking a long ramble across the larger western end of the garden (here more parklike) via avenues and splendid trees to the undoubted reward of the Temple Lawn. On the plan, Anglesey is a garden where delight exacts a certain stoicism.

It is a large enough garden for complete allegiance to the dictum that particular plantings can be appreciated at their particular season, and that part of the garden need not be looked at when *déshabillé*. The Hyacinth Garden gives an apt demonstration. Ten minutes' quiet stroll from the house – across the South Lawn and through trees, along gravelled paths suitably shrouded – brings you suddenly to the entrance of a hedged room astoundingly bedded out with 4,000 soldierly blue and white hyacinths of uniform height and size and overwhelming scent. The hyacinths offer a fairly unbeatable after-lunch treat in spring and they certainly surprise; but is even this spectacle satisfactory? It would be if it were completely enclosed visually as well as practically, but it is not. There is the tantalizing presence, on the plan and over the hedge, of what is called the Narcissus Garden, but the curious visitor who makes a quick dash around the hedge expecting another sweep of scented flowers finds only a disillusioned stone boy.

In warmer weather the performance is staged in the Rose Garden to the south-west of the house. Here 1,000 bushes of modern hybrids are set out in forty square beds, a single variety to a bed. In both design and planting this garden is interestingly modern in concept. The idea of blocks of square beds for flowers, arranged asymmetrically, comes from the 1930s; it was illustrated by Christopher Tunnard in the *Architectural Review* in 1938, and was possibly seen there by Lord Fairhaven. In rose terms, patchy flowering in this arrangement would be a disaster, so the repeat-flowering modern hybrids, such as 'Peace', 'Talisman' (bicoloured scarlet and gold), 'Silver Jubilee' (pink, peach and cream) and 'Fragrant Cloud' (coral scarlet), are excellent successors to 'Frau Karl Druski' (pure white) and 'Shot Silk'. This Rose Garden is clearly spectacular in conception, and excitingly of the 1930s, but asymmetry requires a sound basis in good design just as much as old-fashioned symmetry, and the Rose Garden enclosure is an unhappily haphazard space; the owner's (inevitable) recourse to classical statuary and vases – exquisite items in themselves – only adds to the discrepancy. Modern sculpture would have been much more harmonious.

The other important garden rooms in Anglesey's make-up are the Herbaceous Garden and the Dahlia Garden. They lie, curved back to curved back, in a rather uncomfortable posture to the north of the house, and are ideally approached from the front court through the Winter Dell. This is a sad place, even in summer, a shaded grove of evergreens, butcher's broom, box and hollies, peopled with strange sad stone monks who stare out of the shadows at the one delightful statue – of an unreachable shepherdess. Why is it that I begin to feel that I, and life, are being made a fool of here in this garden?

The Herbaceous Garden is again a hedged enclosure, in the shape of a generous semi-circle, with a splendid semi-circling border for June and July of delphiniums, peonies, heleniums, lupins, lilies, mallows, campanulas, iris, eryngiums – everything. The planting is splendid, the space is splendid, and in the centre (looking a little at sea) is a Rysbrack statue of the Saxon deity Tuw, who named Tuesday. The border is broken with small sitting bays marked with lead flower tubs which 'are said to be copied from some in the Boboli Gardens'. I grab at the Italian reference, for the same thought is beginning to occur to me. Apparently Lady Fairhaven paid a lot of visits to Italy before she married (remember what an indulgent father H. H. Rogers was) and, apart from the statuary and ornament, Anglesey does resemble Italian ideas of gardening, perhaps difficult to comprehend because they are transferred to flat surfaces.

I turn to Geoffrey Jellicoe's *Italian Gardens of the Renaissance*[7] – which was published in 1925 and could well also have been read by Lord Fairhaven – and the semi-circular shape of the Herbaceous Garden springs from the Villa d'Este plan, as the D shape of the Hyacinth Garden springs from Boboli. But in neither case has the idea been correctly, or fully, understood: in the Hyacinth Garden the eye is allowed to roam outside when the view should be contained by screen planting, and in the semi-circle of the Herbaceous Garden the fact that the entrance and exit are in line across the diameter deflects the sense of arrival the instant one has arrived.

Consequently this is not a settled space, no flowery refuge; one merely takes in the sweep of the flowers, the loneliness of the statue, and the eye and mind race on to the exit and the sparkling white paint of Lode Mill in the distance beyond. I would have liked to have said that this was a clever device for movement through the garden, but a feeling of lack of time to stay in restful contemplation of the lovely border is frustrating rather than enticing. Lord Fairhaven is quoted[8] as realizing that people cannot resist seeing what happens around a curve. That is definitely a modern as opposed to a classical notion, as it implies venturing around the outside, convex, edge of a curve rather than being enfolded in the inner, concave, shape. But however it is done, it is the garden-maker's privilege, having heightened expectation in a garden, to pleasantly surprise. Up until now the surprises at Anglesey, if they have occurred at all, have been rather unhappy.

The Dahlia Garden — on the face of it a brilliantly simple modern concept of a garden with a wide grass walk in parallel with double hedges and a wider border of multi-coloured dahlias — should prove the point; perhaps it will even turn the point to illuminate what have been my misunderstandings so far. The entrance is next door to the Herbaceous Garden, the glimpse of the coloured swathe is fascinating, and the instinct is to follow; half-way round, two lugubrious griffins nudge my left elbow and grin, but I am still hopeful. All the way round, to *what*? Some splendid pool or water curtain, or perhaps an ivy-carpeted ante-room with stone sofas from which to contemplate the dahlias? None of these — merely the beech hedge making a backdrop for an inadequate, unnamed bronze of a faun dangling a bunch of grapes, and a narrow path leading to the back of the old farm buildings!

This intensively gardened part of Anglesey is thus full of frustrations, of sequences that don't follow on, of surprises like damp squibs and attempts at asymmetry that come out as lopsidedness. With some brilliant ideas, and all his resources, it seems such a pity that Lord Fairhaven did not talk to someone who would have assured him that even modern gardens have to consider the old rules.

The rest of Anglesey is perhaps best appreciated as a spectacular pleasure park, rather than as a garden. The trees are splendid: four rows of chestnuts march for half a mile to commemorate the Coronation of 1937, there are further avenues of limes, hornbeams and holm oaks and splendid specimens of cedars, rare oaks, pines and beeches everywhere. On the eastern side of the house is the remarkable Emperor's Walk, originally planted in 1955 with quick-growing spruce which was destroyed in storms in 1979 and has, in 1980, been replanted. The trees are thus interestingly young, the scale of the Walk is suitably heroic, and perhaps here is brought home (it is the last view of the garden that today's National Trust visitors have) the superb quality of the statuary collection that Lord Fairhaven made. A wonderful Diana the Huntress launches one on the walk, passing the twelve marble Roman emperors that give it its name. Looking magnificent in isolation, at spacious intervals, are some of the bronze vases by Claude Balin which were originally copied from Versailles for La Bagatelle's garden by Lord Hertford and brought to England as a gift to Lady Sackville from her adoring Sir John Murray Scott, the inheritor of the Wallace Collection. These vases look so different here from their fellows, set with tumbling violas in the cosy confines of Sissinghurst Castle's garden. And most of the statuary at Anglesey can be seen to be wonderful, and when one accepts its use in un-classical ways perhaps it is enjoyable too.

The one feature of the garden that I have no doubts about at all is the Temple Lawn. This was made in the south-west corner of the garden to commemorate the Coronation of Her Majesty The Queen in 1953. A dozen white columns brought from Chesterfield House in London are arranged in a circle, rising from a green sea of smooth lawn; the circle is hedged in dark green yew, its entrance guarded by two Van Nost lions, the temple occupied by a fine copy of Bernini's *David*. Seen as one breaks from the trees, across the sunlit green, the roofless temple is a triumph, the equal of any of the sublime views at Stowe or Studley Royal. But what was it Edith Wharton wrote? Her words come echoing out of Cara Fairhaven's time: '... two dozen twisted columns will not make an Italian garden.'⁹ It is as though Lady Fairhaven heard that echo and her son has answered it. Add a sense of scale and design and an English lawn to the white columns, and, as Mrs Wharton knew, a very effective garden could be made. The Temple Lawn is thus an apt tribute to the robber baron Henry Huttleston Rogers and his wealth, and he would understand.

Anglesey Abbey was given to the National Trust when Lord Fairhaven died in 1966. His obituary in *The Times* was of the briefest: he was known as 'the shy peer' and he also bequeathed a fund, the Fairhaven Fund, to the Fitzwilliam Museum to buy landscape paintings. His brother, Henry Broughton, became the 2nd Lord Fairhaven, and – on the question of gardening legacy – it seems likely that he reflected the paradoxical half of his grandfather's personality.

Henry Broughton had made his first garden at Bakeham House, Englefield Green, in the 1930s. But whereas Huttleston can only ever be imagined dressed in immaculate tweeds, discussing plans with his agent or viewing labours from his Land-Rover, Henry was a working gardener. He worked long hours in his fifty acres of rhododendron and azalea woods, tending his masses of roses, which he liked in romantic disarray, and his seas of gentians, another particular favourite. In non-gardening weather he worked in the greenhouses with his orchid collection; he was a noted expert and a Royal Horticultural Society judge. In the evenings he studied nursery catalogues and books on orchids and hippeastrums. He never put any of his gardening ideas down on paper, but worked directly on the land. His wife, Diana Fellowes, whom he married in 1932, died five years later, leaving him with a small son, the present Lord Fairhaven. His closest gardening friend was his neighbour, Sir Eric Savill, who was making the Valley and Savill Gardens in Windsor Great Park.

Henry Broughton's love of flowers was part of his love of beautiful objects in general, and led to his collecting first books of flowers, then prints and paintings. There is a nice touch of what Vita Sackville-West called holding 'the graces and the courtesies, Against a horrid wilderness' in that his first purchase was in 1939 – an eighteenth-century painting entitled *A Basket of Flowers*, by Mrs Gartside: the major part of his collection was to be made during – and in spite of – the war. One imagines him, when darkness and the blackout kept him from his real flowers, poring over his exquisite collection of little boxes, all flower-covered, and his miniatures of flowers, and his almost secret collection of drawings. After tending his primulas and lilies by day, he spent his evenings amassing delicate amaryllis, lady's slipper and roses captured by Redouté, Ehret, Ferdinand and Francis Bauer, the Dietsche family, Jan van Hysum and Philip Reinagle and any number of lesser-known but wonderful artists. There were glorious sprays of auriculas and parrot tulips, luscious tumbling bowls of every kind of garden flower, rare and delicate botanical studies of trillium and orchis, the strange and the exotic, *Selenicereus grandiflorus*, the Queen of the Night, and *Hura crepitans*, the West Indian sandbox tree. This breathtaking collection, which Lord Fairhaven left to the Fitzwilliam Museum, Cambridge, came as a surprise: Professor Michael Jaffe, then the Fitzwilliam's Director, wrote of the astonishment of 'the sheer quality and quantity of the drawings, thirty-eight albums of them, and about 900 mounted and boxed ... Scarcely any had been published. They came to us uncatalogued and known very incompletely even to specialists.'[10] Since 1974, the Fitzwilliam has exhibited the Broughton Collection in special sequences chosen by John Raven, Honorary Curator of the Collection until his death in 1979, and subsequently by David Scrase.

But let us return to Henry Broughton and his gardens, for the best is still to come. After the war, he renewed his interest in the Barton Stud at Newmarket and in racing, and decided to move from Surrey to South Walsham Hall in Norfolk. It was derelict after Army occupation, so he restored it, moved in in 1947 and began his second garden.

The land surrounding the Hall was a wilderness, a tangle of fallen trees and brambles through which streams, which should have been ordered channels, found their way to South Walsham Inner Broad. The broad is large, calm and quiet; it is tidal (though sea water has never come beyond Acle Bridge), and boats are allowed to enter but not to stay. There is little to detain the Broadland holiday craft, except the quiet and the great skirted trees around the water's rim, and the birds.

Henry Broughton devoted the rest of his life to his new garden. There was an element of assuaging loneliness, perhaps, in his wartime collecting. He married for the second time in 1953 and his collecting faded away. He bought his last drawing in 1958.

In his garden he worked hard as usual. The jungle was cleared bit by bit, the drainage channels were re-directed, and he planted. He planted endless streams of flowers – primulas, primroses, foxgloves, cyclamen, lily-of-the-valley and lilies. They all settled happily into their natural setting, sheltered by enormous oak and beech trees. He planted many other things in his woodland too, and near the Hall there were lawns and roses and borders, and the orchid houses. Among all this the 2nd Lord Fairhaven worked happily until his death in April 1973. South Walsham Hall and its immediate garden were sold, and are now an hotel, but he had made careful provision for the things he really cared about. With his bequest of flower paintings and the drawings, the Fitzwilliam Museum became, almost overnight, a major European source for such things. To care for his woodland garden he had formed the Fairhaven Garden Trust, under the chairmanship of his son, the present and 3rd Lord Fairhaven, who lives at Anglesey Abbey. The day-to-day management of the South Walsham garden and responsibility for its opening to the public through the summer was given to George Debbage, the successor to Jack, Albert and Reggie Debbage of the South Walsham family who had helped make the garden.[11]

Today Lord Fairhaven's woodland garden grows beautifully: from the neighbouring fields or the broad, it looks like any copse of great trees in this fertile Norfolk countryside. The approach from the small car park is along a wide lawn path beside a field of spinach – or at least it looked like spinach struggling through in late May of 1988, when I visited the garden, hoping to catch one of its special performances.

I turn left from the spinach, down a grassy slope into the wood. The oaks are enormous and gnarled, and sprouting their young leaves of luminous green. George Debbage's guide suggests turning right along the length of the wide Beech Walk to the Broad's edge. I know, this time, what I have come for and am too impatient; I turn immediately left towards the first of the narrow wooden bridges over the water channels, and there they are! Unbelievable crowds of Bartley primulas, some above waist-height, sprouting their cerise and pinky-mauve heads from great clumps of leaves, marching into the leafy distances, lining the path's edge and leaving only a single narrow passage through. Bag and camera have to be lifted high so as not to knock the flowers; they are in full bloom, endless subtle changes of the same cerise tone, with not a clashing violet or orange in sight. I wend my way through them, they give way to great clumps of glossy skunk cabbage, *Lysichitum americanum*) in the water, then they crowd the other bank, this time beautifully mixed with pink sprays of *Gaultheria procumbens*.

The dry path on the further bank is of a completely different character, the air is scented with yellow *Azalea ponticum* and there are some species rhododendrons coming into flower, but it is all delicately done. At ground level there are drifts of hostas, lily-of-the-valley, a wine-dark-leaved primrose, 'Guinevere', and several varieties of hardy geraniums. The path continues northwards and westwards to a farther half of the woodland which is a nature reserve and bird sanctuary – Lord Fairhaven developed a great interest in ornithology, especially in the water birds which come to the small Scotshole Broad in the reserve. But the whole garden contains a rich bird population; this afternoon the cuckoo, which I understand is a shy fellow, is persistently close and really rather raucous (or perhaps there are several of them).

I return across the main bridges over the water, and the second act of the primula performance is even more enchanting. It is all a matter of aspiring flowers, fluttering branches and shafts of light, ever-changing, unreal and *exciting*. Excitement settles into pleasure; laughter is the only way out. I soon realize that everyone in this garden is wreathed in smiles; the primulas have that kind of effect.

I turn to the left back on to the Beech Walk and contemplate the placid green lawn which fronts South Walsham Inner Broad. The expanse of quiet grey water is ruffled by a pleasure cruiser which has nosed its way in, but its occupants can't land; poor mortals, they will never see the primulas. I contemplate the garden further along the quiet path beside the broad, where carpets of primroses and anemones have been in flower. The Great Storm damage which has kept George Debbage and his helpers clearing up all winter and most of the spring is evident here, particularly among the Scots pine. But there is a lot of young planting of trees, done in the late 1970s, and the really beautiful beech trees are safe. White foxgloves cluster around the trunks of middle-aged oaks.

I return the way I came but keep to the waterside path which gives a glimpse of the Hall and a curtain call of primulas among leaves of *Iris pseudoacorus*, beneath a 900-year-old oak they call 'King Oak'. He looks like a king.

This is essentially a woodland turned into a garden. It has all its richness of birds, animals and wild flowers, but it has these extra 'flowery incidents' too; sometimes they are rather more carefully staged than incidental, as now, and as in July when the healthy young stands of *Cardiocrinum giganteum* raise their white lily heads beneath the oaks' heavy green. The garden is placidly beautiful at any time of year, but it has the added magic of camellias, hydrangeas, cyclamen, enkianthus, astilbes – these special attractions, as well as the regular repertory of Nature's performance. Nothing new has been introduced since Lord Fairhaven's time; George Debbage operates a management policy of creatively conserving the effects that Lord Fairhaven intended. Perhaps that is the secret of the serenity of this garden: it is old-fashioned, restrained in plant mixes and delicate in colours and contrasts. And it has the integrity of an ancient and rich woodland, which adds the gift of well-being and peace.

PERHAPS at the last we should be grateful to Henry Huttleston Rogers: his memory is not only green, as Andrew Carnegie had hoped, it is multicoloured. His grandson Henry is twice blessed, for the delights of a most lovely woodland garden, and for the penned and brushed delights of the Broughton Collection in the Fitzwilliam

Museum. And we have Huttleston to thank for Anglesey, preserved as he intended. Would that please him? I wonder. He was an arrogant and proud man, with few friends, and neither house nor garden can escape those traits. He used to haunt Newmarket and Old Burlington Street with one particular friend, Earl Spencer; I think Huttleston Broughton would be happiest of all to know that, in the fullness of time, his old friend's grandson will be the King of England. And then the twin shades of Hellhound Rogers and the man who saved Mark Twain really will be pleased.

6

Christopher Tunnard

NOT every grower of zinnias would jump at the chance to tackle the greening of the Sahara, but so often there is, deep in the gardener's heart, an element of miniature endeavour. In the face of war, over Kent and the world, in 1939, Vita Sackville-West wrote of her private battle to defend her Sissinghurst world, the old and the young, the animals and her garden.[1] For her the war was then very close, threatening the white cliffs of Dover, searing through the sky overhead. For us, the horrid wilderness has relentlessly spread within the last forty years. Is it that those of us born to the sound of war are for ever attuned to distant threats? Certainly few of us with gardening sensitivities can ignore the recklessness of the destroyers of rain forests, makers of African dust bowls and polluters of lakes and seas. Yet all of us, merely by existing and consuming for the last forty years, are implicated in the 'greenhouse effect', the deaths of seals, eagles and hares and the coming of acid rain. Crimes of ignorance and innocence? We puny beings can remain sane only by believing that the battle begins at home. A lovely garden *is* a protest. A diet of pulses and home-grown organic vegetables, a hefty tribute to Friends of the Earth, can further assuage our guilt. Many a young gardener will sacrifice home and all that is dear to fight famine and disease, or to make a career fighting for other people's landscapes. When such idealism is allied to a keen sense for good order and design, it produces a rare creature, a philosopher of landscape, a healer of places, a lone voice in the wilderness. Such a man was Christopher Tunnard.

*

TUNNARD'S name invariably inspires a spark of interest in the eyes of anyone in tune with the gardens and landscapes of this century. In England in the 1930s his was the radical, rasping voice preaching Modernism. He is remembered for one book, *Gardens in the Modern Landscape*,[2] published at the outbreak of war, as he left for his native Canada, and eventually America, never to return. Some people who remember him in the 30s think he would not have had the backbone to continue his crusade; unfortunately the timing of his leaving, the tarbrush tendency which equated him with Benjamin Britten and W. H. Auden and so many other talented leavers, relegated him to distant obscurity from that time. For several reasons Tunnard did appear to wish to keep his two lives, his English life and his American life, quite separate. As far as I know he never returned to England after leaving in 1939; as for his second life, I had to go to America to learn about it.

Christopher Tunnard was born in Canada. Little is discoverable of his early life, except that his father was in the Canadian Navy and that Victoria, Vancouver, seems to have been the home of his childhood and of his education. This education, completed in England, was finished in architecture and planning; the connection may well have been Thomas Mawson, President of the Town Planning Institute and the most eminent figure in the planning world at that time, who had strong connections in Canada and became first President of the Institute of Landscape Architects in London in 1929.

If Tunnard came to London under Mawson's wing, he would have been just nineteen. He was tall, fair, with a pleasant, rather soft face and a great deal of shyness and gentleness – not, it seems, the stuff of rebellion. And yet he must have been highly intelligent, articulate, and angry. He was of the generation, as he soon found out in London, that was born too late for the trenches; he shared that urgent bitterness of his contemporaries who blamed the old guard for the war, and he longed to forget it, to forget the tainted Edwardian afternoon and move into the fresh air and clear daylight that the French architect Le Corbusier promised for the new age. He epitomized the kind of young man for whom the Modern movement was meant; he was comfortable enough to rebel.

Aldous Huxley's *Crome Yellow*, with its scorn of cloddishness and cottagey quaintness, was his kind of book. So, of course, was Le Corbusier's *Vers une architecture*, which appeared in translation in 1927, with its battle-cries: 'Modern life demands, and is waiting for, a new kind of plan, both for the house and for the city' and 'The Plan proceeds from within to without; the exterior is the result of an interior' — 'THE "STYLES" ARE A LIE!'[3] Tunnard prepared himself for taking up Le Corbusier's challenge by studying landscape history (so he could avoid the 'styles') and landscape planning, a kind of green town planning which became the Modern version of the old Garden City movement. Tunnard was one of the very earliest landscape architects to champion this cause.

So there he was, a well-qualified, well-connected member of the newest design profession in London as the 1930s began. What did he see about him? Whatever was going on and important was sure to be in *Architectural Review* ('guide-book, totem and art object' of the age), then in its heyday under the direction of de Cronin Hastings and J. M. Richards. The *Review* reflected, having fostered it, a close association between art and architecture, so that the tenets of the Modern movement were seen moving swiftly into all corners of life. Artists and sculptors moving towards 'Abstract and Concrete' — Ben Nicholson, Barbara Hepworth and Henry Moore in the van — were closely in touch with architects Wells Coates, Amyas Connell and Geoffrey Jellicoe. Painters Paul Nash, John Piper, Edward Wadsworth and Edward Bawden, the sculptor Willi Soukup, the potter Bernard Leach and Ben's younger brother, Kit Nicholson, a brilliant young architect and decorator, all came into Tunnard's ken. Geoffrey Jellicoe was teaching at the Architectural Association School (and tried to persuade Tunnard to join him), and the AA became a Mecca for talented refugees from Europe. Erich Mendelsohn arrived in 1933 and went into partnership with Serge Chermayeff, who had come from Russia at the age of ten, been to Harrow, and married the heiress of Waring & Gillow! Walter Gropius, ex-director of the Bauhaus, came in 1934 and worked with

Maxwell Fry. Their white concrete Modern houses began to appear in England.

But what about the gardens? How could Tunnard apply his talent and art and keep up with this galaxy of talented artists? In his eyes the situation must have seemed confusing and fairly appalling. It is neatly encapsulated for us in an exhibition, sporting the label 'International', which was staged by the Royal Horticultural Society in London in October 1928. 'International' must have meant the Empire, for there was apparently nothing in the exhibition from Scandinavia or Europe, where all the Modern design was going on. The vast array was divided, unequally, into five sections. The first was a predictably lavish historical section, masterminded by *Country Life*'s architectural editor, H. Avray Tipping, with *Country Life* photographs of the glories of Hampton Court, Stowe, Kew, Badminton, Bramham and their kind. But hardly the brave new world.

The second section, organized by Mark Fenwick, noted plantsman and gardener and owner of Abbotswood near Stow-on-the-Wold (largely remodelled for him by Edwin Lutyens), was called 'Garden Planning for Town and Country' and showed the work of the big names of the day: Percy Cane (Boden's Ride at Ascot; Little Paddocks at Sunninghill; and Abbey Chase, Chertsey); Edwin Lutyens (Hestercombe in Somerset and the Moghul Garden to Viceroy's House, New Delhi); Reginald Blomfield (Mellerstein, Berwickshire and Apethorpe); Clough Williams-Ellis (Portmeirion); and some gardens by Thomas Mawson's firm, Lakeland Nurseries. They were, without exception, grand – full of long vistas and layered stones, even crazy paving (not Delhi, of course), with massings of old-fashioned flowers basking in the sunshine of that now vanished golden afternoon. Young Mr Tunnard could only have scoffed! A near redemption came from the architects Darcy Braddell and Humphry Deane, who exhibited a rather restrained water garden for Melchett Court at Romsey as a setting for sculpture by Charles Sargent Jagger and Carl Milles – but then instantly damned themselves into extinction with Craft Cottage at Paston, Norfolk, built in 1926 with thatched eaves and peaks and boiled-sweet window panes, crazy brick paths and creeping cottagey flowers. Very un-Modern.

The exhibition had smaller sections on public parks and sculpture for gardens, and accompanying lectures by H. Avray Tipping, the young Christopher Hussey, a fashionable designer of the crazy paving kind, George Dillistone, and Gertrude Jekyll – though the latter, very stout, very blind and eighty-five years old, was most unlikely to have attended in person.

In Tunnard's eyes Miss Jekyll reigned in obsolete isolation. She took no part in the furore that followed the exhibition, when a group of designers formed the British Association of Garden Architects to remedy the parlous state of garden design. A year later the same people decided that they wanted to do more than gardens, and they changed the name to the Institute of Landscape Architects. Tunnard became an early Associate.

But the weight of the Edwardian afternoon on gardens was going to take a lot of moving. There seemed a soporific spell that could not be broken – or perhaps we did not want it broken: in 1925 one of the most influential leaders of the Modern movement, Professor Peter Behrens, a most eminent German architect, pioneer designer of modern factories and electric kettles, designed (from his atelier in Vienna) England's first Modern movement house, New Ways, at 508 Wellingborough Road, Northampton, for the owner of a famous firm of model engineers, Mr Bassett-Lowke. The house is a shrine – simple, white, flat-roofed, with large, plain windows. Professor Behrens also designed the garden; the plans are highly treasured in the Drawings Collection of the Royal Institute of British Architects[4] – for they really do represent (like the treasures of Palladio and 'Capability' Brown) the touch from Olympus. But I would have thought that the great Professor Behrens, whose factories and kettles are classics of their kind, would have given a little thought to the Modern garden – and, astoundingly, he has not. He has surrounded, in his own hand, his Modern little New Ways with old-fashioned, cute, quaint, kitsch crazy paving!

Young Mr Tunnard was clearly on his own. All these slogans and battle cries that came from Europe, from Le Corbusier, Mies van der Rohe and Bruno Taut, clearly could not reach English

119

gardens; even Frank Lloyd Wright, calling from across the Atlantic
about his houses that grew out of their contours, giving form and
meaning to the natural landscape by their subtle presence, could
not budge the pergolas and terraces of Edwardian taste. Even Oliver
Hill, an older English architect who had won a Military Cross in
the First World War and whom I see as a brilliant exponent of the
tricks of the Modern movement with his white houses, clean steps
and terraces, picture frames and curving drives, must have seemed
too facile in Tunnard's eyes. In 1925 Hill designed both Joldwynds
on Holmbury Hill, an eye-opening Modern movement house and
garden, *and*, in the same village, Woodhouse Copse, thatched and
cottagey with a tiered and terraced dry-wall garden planted by
Gertrude Jekyll.

The landscape and garden arts, far behind as usual, were not even
to be taken seriously in England it seemed. Not surprisingly, but
with great foresight, Tunnard packed his bags and left for where he
could see some real Modern gardens – Europe.

Of what he saw I am by no means certain, but from what he later
wrote, some assumptions can be made. The leaders in French garden
design were the Vera brothers, André and Paul; though Le Corbusier
had inferred their damnation as 'decorative artists' and 'intolerable
witnesses to a dead spirit', the brothers were the best-known garden
designers with anywhere near Modernist thoughts. During the
1920s they made their own garden on a 300 ft × 300 ft × 200 ft
triangle between Rue Quinault and Rue Duigan Trouin in St Germain-en-Laye. The house faced Rue Quinault at the widest end of
the triangle; the rest of the layout seems conventional enough, a
clean arrangement of rectangles, triangles and semi-circles to fit
garden and lawn plots into the site. It is in the detail that the
brothers' very twentyish sense of humour, witty and mocking at
tradition, is endlessly evident: grass triangles of brilliant green,
sharply angled and cut, were edged with white gravel paths, the
box 'parterre' on the rectangular lawn was of immaculate squat
hedges, twice as wide as they were high (i.e. six inches high by a
foot wide – exactly the opposite of the traditional kind) – and this
was succeeded by a layout of white concrete zig-zags, about six

15. Huttleston Broughton, 1st Lord Fairhaven (1896–1966), the chief maker of the garden of Anglesey Abbey. A portrait by A. Christie, 1941.

16. Anglesey Abbey, the garden in the making: setting out in the landscape style, with surveyor's staves for positioning the statues and planting, was a rare sight in gardens of twentieth-century England.

17. Anglesey Abbey, the south-west of the house and part of the rose garden.

18. Planting Fields, Oyster Bay, Long Island, New York, the house built by William Robertson Coe and his wife Mai Rogers, sister of Cara, Lady Fairhaven.

19. Anglesey Abbey, the Temple Lawn: this was made in 1953 from Corinthian columns from Chesterfield House in London, to commemorate the coronation of Queen Elizabeth II. It is one of the most successful features of the garden.

20. Anne Jemima Clough
(1820–92), the first Principal of
Newnham College, Cambridge,
and the inspiration of its
garden.

21. The Newnham staff in the garden in 1896: from left to right they are
E. M. Sharpley, M. Greenwood, A. S. Collier, P. G. Fawcett (seated), Helen
Gladstone, A. Gardner, Mrs Eleanor Sidgwick, H. G. Klassen, I. Freund, M. E.
Rickett, L. Sheldon, M. J. Tuke, Katharine Stephen, E. R. Saunders and Blanche
Athena Clough (seated). From the beginning their garden was an essential
part of the background to college life.

22. The garden of Newnham College, as made in 1895 by James Backhouse of York. The Observatory was presented to the College by Mrs William Bateson, the wife of the Master of St John's College and the mother of Anna and Mary: Anna ran a market garden enterprise at New Milton in Hampshire which was much admired by Frances Wolseley.

23. Bentley Wood, Halland, Sussex, the garden designed by Christopher Tunnard. The plinth was specially built to hold a reclining figure by Henry Moore, which was delivered to the garden in 1938 but subsequently returned when the client, Serge Chermayeff, left for America at the outbreak of war. The sculpture now belongs to the Tate Gallery.

24. St Ann's Hill, Chertsey, Surrey: Tunnard's modern garden theory reduced design to two elements, that of 'prospect' and 'picture'. The 'picture' device is here illustrated in his most famous English garden, made for a house designed by Raymond McGrath in which Christopher Tunnard and Gerald Schlesinger lived briefly before the war.

25. Gertrude Jekyll in old age,
photographed in her Spring Garden
at Munstead Wood, near Guildford in
Surrey.

26. Gertrude Jekyll's workshop, which gives an idea of the range of her
talents. The paintings and photographs are mostly by her, and so is the inlay
work, which survives as a cupboard door in her house. The plan chests
originally held her paintings and garden design drawings; most of the latter
now belong to the University of California at Berkeley.

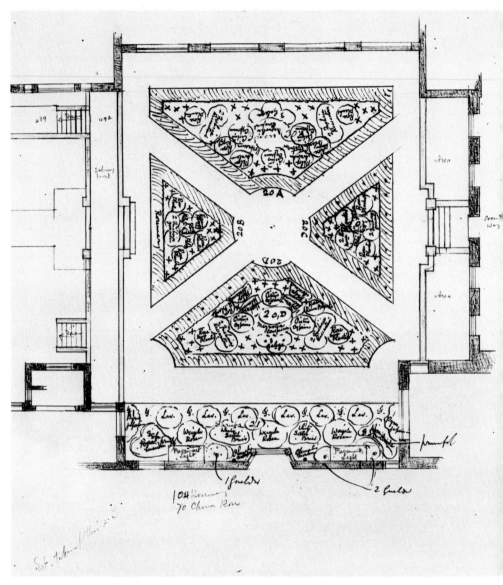

27. The West Rosemary Garden for King Edward VII's Sanatorium, as planned and drawn by Gertrude Jekyll. The small courtyard garden has rosemary hedges surrounding pink China rose bushes, cistus, galega, fuchsia, Jerusalem sage and 'Madame Plantier' roses. It shows the type of simple, scented planting that would benefit hospital patients in small gardens where they could also do some gentle gardening.

inches high, two inches wide, which crossed the lawn, partnered by ribbons of *stachys* on their inward sides. The brothers were specialists in 'green architecture' – little containers of box matched to rectangles of white stone, wire-framed structures 'made' of ivy, in particular the twisted spires, which somehow intimated, merely intimated, a seal, with a ball of ivy on top. Their garden was full of jokes and surprises, within an overall sublimely simple and accurate asymmetry.

In *Modern Gardens*, Peter Shepheard refers to the 'radical turn of thought'[5] which made the Vera brothers attractive to Modernists. In 1926 they had built for that great gardening enthusiast, Vicomte Charles de Noailles, a fantastic little triangular garden enclosed by a mirror wall. The mirror reflected the splintered wedges of pavings and plants that fanned alarmingly across crazy 'rectangles' that had none of their angles the same. It must have been an experiment, for the garden was subsequently destroyed and Tunnard was more likely to have seen what was probably its successor. Vicomte Charles was employing the French architect Robert Mallet-Stevens to alter his medieval château at Hyères, and Mallet-Stevens brought along a brilliant young garden architect from his office, Gabriel Guevrekian, who was to make the most famous Modern movement garden of all.

Guevrekian, a refugee from Russia via Turkey, had designed a triangular garden for the Decorative Arts Exposition in Paris in 1925 (at the age of twenty-five), and he transformed this idea for Hyères. This was a triangle walled in white concrete, viewed from the base, with the eyes channelled to the apex, where a figure sculpture by Lipschitz was set against the distant horizon. The triangle was filled with brick boxes of flowers, chequerboarded with paved squares, with triangular planters filling in along the sides; the whole effect was rather psychedelic, with blocks of flowers – simple plantings of tulips – 'marching' towards the statue and the view. The brothers Vera had their vegetable plots at St Germain-en-Laye set out in simple squares and rectangles: the simple square for flowers or vegetables, boxed or level with surrounding paving or grass, was to become one of the abiding features of the Modern movement garden. The little triangle of marching squares at Hyères somehow indelibly printed the idea on the mind's eye. Guevrekian went on designing houses with gardens in France and Iran, but he never again matched the magical impact of the little garden at Hyères.

Like many a Modernist pilgrim, Tunnard saw Hyères, but he found his most worthwhile contact with the Belgian garden architect Jean Caneel-Claes. At the time of Tunnard's visit, Caneel-Claes was working on a garden at Liederkerke, on a hillside site sloping down to the valley of the river Dendre. His *forte* was in the use of mass-produced concrete paving slabs (which were *not* pretending to be stone); he placed them in pairs, first down a ramp from the terrace which crossed the whole front of the house and took a hairpin bend, then in pairs marching directly down the lawn to a paved and walled sitting bay at a lower level. The paviours were set flush with the lawn so that they could be mown over, and with wide spaces in between through which grass or creeping herbs could grow.[6] Caneel-Claes did endless variations on his paviours. Large ones made a single path directly down the garden, with smaller ones leading off around planting bays of square or rectangular form; just to leave out a paviour, of course, created a flower or herb bed, to leave out two, three or four on a paved terrace gave one a pool. The fun was in the subtly changing textures of the horizontal plane, all with the same loyalty to simple geometric form.

For vertical interest Caneel-Claes used a very plain squared wooden trellis, painted white, standing up vertically to hold plants, or laid on top of plain square white concrete posts to form an arbour. He also constructed angled screens, four in a row, which made interesting geometrical shadows on the ground and formed perfectly serviceable though 'broken' or staggered screens for privacy. Lombardy poplars and rows of cypresses were also favourites for vertical accents to balance out the horizontal design. Existing trees were carefully preserved in any scheme and used as focuses in the design; all Modern garden designers seem to have heard the echo of Frank Lloyd Wright and the famous house in California which he curved around an ancient tree — this regard for sitting tenants of the site was very much in the true Modernist philosophy.

Tunnard and his new-found ally, Caneel-Claes, may have visited Sweden, and they certainly discussed the Swedish philosophy of Modern garden design that was beginning to be demonstrated in Stockholm's parks and gardens. Swedish architects were striving for a contrast between simple architectural forms and designs for terraces, paths and pools, and 'free and luxuriant vegetation'. This vegetation – it was an important emphasis – veered towards the native and natural, rather than the highly contrived or gardenesque; here Modernism was growing hand in hand with ecological gardening in the years before the Second World War.

When Christopher Tunnard came home, armed with all these ideas, he and Caneel-Claes issued a joint manifesto – obligatory in the 1930s. It sounded only too manifesto-like: 'We believe ... in the reliance of the designer on his own knowledge and experience and not on the academic symbolism of the styles or outworn systems of aesthetics, to create by experiment and invention new forms which are significant of the age from which they spring.'[7]

The manifesto was more widely read when it was turned into a series of articles for *Architectural Review* in 1937 and 1938; these were in turn adapted into Tunnard's book, *Gardens in the Modern Landscape*, also published in 1938. It is now out of print (and I have twice failed to persuade the publisher, the Architectural Press, to resurrect it), so a few battered copies of the original are all we have to commemorate Tunnard. It is, I am not alone in thinking, a most remarkable book.

When Tunnard came back from Europe after seeing the ideas of European designers he must have felt very angry at the smugness of old England; he probably needed little editorial encouragement from the *Architectural Review* to be controversial, and he launched into a caustic attack on the most sacred symbols of 200 years of English landscape history. He blamed Addison and his *Spectator* essays, written in Queen Anne's reign, for inspiring 200 years of confused interaction between the arts of painting and gardening: he exhorted his fellows to see that brother artists, 'in almost every sphere of aesthetic activity, have wiped the mud from their shoes and set off on a straighter road towards a more clearly defined horizon'.[8]

It was Tunnard who began the now familiar criticism of 'Capability' Brown for sweeping away old flower gardens. He questions Brown's skill in planting — he has a point in suggesting that our great thankfulness for the sheer number of trees Brown planted has blinded us to their 'ill-assorted' groupings, which are not so technically sound as to warrant our uncritical preservation and adoration of his works. He sees the Gothic and Oriental, 'with Classic, a pale shadow, struggling behind', as concepts in gardens and ornaments, mocking the new and echoing a vanished past: 'Symbolism is dying, and devotees of the new cult seek to justify the use of grottoes, caves and ruins by concealing in them cattle sheds and herdsmen's hovels or by designing them in a manner naturalized to the trees and woods.'[9]

He carries on through history in this angry, waspish mood, but his is the hurt anger of a favourite nephew who has been left out of his rich aunt's will. He cannot stop loving the great landscape art of England — Blenheim, Stowe, Painshill (still in a good state of repair in the 1930s), and even the Victorian gardens, like Redleaf at Penshurst — but he hates the thought of all those other artists (other than landscape architects) who have subjected his beloved landscape to their arrogant and muddle-headed excesses: Pugin and Ruskin and their 'world of make-believe ... [that] was not conducive to artistic progress', the 'exalted Victorian mind [that] had not learned to compromise; in consequence it botched', producing such 'grotesque indecency' as 'A cedar of Lebanon, a clump of plumous pampas grass and some pieces of rockwork ... used to make a miniature landscape on the front lawn with a crescent moon and stars carved out of the turf for bedding at the back.'[10] Even worse in Tunnard's view, was John Claudius Loudon, offering to the 'modern' designer of the 1850s the complete bounty of Classic or Gothick, with a dash of Hindoo, Elizabethan, Italian ... '... the landscape-gardener who would lay out grounds at the present-day, may adopt either the oldest, or geometrical style ... or he may adopt the modern or irregular style ... and he may further combine the two styles in such a manner as to join regularity and irregularity in one design.'[11]

Finally, Tunnard sets about Gertrude Jekyll and her world. The Miss Jekyll he met in Francis Jekyll's *Memoir*, which was first published in 1934, was a reactionary, preferring animal to human society and deploring the advance of science and of civilization, happy in her cottagey and wild gardens. Only when Impressionism was fifty years old did she start applying it to garden colours (another dead artistic influence), and then she failed posterity because she was not a good enough painter to put her ideas about flowers and colour and light on to canvas! Tunnard is contradictory and ambiguous about Miss Jekyll – she had died only at the very end of 1932 and his was the first less than adulatory assessment – he credits her with 'a careful and accurate estimate of colour effects through observation and experiment' but goes on to imply that her sophisticated and painterly taste for subdued and graded colours is not relevant to traditional English taste. This taste, says Tunnard, may be primitive, but it is our own – for the strong bright reds and blues of the national flag, 'egg yellow, the tobacco brown which with white and emerald green still decorates our pleasure boats, the burnt sienna of the sails of fishing smacks and the vermilion of the pillar box'. These are the English tradition, and the sophisticated arty-crafty tastes of decorators and dressmakers should not make us ashamed of them – 'pure structural colour' is nothing to be afraid of.[12]

All this turmoil, page after page of invective, not always rational, made good shocking reading – and so much of the Modern movement was about being shocking – in the late 1930s. But Tunnard did add a positively creative half to his book. If he agreed with Le Corbusier, 'The Styles are a lie', he had made his point. That it wasn't so much that the past was lying, but much more that a new style was needed, is now clear to us with hindsight. Young Mr Tunnard, having stripped his English landscape inheritance of all its mossy pretensions and excessive fantasies, is content with two legacies, a picture – in a frame – and a prospect. He then declares that there are three justifiable sources of inspiration for modern

designers – that of fitness for purpose (the much vaunted func-
tionalism of Modern Architecture), the influence of modern art, and
the influence he personally felt the strongest, that of Japanese
gardens. He has, of course, fallen into traps, merely different ones,
just as the indolent Shenstone, the capricious Chambers and the
reactionary Miss Jekyll did, but I forgive him – we must, for there
is no other way.

The rest of his book is devoted to the Modern movement style
of garden designing. He does indeed banish the clutter, slim down
good design to ordinary sized gardens, face up to modern materials
and primary colours and introduce Japanese occult symmetry in
place of 'that most snobbish form of Renaissance planning', the axial
vista. He produces gardens to please Adolf Loos's dictum – 'To find
beauty in form instead of making it depend upon ornament, is the
goal to which humanity is aspiring'; and in line with Raymond
Mortimer's by-line from *New Interior Design* (1929) – 'Graceful-
ness, in things as in persons, results from an elimination of the un-
necessary.'[13] They were gardens which came from his own
experience and were honest in their own time, but, for good or
ill, they are of just another Style.

What were Tunnard's Modern gardens like? Two were made in
England and survive to explain his philosophy. The first is the
garden of Bentley Wood at Halland in East Sussex, made for the
house which Serge Chermayeff designed for himself and his wife in
1934. The Chermayeffs' site was part sloping downland field, part
copse, with a view over more fields and downs to the south and
towards the sea. Tunnard was involved right from the beginning,
carefully marking out the trees to be saved in the copse so that
garden could melt into woodland to the side of the house.

The completed house, a steel-framed, weatherboarded and glass
'box', was approached by a winding concreted drive from the east,
through bracken and a few trees. From this direction the whole
garden and house was surrounded and masked by a wall of yellow
brick about six feet high, above which the cedarboarded second
storey of the house rose; the Canadian weatherboards faded, as
intended, to soft mauve. Inside the court on the north side of the

house, the main door connected to a garage block by a wooden-framed, glass-roofed verandah; the house door had accent planting of purple and evergreen shrubs. Inside the house the main living- and dining-rooms, and the main bedrooms, faced south, with glass sliding doors that meant the dividing walls became almost invisible on fine days; this ease of passage, from the indoor room to the outdoor room, is an aspect of Modern design that has been whole-heartedly adopted, often with disastrous results for visual harmony, by so many timber-framed cottages and mock Tudor semi-detached houses.

Outside, one stepped on to a large, simply square-paved terrace, to be used for sitting or eating in the 30s concept of outdoor, sun-loving living. The steel-framed façade of the house was structurally divided into rectangles, the bedroom windows were set back so that these 'frames' enclosed pictures of the distant landscape, and the device was repeated at the 'bottom' of the garden – at the end of a paved catwalk which extended from the terrace – by a free-standing viewing frame which closed this green gallery of garden. The green was provided by mown grass beside the catwalk, minimal shrubs against the long east wall and a single maple, saved from the original ground level. Otherwise Bentley Wood's garden, to the west, was mown grass fading into birch copse, with a little paving of paths into the copse.

It is a spare and functional garden, demanding little upkeep, taking due note of its surrounding landscape; apart from an oil jar of spiky planting and a few deck chairs, the only decoration used to be a Henry Moore reclining figure, for which the plinth at the end of the catwalk was designed and made (in a way, the whole garden was designed for this work of art) – but, of course, the figure has long since vanished from its home. Tunnard's faithfulness to his artist contemporaries was expressed by the works of Moore, Willi Soukup or perhaps Carl Milles finding starring roles in his designs.

The second garden is more complex. It is the garden of St Ann's Hill near Chertsey in Surrey, a house – which we would regard as looking more like the superstructure of an ocean liner – built for Tunnard by the young Australian architect Raymond McGrath.

St Ann's Hill was Tunnard's English swan-song, and it is also a strikingly beautiful and deservedly much-admired 30s Modern house. It is large and fairly grand and it occupies a hillside site, as its name indicates, in an eighteenth-century landscaped park, once the home of Charles James Fox.

In the 30s the park still had a classical temple or two, some magnificent Lebanon cedars, and a mass of nineteenth-century rhododendrons. McGrath apparently adopted the circular plan form of the venerable cedars for his design; the white, steel-framed, concrete-rendered house occupies just over half of the circle, the completion being made on the garden side by a curving paved terrace. The circle is given a tail: partly glass-walled garden room, partly walled and paved garden court. The structural girder frames are left standing to make, similarly to though rather more flamboyantly than at Bentley Wood, picture frames for viewing the landscape from curved bedrooms or sleeping balconies, and the walls of the garden court are also cut with large picture frames, which perfectly enclose a view of a most elegant cedar on the lower slope of the lawn.

The garden court is cleanly paved, with single paviours omitted and plants put in to make flower beds; the focal point of the court was a circular pool, the setting for a Willi Soukup fountain in Hopton Wood stone, which in turn was framed against the plain doorway opening in the end wall of the court. This doorway and its wall were a little Tunnard time-trick — for on the inner side they appeared white, pure and present-day, while on stepping through into the remnants of the eighteenth-century copse surrounding the temple, the reverse guise of the wall was of Georgian brick and fragments of stone ornament.

A further trick was played in the garden, this one even more surreal. Tunnard turned upside down the accepted idea of soft vegetation clothing hard form which is expressed in every rose-draped balustrade, creeper-clad house or urn. There was a mammoth and venerable rhododendron clump on the lawn to the south-east of the house; he designed a raised and curved paved platform, holding a pool and formal flower gardens, around the rhododendron. This substantial structure moulding itself around a soft and (seemingly) ephemeral plant epitomized his assault on conventional wisdom and received traditions.

As a house in a modern garden, St Ann's Hill fulfils all Tunnard's beliefs. In taking the motif of the past, the circular form of the cedar tree, and playing with it in modern concrete, steel and glass, and in circular plantings and cuttings and paths through the larger area of the garden, McGrath and Tunnard asserted their own invention and experience in a design that owed nothing to past 'styles'. They were so delighted with the house and garden in plan that this was incised upon amber glass as the chief decoration in the circular (what else?) entrance hall of the house. From the bedrooms, roof terraces and garden court the garden and landscape offered a variety of views and prospects, framed in white steel. The garden court was a useful and sheltered outdoor room; the whole effect was clutter-free and pure of form, worthy of contemplation, with planting used according to the Japanese inspiration, seen with the sensitive eye of a Zen Buddhist who revered such simple things as a branch of blossom against the sky or a single ivy trailing across a plain wall. It was in his planting philosophy (and remember he was really a historian and a planner, and only became a plantsman as he practised) that Tunnard was influenced by things Japanese.

Tunnard may have visited Japan — or have had long talks with Bernard Leach — and he must have been a very early advocate of Zen aesthetic beliefs (as opposed to Japanese tea-houses, stone lanterns and decorative gardening ideas) among English designers. But it was odd that he should so enthusiastically adopt someone else's age-old traditions, having so energetically refuted his own! Around Japanese houses, he discovered, plants were used with great economy, and with a consequent appreciation of each plant's distinct form and line. He noted that there were 'no great waves of vegetation beating on a wall', 'no barbaric massings of colour', but that designed features and carefully chosen plants existed together in a mutual respect. From these Japanese experiences, from the researches of a Swiss plantsman called Correvon who had identified some 'formes architecturales', and with the distinctive illustrations of Gordon Cullen, Tunnard laid down the basis of modern planting design for his own gardens and for generations of professional designers to the present day. Interesting leaf shapes, colours and textures, elegant form and the ability to produce decorative autumn fruits, were of much greater importance than mere flowers. These architectural plants had to be hardy, tolerant of dry sun and/or wet shade in order to survive in their predominantly man-made environments of paved courts and terraces, roof gardens and wall bases. They had to be good value, all-year-round performers, for they, unlike their ancestors in the wilder recesses of Munstead Wood, would be on show every day of the year. It was Tunnard who, on this basis, forwarded the fortunes of *Vinca major elegantissima* (golden periwinkle), *Pachysandra terminalis*, hebes, ivies, the famous *Fatsia japonica*, many a berberis and cotoneaster, especially *C. horizontalis*, bamboos, New Zealand flax, *Viburnum davidii*, all kinds of hosta varieties, euphorbias, *Tiarella cordifolia*, and lots of grasses and herbs which became the approved plants to appear on modern patios and terraces and in architectural scheme illustrations. They also became the basis of the Institute of Landscape Architects' Basic Plant List, a lifebelt for many young designers and architects entering stormy horticultural seas.

Christopher Tunnard's garden philosophy was, apart perhaps from buying Henry Moore or Willi Soukup (although they were young and struggling then), a democratic way of gardening. His materials were mass-produced concrete and manufactured joinery, and his plants were few and more likely to survive than many a flimsy exotic. His view of Modern gardening was, for the first time in history, an effort by a first-class designer to produce an ideal for the ordinary garden, whether long and thin or quirky and triangular. He was designing gardens to suit Modern houses and Modern lifestyles, ideal gardens for all those houses with Crittall windows and sunburst front doors that were streaming along the suburban closes and arterial roads. What went wrong? The houses exist, so why don't the gardens of true 30s style exist also? The sad and simple fact was that Christopher Tunnard was crying in the wilderness, and not just into the empty air of the 30s world heading irrevocably towards war. With a very few exceptions, the readers of *Architectural Review* and the buyers of books on good design were only too comfortably ensconced in their Georgian squares and Jacobean manor houses to contemplate with any seriousness building Modern houses with Modern gardens; and the eager young couples only too happy with their Modern semi-detached houses, or even detached white villas, were hardly likely to be readers of the *Review*. Their idea for their garden was cosy crazily paved paths with a sundial and a fishing gnome on the rockery! Poor Mr Tunnard had no audience, no effective audience, at all.

Gardens in the Modern Landscape showed three more of Tunnard's designs, all of which tantalizingly illustrate just how his thinking would have solved our post-war need for labour-saving gardens, gardens which would fit into busy lives without demanding too much energy or expense. For a house at Walton-on-Thames, on a square plot with the house in one corner, Tunnard divided the garden asymmetrically with a loose zig-zag hedge separating off a working area (easily accessible from the drive) from the main garden. A small concrete paved terrace fanned along the garden front of the house, with the flowery interest confined to rows of square beds in threes ranged parallel with the hedge and following the zig-zag. The beds were planned to hold tulips and roses, but were adaptable to herbs or shrubs if preferred; as they were about three feet square they were not a burden and the number could be reduced or increased without upsetting the balance of the design. The rest of the three-quarters of an acre of garden was lawn, partly smooth, partly rougher grass with spring flowers melting into shrubs and trees on the garden boundary. The only formal feature was a circular space enclosed by hedges, which provided a small green gallery for a piece of sculpture.

For Land's End, Garby, near Leicester, a modern country house by Raymond McGrath,[14] Tunnard provided a large hedged enclosure divided into flat chequerboard squares of planting, grass and paving; again there were infinite choices as to how complex or simple this planting could be. The south side of this house sheltered a circular plunge pool, open to the sun and the surrounding country views but separated from the rest of the garden. Tunnard seemed to be good at handling the swimming-pool, a feature which has defeated so many modern designers and ruined so many gardens: in another and quite small pinewoods garden at Cobham, Surrey, he made a boating lake cum swimming-pool on the lower slope of the hillside, with sandy banks for sitting and sunbathing. The pool was given waterside planting, but otherwise there was merely a paved path which approached it through grass and trees, and the rest of the garden was light woodland for minimal maintenance.

In June 1938 the young garden designers of the Institute of Landscape Architects held their first exhibition of work at Broadway in Worcestershire, with the help of Gordon Russell the furniture-maker, a friend of Geoffrey Jellicoe and of the profession in general. But Christopher Tunnard was already in America, though his garden for St Ann's Hill was given pride of place in the exhibition. It really was, as time would tell, a case of the most brilliant bird having flown.

Tunnard had gone to the prestigious Harvard School of Land-scape Design, where he had been offered a teaching job. As a consequence, New England also has a sprinkling of Tunnard gardens. The best was a small garden, sixty-five feet by forty-two, with 'a hint of luxury', at Newport, Rhode Island. This is a garden of asymmetry and occult balance within its walled rectangle. A loosely triangular lawn spreads from the house terrace, narrowing to an angled and off-centre free-standing hedge of clipped box. In front of this hedge is a rectangular black pool with a golden bronze lacquered abstract sculpture (a 'chimerical font') by Arp towards the right-hand end, balanced by clumps of clipped yew at the other. The left-hand side of the lawn has two semi-circular bays of yew hedging around circular pools (shallow to attract the birds), with fountains, low box edgings and sinuous beds of ivies between them, and the right-hand side of the lawn has a larger but similar pool with a fountain. Small-leaved limes have been planted – with an intention that they will be pleached – behind the two pools and at the end of the garden, and they are balanced by a tight row of thuyas on the right behind the larger pool. Thus the basic concept of the garden is concerned with form, light and shade, with a limited palette of plants that are used architecturally and clipped into strong shapes. Summer prettiness is not forgotten, however, and the designer planned for sproutings of purple and white petunias, carnations and lemon-yellow thunbergias.[15] I think this was the most charming of Tunnard's designs that were published. It has all the restraint, Modernity and individuality that he believed in; it needs only clipping and mowing unless flowers are chosen – the great thing is to have the choice.

This Newport garden was made after the Second World War, and at about the same time a revised edition of *Gardens in the Modern Landscape* was published, with pictures of more of Tunnard's work in America. These included a large garden at Lincoln, Massachusetts, near Thoreau's Walden Pond, and a tiny town garden in Cambridge, which he made appear larger by diagonal emphasis within the walled rectangle. He also designed a terraced garden in Farmington, Connecticut, for James Thrall Soby, an art collector who possessed an Alexander Calder mobile for his garden, and a projected garden for an extension to New York's Museum of Modern Art by the architect Philip Johnson.

However, Tunnard was already turning away from gardens towards landscape planning, for community housing schemes he was working on with students at Harvard. On professional terms one could not blame him – landscape for the masses was a far more noble aim than gardens for a privileged few – but there is also a hint that this change of heart was not for purely practical reasons. This second edition of *Gardens in the Modern Landscape* includes a warning note in the guise of an addendum by the eminent Dean of Harvard, Joseph Hudnut. Dean Hudnut expresses himself as 'impatient', 'out of sympathy', and bored by garden designers intending 'assertions of modernity', as well as by those seeking a closeness with nature to the point of inviting the 'natural landscape' into the garden. In that wonderful wordiness that only eminent American academics can master, he actually claims only failure and lack of understanding for modern houses and gardens thus far – and as he was writing in 1948 it was to be thus far, and no farther. He sounds an eloquent death-knell for a movement hardly born; he voices the advanced modernism of liberation from the *tyranny of structure* for modern buildings which no longer confine space but model it, direct its flow and define the volumes into which it is only lightly divided. Then he states that 'Gardens, like houses, are built of space', and announces the new god, 'space' (and he was not anticipating President Kennedy and NASA's Apollo programme): 'So varied, powerful and unhackneyed a medium cannot be forever neglected by the landscape architect.' His final paragraph *cannot* be paraphrased:

Our new space proclaims as eloquently the evolving scheme of our lives, the new patterns of idea and manners, the changed tempo, the wider horizons. Into these new orderings of space there has been translated the grace and order and completeness which the architect has discovered beneath the infinite complexities, the speed, the vast dimensions, and the harsh mechanizations of our world. That which the house tells us, the garden must reaffirm.[16]

I can only imagine that Christopher Tunnard printed this with his thumbs in his ears, yah-booing at the reactionary English establishment which had now been *told*. There was no doubt about it, he was the only English designer who understood the great blessing that Modern gardens could have conferred on modern life. He had done just what this eminent American academic was driving at. And the eminent American academic had as good as told him that he was wasting his time. We are still crying in the wilderness, as Dean Hudnut did, for that unreachable genius of Villa Caprarola, Vaux-le-Vicomte, Stowe, or 'our new space'. We are still, as Dean Hudnut was, too preoccupied to notice when the genius does return.

But, on the other hand, in the aftermath of the Second World War there were more important things to be doing than gardens. Design on the land in any form was at a low ebb; re-development was all the rage. Tunnard did not stay long at Harvard, but moved to Yale, where he was given a small department of City and Regional Planning. His budget was minimal but his students were keen; he had married, and was well looked after, well organized and surrounded by friends. He could have been comfortable and quiet for the rest of his days. There were to be no more manifestos or attempts to shock – the mature Tunnard would go on speaking in a quiet voice.

He must soon have realized that all he had achieved in England was based on a ruthless sifting out of the best of history, and the histories of ancient civilizations such as Japan and Europe. In America he had found a gangling ugly duckling of a country, whose people – at least his students – were hungry for a past of their own, on which to base a future. In 1950 Frederick Law Olmsted was yet to be rediscovered (Laura Wood Roper, his biographer, was beginning to catalogue the vast collection of Olmsted papers, writing preliminary articles on what she found), few even thought of the great ecologist George Perkins Marsh and his warnings of the effect pioneering with vigour had had on the American landscape, and Norman K. Newton's classic *Design on the Land* was yet to be published.[17] Post-war Americans, prosperous by European standards, were taking to the freeways and the suburbs, distance being no object; city centres became redundant ghettos, fine natural landscape was spread with large lots and large houses. The guardians of the heritage landscapes, the great Federal Park and Forest Services, were at loggerheads, quarrelling in front of their supporters and their adversaries; any kind of bureaucratic planning in regional landscape terms, based upon natural systems, was anathema to the all-powerful States and to every good freedom-loving nephew of Uncle Sam.

Tunnard's reaction was quietly to show America good landscapes. His book *The City of Man*, published in 1953,[18] was simply an appraisal of cities as the most sophisticated and desirable of human creations, and he added American cities to the world's score. His next book, published in 1955, was written with Henry Hope Reed, the sometime curator of New York's Central Park, and was called *American Skyline*.[19] Tunnard invited, or attracted, all his eminent friends to Yale – Americans like Reed and Lewis Mumford, as well as the celebrated émigrés Walter Gropius, Erich Mendelsohn and Serge Chermayeff, whom he had known in England.

Tunnard's most noted book, *Man-made America: Chaos or Control?*, was written with Boris Pushkarov and published in 1963;[20] the authors were presented with a National Book Award for one of the most distinguished books of the year, a book that was concerned with the 'proper business for every responsible citizen'. This proper business was cool illustration and analysis by Tunnard of the advantages of cluster and community housing design, the separation by plan rather than chance of industry and housing, the good design and planting of freeways and the preservation of integrated greenways, for the protection of rivers, woods and wildlife within the fabric of man-made America. The point was also made that there was much of man-made America, in old towns and cities, that was worth preserving. Ann Satterthwaite, Tunnard's ex-student, and now a very eminent landscape historian and landscape planner, who worked on this aspect of the book, remembers that the idea of historic preservation was a luxury then, little thought of or appreciated; it was Tunnard himself who gave his spare time to start things moving in New Haven and Providence, two places now so proud of their restored streets and buildings.

Whether Tunnard disturbed American consciences is hard for me to say. President Johnson did make that memorable address to Congress in 1966: 'Let us from this moment begin our work in earnest – so that future generations of Americans will look back and say: 1966 was the year of the new conservation, when farsighted men took farsighted steps to preserve the beauty that is the heritage of our Republic.'[21] The planning profession seemed to take the word 'farsighted' literally: planning moved off into space with NASA, and the satellite camera's view and the computer print-out became the tools of a new science that wanted nothing to do with old art. In the absence of a historical or aesthetic base for judgements, the manipulators of these systems took to *zoning* from their heavenly heights, and were more than ever brought down to earth by the individual American's vigorously defended right to profit from the land he owned. Tunnard's City and Regional Planning Department at Yale was closed in the late 1960s; his was not the kind of disruptive voice that was wanted.

Christopher Tunnard was left in peace to write his last book, *The*

World with a View: an enquiry into the nature of scenic values, published in 1978, the year before he died.[22] His clean-sweep mind had lost none of its clear vision; his prose was more elegant and persuasive than ever. He pursues, delightfully and intellectually, the scientific, artistic and literary bases for appreciating one's surroundings (not forgetting to introduce the American dimension in every case), he makes a brilliant journey through the influences that gardens exert on us, and he explains the values of good urban surroundings and the desirability of preserving these qualities, not just the buildings themselves. His conclusion, 'The All-Embracing View', searches poignantly (in view of his own story) for the evidence that his view of our world will go on being seen. What immediately becomes clear is that he has held true to his finely judged vision across forty years. He is still heading for his clear horizon:

Among the most important of human rights is the right to see beautiful things wherever one may find oneself.[23]

He is more than ever certain that this kind of beauty is not found in any élitist adoration of the past; it is available and necessary to everyone, a summation of natural human curiosity and observation: 'Taste will develop, for taste is knowledge and not to be mistaken for fashion.'[24] Such taste will be refined from an awareness of the past, a deep sympathy with nature, and a landscape's fitness for its purpose.

All elements of society must come eventually to realize that scenic values are an essential part of the cultural life of nations, that their desecration is a crime against the people, and that they can be cherished and enhanced only by the development of esthetic judgement.[25]

In the end, it seems, a world as crowded as ours is not unlike a garden. The welfare of its waters, woods and wildlife depends upon our care, we want it to be neither a slavish imitation of some historic style, nor covered in concrete and filled with gadgets; we want the happy beautiful medium, a design that fits our own time and our purposes, that gives us a pleasure that we can share in understanding with our neighbours.

At the last, Tunnard saw hope. That the 'new planning' would overcome possessiveness and greed to establish the values of 'A World with a Lovely View', and that the first world would teach the third, with the setting up of a secretariat of the environment by the United Nations in Nairobi. He ends:

A beginning has been made to bridge a gap wider than the Gorge of Tempe – the yawning chasm between the unbridled exploitation of technology on the one side and full development of the cultural patrimony on the other. The gap will only be bridged when the aesthetic values of society are properly understood.[26]

7

Gertrude Jekyll – At Home and Abroad

EOPLE keep asking me the same questions about Miss Jekyll, with whom I have been acquainted now for about fifteen years.[1] Is it true that she had fourteen gardeners? How do you feel about her? Why are her drawings in America? What will happen to Munstead Wood? Here are some attempts at some answers.

The question about how many gardeners she had annoys me; it is a 'think-of-a-number' game, starting with a vaguely plausible figure of six or eight, rising to fifteen or twenty, then soaring to the sky with unlikely guesses that may be fifty or ninety-nine. The implication is that Jekyll gardening is an impossible dream, and she is dismissed as irrelevant to our time. In fact she was running a nursery business at Munstead Wood from around 1888 until her death in 1932, a nursery just like Mr Kelway's or Mr Jackman's, and no one quibbles over how many staff *they* might have employed. Miss Jekyll published a nursery catalogue, printed by Craddocks of Godalming, with 'the best hardy plants' for sale, and she provided plants for the majority of her 350 private garden design clients. She ran a professional garden, but her wealth of ideas contains something for every amateur.

But I suspect there is still an intimidatory glow about her, because of her legendary achievements as well as her supposedly complicated gardening. First, her achievements.

Gertrude Jekyll was born in 1843 and brought up in a grand but very ugly house in Surrey parkland near Guildford. She was initiated into a ladylike life of fine sewing, piano playing, drawing-room conversation and a little compulsory singing in French and Italian; but she was also a tomboy, playing cricket with her brothers, riding on the heath, sculling on the lake and generally running wild out of doors, until all hours, all summer long. She could hold her own with crusty generals (friends of her father) or princesses of the blood, but she was also — unusually for her time and class — equally at home with the blacksmith in the village or helping the lock-keeper's wife with her laundry.

When she was eighteen Gertrude was not the first, but about the fourth, woman to go to Henry Cole's School of Art in South Kensington. Without hesitation, she then bearded John Ruskin, George Frederick Watts, Edward Burne-Jones, Simeon Solomon, Dante Gabriel Rossetti — many of that rather risqué Pre-Raphaelite circle — on the subject of her art. She travelled to the remotest Greek islands and to Africa, sketching all the way, and she returned to copy Turners and Van Dycks and to make her way into their profession.

She changed tack in a wider cause, embroidering for Lord Leighton, decorating for the Duke of Westminster, making silver necklaces for Burne-Jones, painting a prancing White Horse for the inn at Hascombe, and exhibiting a painting of her brother's dog at the Royal Academy. The impression she made on her neighbours at Wargrave, Berkshire, when she was around thirty years of age and on enforced absence from her beloved Surrey, is given by a rather breathless George Leslie:

[She was] clever and witty in conversation, active and energetic in mind and body, and would at all times have shone conspicuously bright among other ladies ... there is hardly any useful handicraft the mysteries of which she has not mastered — carving, modelling, house-painting, carpentry, smith's work, repoussé work, gilding, wood-inlaying, embroidery, gardening and all manner of herb and flower culture.[2]

On returning to settle in Surrey 'for good' in 1878, at the age of thirty-five, Miss Jekyll proceeded to plan and make a large garden for her mother's newly-built house and then to buy a plot of fifteen acres for herself. She took up gardening, gardening friends and gardening writing and photography; she made her garden at Munstead Wood, and launched herself on a new career of writing. She produced sixteen books and no fewer than 1,032 articles, mainly for *Country Life*, *The Garden* and *Gardening Illustrated*, between 1881 and her death in 1932.[3] She ran her nursery, took photographs for all her books, and carried out about 250 private garden and planting design commissions (some of which entailed a dozen detailed plans); there were another 120 commissions in partnership with Edwin Lutyens, whom she was largely responsible for launching on his career as the greatest English architect since Christopher Wren. Miss Jekyll believed profoundly in, and worshipped regularly, a benevolent God, and felt it was her bounden duty and her joy to work while He gave her light. She worked almost up until the day she died, with the dying year, on 8 December 1932. At her funeral the church of St John at Busbridge, just across the road from her home, was packed with eminent and famous personages, but it was her gardeners and garden boys, four of them, who lowered her into her moss-lined grave.

THIS panegyric has been written many times before, and is the substance of Miss Jekyll's legend. It is always a good thing to have the measure of a person with whom one would like to become acquainted; but friendship is furthered by pushing such facts aside, for they are not the subject of everyday conversation. Much better to be invited home, as the young Edwin Lutyens was, to meet the lady on her home ground and find out what she was really like. He was amazed at her homely appearance, in an apron and blue skirt that 'in no way hid her ankles' – which was thankfully the kind of revelation that made them friends, rather than frightening him off. Out of the friendship came her house, built solidly with double walls of Bargate stone outside and brick inside, with the finest craftsmanship in the best old traditions, so that it appeared not to be a new house, but 'took on the soul of a more ancient dwelling place'.

But what was Munstead Wood really like, as a home, in Miss Jekyll's day? It is an important question, for we are very conscious of interiors and exteriors now, and the two are so much more interdependent than in the past. How can we really know the atmosphere of Miss Jekyll's garden if we have little idea of the much more tangible atmosphere of her house? In several years of looking at Lutyens's houses, with or without Jekyll gardens, it has become brilliantly clear to me that if the owners have not got the right idea inside the house, then the garden hasn't a chance; but I know only a handful of houses and gardens in their part of Surrey that both Miss Jekyll and her young architect friend could happily return to and feel justified. From these, from the 6d auction catalogue of Alfred Savill & Sons for the sale of the contents of Munstead Wood on 1 and 2 September 1948, and from my own knowledge, I want to try and visit her at home. After that will come a little Jekyll gardening.

MUNSTEAD Wood was to be approached on foot; wheels, of whatever kind, could be left elsewhere. Miss Jekyll's home is reached via the sandy, tree-shaded lane which cuts off the corner from Busbridge church to Munstead Heath Road: she told us herself of the 'close-paled hand-gate',[4] swinging easily to the iron latch, through which one enters, to a rolled sand path between grass banks that winds to the front porch. To the left of the path is her large woodland garden, with paths edged with ferns leading off into it; to the right is the green glade, sheltered by oak trees, where the bunch primroses bloom in spring.

The house presents a sedate façade. Two narrow bands of dark-eyed windows stare sombrely from the golden sandstone wall, beneath a modest roof. The steady gaze of the windows comes from their being set almost flush with the stone wall, to give the largest possible window-sills inside. There is no door, at least no doorcase, merely a round-headed arch in the wall at the left-hand end. The arch leads to Miss Jekyll's 'long porch', for shaking off in wet weather; through a second arch is a glimpse of lawn glade, broad stone steps, and the hedge of Scotch briars on the south front of the house. From the easy lawn (Miss Jekyll was not one to go in for striped lawns), the wide grass path known as the Green Wood

Walk leads off into the woodland of rhododendrons and birches, with clumps of white lilies at their feet.

Under the porch to the right is the entrance door, of heavy natural oak. Inside is a spacious 'vestibule' or outer hall, with a window on the right and a brick fireplace set diagonally on the left. This offers a cool shady welcome in summer, and a warm welcome in winter. Beneath the window, with its dark blue repp curtains, is a narrowish oak refectory table on which brass gleams against blue velvet; more polished brass gleams from a little carriage clock on the mantelpiece, and there are brass plates for wall lights. In the centre of the hall is an oval gate-legged table; two chairs, generous Queen Anne chairs of walnut with brown hide seats, stand either side of the fireplace, and on the opposite long wall is a Jacobean oak dresser, bearing blue and white and green Chinese and Italian pottery bowls and plates. The greenery – Miss Jekyll regarded the entrance hall as the place for a 'good mass of greenery'[5] – is provided by a large fern, a maidenhair or a tender pteris, in a blue and white Flemish jardinière on the dresser, and perhaps a blue and white bowl of ivy and polypody on the table.

In the hall, feet are scuffed on matting and coats taken off to be dried, or hung in a tall oak cupboard; this entrance from the outer world is a placid place, lit by morning sun which makes the polish on Miss Jekyll's treasures gleam. In the afternoon it is more sombre, though then the light beckons from the opposite direction, from the corridor with the long red Persian carpet which leads into the sitting-room.

On the way through the oak-panelled corridor a door on the left leads into the large, light and almost square dining-room. It is actually twenty feet long by fifteen deep, but cupboards each side of the fireplace, at the left-hand end, foreshorten it. A long refectory table with oak ladderback chairs with rush seats and red cushions (three each side, a carver at each end) is parallel with the bright southern casement which looks out over the briar hedge and the lawn. The scent of briars comes into the room; perhaps the short blue curtains (the same blue repp as in the hall) lift in the breeze. It is a light room, with pale plastered walls hung with dark-framed pictures of Italian ruins, bridges and arches. At the opposite end to the fireplace is a finely carved oak dresser, well polished, loaded with a precious hoard of pewter plates, jugs and tureens. Around the corner, on the right inside the door as one enters, is a simple refectory table covered with white linen, holding a small electric hotplate. On the shelves beside the fire is a collection of blue and white Chinese porcelain. Miss Jekyll owned a plain white dinner service, perhaps for everyday use, and also a large collection of Johnson's 'Rose Dawn'.

Back in the corridor, a wide oak arch to the left, hung with heavy Genoese velvet in winter, opens into the sitting-room, the main room of the house. It is, as Miss Jekyll says, 'low and fairly large, measuring twenty-seven by twenty-one feet and eight feet from floor to ceiling,'[6] – it is a warm, pale room, flooded with southern light from a long range of windows, and in the afternoon the western sun comes pouring down the stairs at the far end. It strikes as an odd arrangement to have the enormous canopied fireplace next to the stairs, but Miss Jekyll quite simply wanted to be able to enjoy as much as possible the fine workmanship of the staircase, its low and broad treads and its finely turned finials set on angle posts that 'go right down and rest on brick masonry'[7] or hang from the decorative underside of the upper flight. These open stairs set the airy mood of the house in summer; with traditional English stoicism Miss Jekyll would survive far into the autumn, well passing Michaelmas, before having the heavy velvets hung across the arch.

This room thus presented quite different aspects in winter and in summer. In winter it was closeted and muted with heavy hangings, a roaring log fire and blue and white Italian ware table lamps making wood and ornaments gleam in the cosy dusk. But in summer, when the heavy velvets were banished, with apricot satin curtains at the windows and light flooding in all directions, the garden door open to the scents of rosemary and briars, how could anyone say that Miss Jekyll only wanted a dark house? This annoying legend (which has given *carte blanche* for too many Lutyens houses to be cursed with more and bigger windows) seems to be mistaken. Lawrence Weaver, in *Houses and Gardens by E. L. Lutyens*, writes of the 'perfect understanding' between Miss Jekyll and her architect and that 'if the light is subdued in some rooms it is precisely because that was desired,'[8] but the lady herself says: 'I disliked small narrow passages, and would have nothing poky or screwy or ill-lighted.'[9] And it is not; it is merely that the light is controlled to time of day and season, for with a philosophy of living close to nature she liked to know what the weather was like; she put on and took off her extra layers accordingly, and her house did likewise.

Through the sitting-room's seasons, the objects around its owner remained constant. This was a room of muted warm colours: a lot of pale, polished warm oak, a browny patterned Axminster rug covering the sitting area, with a chesterfield and easy chairs covered in beige and fawn striped fabric. Small oak tables of great age – a strange rounded one on three legs – and wooden stools, were placed beside chairs. As in almost every room, there is a long oak refectory table, this one holding treasures of Miss Jekyll's own making – an embossed and inlaid glove-box, her silver-plated repoussé dishes, and perhaps a bunch of white lilac in a bluish glazed jug, or a tumble of roses or peonies in a porcelain bowl, according to the season. She thought flowers in the sitting-room should be of rarity value – she said she had seen too many drawing-rooms resembling thickets!

The walls were hung with many paintings: landscapes of her own, Algerian landscapes by her friend Barbara Bodichon, and impressionist watercolours by H. B. Brabazon. Conspicuous in this room was a Holbein-like portrait of Henry VIII in a black and gilt frame, a likely family heirloom. At the end of the sitting-room (along the walls of which were a fairly continuous but uncluttered stream of elbow chairs and oak chests) was an inlaid marquetry cabinet of many drawers and alcoves.

Under the stairs is the door to the workshop, where the lady is most likely to be found. She describes her stores of wood and tools, her collections of textiles and pottery, in *Home and Garden*,[10] but the sale catalogue reveals more: her Collins camera with Dallmeyer lens and tripod (with which she photographed her garden for thirty years); brass scales for weighing her letters and packets of plans; a

Rippingill's oil stove, pale blue, for her late suppers, with electric toaster; and her own stained oak sloping-topped work desk, with a rack for paper and envelopes at the back. A Steck pianola (Mary Lutyens remembers how Miss Jekyll enjoyed playing Mrs Merton's pianola at Folly Farm in the summer of 1916), a metronome, her lap desk for writing letters on the chesterfield (this one covered in green canvas) by the fire. Here also were her plan chests, though they do not appear in the sale catalogue. Had they already been snapped up by some roving architect who had bundled their contents into a wheelbarrow, from where they would be rescued in the nick of time and taken to America?

This large workroom held so much of Miss Jekyll's life and work. As well as her collections (she was a real hoarder), there were more things she had made — brass repoussé dishes, her inlaid ivory and mother-of-pearl panelled cupboard, a turned oak oblong stool with tapestry seat, a needlework picture of the British Isles (product of industrious youth?), velvet appliqué stuffs, shell pictures, and more paintings by herself and her friends. Beyond the workshop is the small garden lobby, with her flower vases (the special glass ones she designed and had made and marketed as Munstead glasses), her folding steps and canvas-seated garden chair, and, I presume, those large and capable gardening boots.

Back on the stairs, the book room is entered from the half-landing, through another velvet-curtained arch. Miss Jekyll describes this herself: ' ... the south wall is mostly window, the west wall is all of books; northward is the entrance arch and an oak bureau, and on the fourth side is another bookcase and the fireplace.'[11] The window curtains are of heavy red felt; there are short blue and yellow folkweave curtains to keep the sun off some books. One easy chair and a Turkey hearthrug complete 'the precious feeling of repose' that she cherishes in here. The pictures are for memories and contemplation — *The Sea at Hastings* and her own garden at Scalands in Sussex (Miss Jekyll's first commission) by dear Barbara Bodichon, a vase of flowers by Brabbie, and her own copy of Sir Joshua Reynolds's *Miss Bowler*.

If you can tell a person by their books, then the volumes of

John Ruskin, George Eliot, Disraeli, Browning, Shelley, La Fontaine, Macaulay and Gibbon will be expected, along with all the eminent floras and her own books and manuscripts. But there are also Lewis Carroll, Thoreau's *Walden*, Stephenson and Churchill's *Medical Botany*, Helen Allingham, Mrs Earle, a signed copy of the popular novelist Norman Douglas's *Nerinda*, and a proof and a few pencil drawings of her own unpublished book on primulas. A catholic collection for a lady of generous mind.

Miss Jekyll writes of how she chose her bedroom 'near the further end' of her famous upstairs gallery, so that she could more often enjoy walking its length.[12] The gallery is sixty feet long and ten feet wide; it is arched with massive oak beams, and the windows on the left look out northwards into the garden court and along the nut walk. On the right are cupboards filled with more of the treasures she has collected, which she also describes in *Home and Garden*. But, of course, she does not mention her bedroom, which is, as far as I can make out, the room on the right at the end of the gallery, above the dining-room, looking south over the garden. Here she slept in her carved and panelled 3ft 4inch oak bed, designed for her by Edwin Lutyens, with hair mattress, feather pillows, green and cream silk-bordered blankets and green quilt. More Jacobean oak tables and a chest, a blue Axminster carpet, green damask curtains, a day bed with yellow and green art tapestry cover, a small mahogany swing mirror and some decorated Lowestoft ware for her morning tea complete the picture.

Finally, the kitchen, a room as large as the workroom at the opposite end of the house, in the east wing. Miss Jekyll would not have expected her faithful housekeeper to be short of comfort; here too are heavy blue curtains, a cheerful red oriental carpet and mahogany armchairs, flower pictures, a hassock, a good grandfather clock and a pretty green and gilt corner cupboard for china. The rest of the kitchen would have had Lutyens's usual painted cupboards, with long working tops and glass-fronted cupboards above. Outside there was a large pot-pourri tub, with cover.

*

IN the building of her house, the most seriously studied undertaking of her life, Miss Jekyll had sought to imbue the new building 'in some mysterious way' with 'an expression of cheerful, kindly welcome, or restfulness to mind and body, abounding satisfaction to eye and brain'.[13] She seems to have achieved this wonderfully well; the beauty of the building went a long way towards it, and she had her architect to thank for that, but her reverence for the hand-finished natural oak was important too, and the presence of lovingly polished Jacobean furniture added the necessary patina of age. But there was plenty of comfort too, in plump red-cushioned seats, well-padded sofas and warm velvet curtains. And it was not a house of the past alone, for though she would not accept a motor car, a telephone or a motor mower, she enjoyed her radio and gramophone, with an extra large speaker because she especially liked the percussion.

Perhaps the most important thing to notice is that having created, at considerable cost and effort, the sense of refuge and peace, she furnished and used the house in such a way that this was fostered. She did not fill the rooms with garish colours, a whole flower show of chintzes, bibelots, gleaming objects on every surface, skirts and tassels, drapes and sashes, or even masses of flowers. How unrestful all that subsequent interior taste seems in comparison with the restful delights of Munstead Wood, where in predictable yet often breathtaking ways the light, intensified by deep casements and dark curtains, picked out the glow of polished brass or ebony picture frame, dappled the Bokhara rugs on polished floors, flooded the summer sitting-room with a beigey-apricot glow or peeped into the firelit gloom of the book-room. Resting on the basis of a perpetual harmony, each room had a character that cosseted and pleased its user; is it therefore surprising that this harmony and pleasure were also the key to the garden?

And of course they were. Miss Jekyll's gardening philosophy is an echo of the intentions of her house. She liked quiet entrances, with masses of good greenery in shrubs and hedges and on walls. (Don't mass the geraniums by the front door!) Her intention, rather than to shock or dazzle, was to put the visitor at ease, to provide a direct, dry path to shelter while one rang the bell, before the calming, warm reception of the entrance hall took over. The garden, as seen from the sitting-room, was also of complementary character — pretty, inviting, offering scents and diversions, or a sunny terrace or lawn background to conversation. For private retreats the book-room, and the hidden garden, a green glade for hiding with a book, were matching concepts. And there were the high-points: the great gallery on the first floor was her pride, and so was the great herbaceous border which crossed the centre of the garden in front of its high sandstone wall, in the same way that the gallery crossed the house. They were both so placed that each had to be encountered, and admired, in the course of almost every journey. Of course, we cannot all have Lutyens houses, fine galleries and magnificent herbaceous borders; nor do we need them. (In fact, many of us have houses older than or as old as Miss Jekyll's, and all houses built before the 1939 war have a patina of age, if it has not been frightened off.)

I hope Miss Jekyll has made her point. It is her fine example that makes her philosophy so clear; it is her philosophy that we need so badly to bring calm into our rattletrap lives, for she can give us a gentle progression through living, rather than a helter-skelter ride. Just as her workroom was crowded with the achievements of her life, so a large part of her garden was filled with her collections of special plant treasures, for propagation, seed-collecting and hybridizing. Workroom and work-garden were her private achievements. She expected that the rest of us gardeners and would-be gardeners who come to her would take advantage of her philosophy and skills, and then develop for ourselves. Like all good teachers, she contained an infinite capacity to be drawn on according to the needs and capabilities of her clients, or pupils. Once you have created your calm progression of quiet entrance, delightful outdoor sitting-room and garden 'book-room', with perhaps an area for vegetables, fruit and cut flowers, she will advise you — as she did so many — on suggested ways to plant your spaces.

To prove that she does *not* intend you to plant a colour-graded

border fourteen feet deep and a hundred and twenty feet long, with
the complete contents of the Chelsea Flower Show tent in it, here
are some of her plans.

THE gentlest of planting schemes, for the frail and ill to enjoy, a
'book-room' of a garden, full of familiar old friends, was the West
Rosemary Garden, planned in a 30-foot square space enclosed within
the buildings of King Edward VII's Hospital at Midhurst.[14] The
rectangle was divided into four wedges of garden, each bed hedged
with rosemary; Miss Jekyll probably used *R. officinalis*, but 'Miss
Jessop's Upright' is the one often used for hedges now – the choice
is yours. Inside the hedge was a mixture of *Cistus cyprius*, which has
white flowers with purple splotches (purists could use *C. 'Albiflorus'*,
all white), *Verbascum plumosa*, a white phlox, a white tea rose, 'Reine
Blanche', and spraying arches of the creamy-white rose 'Madame
Plantier' – all these in balanced pairings within the beds. Miss Jekyll
added *Galega officinalis* (blue goat's rue), a group of three in the
front of each larger bed, flanked by *Fuchsia riccartonii*, her favourite
deep scarlet *F. magellanica*, and *F. gracilis*, its smaller fellow, in the
smaller beds. The large beds had a single *Magnolia conspicua* (we
now call it *M. denudata*), with very fragrant, pure white flowers. All
the spaces were filled with groups of three 'Old Blush China' roses,
the rose that blooms till Christmas.

A little more complex in arrangement, a sitting-room border to
be contemplated from a window or terrace, is the famous border
for the lawn terrace at Edward Hudson's Deanery Garden at Sonning
in Berkshire.[15] The colour scheme of delicate pinks, pale blues and
silver, with a dash of purple and late yellow, is highly sophisticated
yet contains nothing rare or difficult. The south-facing border, which
could be used against a house or small wall, is 8 feet deep and 50
long. A drift of rosemary marks the beginning, matching a clump
on the other side of a short flight of steps; the use of such a plant
in balancing situations (for instance, on either side of a door) brings
harmony to planting, but don't use the same plant at each end of a
border – that equals boring repetition.

After the rosemary, along the wall, come a large yucca

(*Y. recurvifolia* would like this warm dry spot), two 'Old Blush China' roses, a clump of steely *Echinops ritro* (globe thistle), tall pink hollyhocks and more thistles with *Clematis jackmanii* – a large violet-purple-flowered clematis, and *Clematis flammula*, whose small, scented white flowers will climb over twenty feet in a summer, rambling behind and into them. In front of this array of spikes and pink flowers Miss Jekyll masses pale blue delphiniums, with the clematis and echinops, more China roses, lavenders, and a small, bushy species hydrangea, possibly *H. arborescens* or *H. chinensis*, but any modest-flowering one in pinky-blue or cream would do. Miss Jekyll had a soft spot for hydrangeas, and the biggest, bluest mop-heads in pots of luxuriant greenery adorned the North Court at Munstead Wood: in that position their exuberance and scale were right, while in this border something sophisticated, but perhaps more delicate, is demanded. The rosemary and hydrangea are allowed to tumble to the front of the bed, to be followed by pink rock pinks, masses of santolina and a dash of white daisy.

The opposite border, of similar proportions, is next to the lawn, with complementary rosemary, small blue irises, mignonette, more irises and blue pansies at the lawn edge. The other side of the bed tumbles over the top of a dry stone wall, with rosemary, catmint, pink rock pinks, pink snapdragons, white valerian and santolina mixed with white snapdragons all turning a vertical into a horizontal garden. Along the centre are more pink 'Old Blush China' roses, pink hollyhocks, pale blue delphiniums, *Echinops ritro* and a clump of another favourite, a creamy-white meadowsweet.

These borders, with their steadfast rules about delicate colours (soft pinks, perhaps with a purple veining somewhere that picks up the clematis colour, delicate lavender mauves and rosemary blues, the silvers and greys) and textures (clumps of good foliage in the hydrangea and catmints, spiky yuccas, soft lavender cottons), allow for endless variations on a theme, as each year brings good plants of a particular species, or perhaps an opportunity to experiment with pinky meadowsweet instead of cream, or purple violas instead of blue. The basis of restraint, regard for the cardinal rules, keeps the harmony and atmosphere of the scheme yet allows for little flutters of surprise; why should not a good flower border be like a comfortable sitting-room, a familiar friend, constantly re-visited, with sometimes a new picture or cushion cover, or the furniture moved around a little?[16]

THOUGH she worked until her last days, Miss Jekyll's final years at Munstead Wood were quiet ones; she lived on into the serene obscurity of old age while the younger, faster world flapped its short skirts and shorter haircuts well out of her fading sight. In October 1932 her beloved brother, neighbour and counsellor, Sir Herbert Jekyll, died. After the funeral Sir Edwin Lutyens found her self-possessed but frail, in her room 'with a delicious dark blue felt cap on her head';[17] it was his last sight of her, for she died peacefully on 8 December, a few days after her eighty-ninth birthday. A large congregation of respectful eminences crowded into St John's churchyard, just across the road from the end of her garden, and watched her gardeners lower her into her moss-lined grave.[18] The moss had been raked up from the Munstead Wood lawn that morning.

Munstead Wood was tidied and made ready for Francis Jekyll, who was to come and write his aunt's biography, but he preferred to live in The Hut. Nothing in the big house was touched, but he took all her private letters, diaries and notebooks away to work on. Lady Jekyll, Sir Herbert's widow, let Munstead Wood to Elisabeth Lutyens and her husband, Ian Glennie, the following summer, and to Mary Lutyens in the autumn and winter. Mary remembers that Miss Jekyll's clothes still hung in the cupboards, and she was most impressed by the 'meticulous neatness' of the workroom: ' ... the small drawers in one chest held all the necessities for her shell pictures – the shells and pieces of coral carefully graded as to size and colour.'[19] Miss Jekyll's friendly presence continued to fill the house, 'which still seemed to give off the scent of new wood'. Outside the garden was beautiful, but fading fast.

Francis Jekyll's *Memoir* of his aunt was published by Jonathan Cape in 1934. Lady Jekyll died in 1937, and the last guardian of the quiet world of Munstead was gone. Munstead Wood was let to various sympathetic tenants during the war; afterwards it was sold, and the contents were carefully catalogued for auction by Alfred Savill & Sons on 1 and 2 September 1948.

Those sale dates are the last certainties in the story before passing time consigned Miss Jekyll's real life first to obscurity, and then – through hazy recollections and conditioned memories – into legend. Is there the slightest chance of recalling the truth?

In the drab 1950s no one was interested in gardens, least of all in the elaborate plantings of that lavish and vanished world of Miss Jekyll's heyday. She was left in peace, largely irrelevant to the small world of gardening, which had opted for the revival of bad taste – masses of labour-saving shrubs, azaleas and heathers in garish magentas and oranges, the martial bedding of boring tulips and seas of forget-me-nots, and narrow preoccupations such as perfect emerald lawns or cactus dahlias. The art went out of gardening; Jekyll theories were kept alive in a few quiet places – at Waterperry under Miss Havergal's regime and at Swanley, where they were learnt by two young landscape architects, Brenda Colvin and Sylvia Crowe. Brenda Colvin later passed her theories on to the young Anthony du Gard Pasley.

In the wider world of west Surrey a fresh wave of commuter prosperity swept across the heaths and into the villages that Miss Jekyll had known. An added attraction for commuters was the carefully conserved, cobble-streeted luxury of Guildford, the smartest shopping town in the smartest part of southern England. The best and most desirable London stores – Heal's of Tottenham Court Road, the Army & Navy, Russell & Bromley – jostled with boutiques, La Boulangerie and the indispensable green welly shop, Jefferies, in the High Street. Property prices boomed; every cottage was enlarged and given a second bathroom and a granny flat. Munstead Wood itself was divided, and Miss Jekyll's Hut, her stables and her gardener's cottage became separate residences. A new house was built on the kitchen garden site of her pigsty. Among all this prosperity, 'Old West Surrey' crept into the confines of Castle Arch in Quarry Street, the stronghold of the Surrey

Archaeological Society, a group of serious and stoical guardians of Surrey's past. Among their concerns for the Pilgrim's Way and Bronze Age excavations, they had a regard for recent history that was far in advance of the time. It was through an outing to Munstead, Tigbourne Court and Orchards that I first heard about Miss Jekyll and Edwin Lutyens, in the early 1970s.

In 1966 Country Life Limited, for ever loyal to the memory of both Lutyens and Miss Jekyll, had published Betty Massingham's *Miss Jekyll: Portrait of a Great Gardener*. Mrs Massingham wrote a charming book; she knew the familiars of Miss Jekyll's world and consulted Lady Emily Lutyens, Oliver Hill and Harold Falkner, Christopher Hussey and the great-great-niece of Hercules Brabazon. But biography was a very gentle art then, in the last days before the gloves came off with landmark publications such as Michael Holroyd's *Lytton Strachey* (1967–8) and Nigel Nicolson's *Portrait of a Marriage* (1973). *Portrait of a Great Gardener* is full of delightful anecdotes and memories, scraps of correspondence, and a re-trimming of the facts from Francis Jekyll's *Memoir*. Mrs Massingham made much of Miss Jekyll's favourite flowers, her cats and her latter-day penchant for 'a good-natured battle of words',[20] but from behind this façade of charm a mystery begins to emerge. Whereas Francis Jekyll had had all Miss Jekyll's diaries, notebooks, drawings and correspondence, Mrs Massingham had none of these. Why not?

No diaries or letters have ever come to light. It is easy to assume that Francis Jekyll destroyed them after he had finished his task; or might he have packed them away in a dark corner of the attic at Munstead House? It was as a result of her book that Betty Massingham heard, in the kind of nightmare that biographers dread, that there was an enormous collection of Miss Jekyll's drawings resting safely in the Library of the College of Environmental Design at the University of California's Berkeley campus. And how did they get *there*? That is not a simple question to answer.

In those days of the 'discretionary' biography, and before the octopus tentacles of the Humanities Foundation at Austin, Texas, reached over Europe, it was quite usual to destroy private papers once the parts deemed printable had been published. Because of his apparent homosexuality, Francis Jekyll was sensitive to family opinion and the innate English sense of privacy probably prevailed. But the drawings were a different matter; he used them to compile a list of his aunt's commissions which was included in his *Memoir*. Did he then feel he had no further use for them? The drawings are bulky: they had filled Miss Jekyll's large plan chest, which was a dominant feature in her workshop but does not appear in the Munstead Wood sale catalogue. Did one of Francis's architect or artist friends covet the plan chest? Had one of his dealer friends an eye for the possible value of the drawings? The latter suggestion has possibilities, because Michael Laurie, Professor of Landscape Architecture at Berkeley, records Beatrix Farrand's note that she bought the drawings collection 'for a moderate sum' from a London dealer during the war.[21]

What happened after Mrs Farrand acquired the drawings is known.[22] In the late 1930s she and her husband, the distinguished constitutional historian Max Farrand, had set up an archive and library 'dedicated to the appreciation of natural beauty, plant and bird life and a taste for gardening'[23] at their country home, Reef Point, Bar Harbor, in Maine. Mrs Farrand, then at the peak of her own distinguished career as a landscape and garden designer, was a great admirer of Miss Jekyll's work and writings, and in terms of sympathy, foresight and understanding she was uniquely appreciative of the value of the drawings, far more so than anyone in England would have been at the time. After Max Farrand's retirement in 1941, he and Beatrix devoted more and more time to their project, collecting much valuable material, and intending that Reef Point Gardens should live on as an environmental teaching centre after their deaths.

Max Farrand died in 1945, knowing that the project was a success; 50,000 people had visited Reef Point and it was widely known as one of the best sources on the history of garden design. Ten years later, however, rising costs and uncertainties made Beatrix consult her wisest friends on the best course of action; she was advised, and she followed the advice, that the resources of Reef Point should be dispersed and that the archive material and library should go to a teaching institution which would value them. She chose the Department of Landscape Architecture at Berkeley, and the Reef Point Collection was duly dispatched on its journey across the continent by special lorry. Mrs Farrand died four years later, in 1959.

The Jekyll drawings, which included many Lutyens drawings sent from his office to instruct her on garden designs and schemes, and letters to and from clients, had been catalogued and labelled while at Reef Point, and stored in flat folders. In 1964 the Berkeley Department of Landscape Architecture was amalgamated with architecture and city planning into one College of Environmental Design at Wurster Hall, and the drawings took their place in the new combined library. After the publication of *Portrait of a Great Gardener*, Betty Massingham went to Berkeley and spent a great deal of time re-cataloguing the collection, and considerable cross-referencing and annotation has been done since that time. The drawings are kept in fine conditions in metal cabinets, and a programme of paper conservation is being carried out on them. They have a very good home, even though they are far away; perhaps, though, in a climate so very different from either Maine or Surrey, and in a West Coast state with its proud new westwards-looking direction, they are of rather less use than either Beatrix Farrand or Gertrude Jekyll would have hoped them to be.

Lot 217 in the September 1948 sale comprised six volumes of albums containing a collection 'of the late Miss Gertrude Jekyll's photographs of flowers, bouquets, gardens, buildings, styles of architecture; in all above 2,000 photographs'. These blue albums also went to Berkeley from Reef Point; Mrs Farrand noted in her 'Report of Progress 1949–50' that she had bought these six albums for £18.[24] Beatrix also told Mildred Bliss, her friend and client at Dumbarton Oaks in Washington DC, on 21 May 1948, that she had had the 'good fortune' to find the Jekyll drawings at a sale of the Massachusetts Horticultural Society.[25] Mrs Farrand was in constant contact with London book dealers and her interest in garden material was widely known, but exactly how the drawings, which were not in the sale, and the albums, which were, arrived with her, is open to speculation still. There are also plenty of English stories, from the memories of those who were at the sale, of wheelbarrows of drawings being rescued – from a bonfire? from a Red Cross sale? from a waste-paper drive? The truth is probably lost for ever.

However, it matters not too much, for the drawings have a good home. Betty Massingham returned from her Californian trip, with the news of their existence as an almost complete record of Miss Jekyll's 350 design commissions, to find that another resurrection was in hand. Miss Jekyll's young architect friend, who had grown to be the builder of Viceroy's House, New Delhi, great City buildings, the Cenotaph, the British Embassy in Washington, Queen Mary's Dolls' House – in short, the most famous architect of his day – and who had died on New Year's Day 1944, was also due for a revival.

Lutyens's reputation had also been loyally kept alive at Country Life Limited (where the vast, three-volume *Memorial* and Christopher Hussey's *Life of Lutyens* had been published in 1951), but his work was regarded as largely irrelevant to modern architecture. Interest began to grow gradually in America, as architects there, Philip Johnson and Michael Graves among them, found in Lutyens's quirky genius for his own form of classicism a recipe for the rise of Post-Modernism. Lutyens's reappraisal in America was picked up by critics here: Gavin Stamp wrote a timely piece, *The Rise, Fall and Rise Again of Sir Edwin Lutyens,*[26] and Colin Amery of the *Financial Times* persuaded the art establishment that architecture was a fit subject for popular acclaim and that Lutyens was the man whose personality and work exhibited the desired qualities of sweetness and light.

The Arts Council, though more comfortable with a genius of known quality like Pablo Picasso, took the bait, and the Hayward Gallery was booked for three months in the winter of 1981–2. Mary Lutyens, the architect's youngest daughter, contributed invaluable encouragement and family knowledge, and the vast RIBA collection of drawings was accessible and had been recently catalogued by Margaret Richardson. These people formed the nucleus of the Lutyens Exhibition Committee, and though I may be biased, that committee seemed to offer the final exception that proves the rule that a horse designed by a committee is not a mule, but a Derby winner!

One hundred thousand people crowded to the exhibition, which made an impact beyond its time and existence. Piers Gough, the architect/designer, filled the Hayward with evocations of country houses, castles and Imperial India. Visitors could experience what it was like to be in a Lutyens room, complete with its black ceiling and emerald green walls, and examine his architectural games; only Lutyens had the temerity to invent his own architectural order, with bells on, for New Delhi. Finally, there was his death mask, a fragile effigy; everyone marvelled that such a small, domed brain could contain all he had built. The exhibition was a triumph, and raised its subject to the status of a popular hero; it made him what he would most have wished to be, an architect as well known as Sir Christopher Wren.

Miss Jekyll had her own prominent place in Lutyens's life and career, and her place in the Hayward Gallery exhibition was assured, but it was inconceivable that she should not be accompanied by flowers and living plants. The arid concrete jungle of the South Bank, and the particularly alien confines of the Hayward Gallery, were not designed for such indulgences, and it was entirely due to the skills and energies of Merrist Wood Agricultural College that the exhibition's evocation of Munstead Wood included the scent of lilies and lush greenery, which left a powerful memory in many minds.[27]

At the same time as Miss Jekyll was playing her part on the South Bank, she was present in her own right at a small exhibition staged by the Architectural Association in Bedford Square. She would certainly have felt at home in that elegant Georgian exhibition space, one of the loveliest in London, and it was no trouble at all to install her shade happily. What was surprising was the number of people, total strangers to the Architectural Association as well as devotees of the more usual flights of architectural fantasy exhibited there, who came. They came to peruse the little silver casket and the salvers that she made, to look at her shell pictures, her paintings, and some of her garden design drawings, brought from California and being seen in London for the first time. The British public, and a surprising number of visitors from abroad, took this down-to-earth artist craftswoman to their hearts, and she remains firmly installed there.[28]

Gertrude Jekyll has now been approached from almost every angle of her multi-talented career. Her books on gardening, now mostly available reprinted, offer enough ideas to fill ten gardening lives; they have been expertly distilled and related to gardening in our time by Penelope Hobhouse and Christopher Lloyd. Her photographs of her garden, the most vital image of her life, have been presented anew in a volume called *A Vision of Garden and Wood* by two eminent Americans — Judith Tankard, a lecturer in landscape design history at Radcliffe, and Michael van Valkenburgh, a landscape architect and teacher at Harvard Graduate School of Design.[29] Her gardens, large and small, in Britain and including one she never saw, for the Glebe House, Woodbury, Connecticut, are being enthusiastically replanted, and she is emulated and admired on the other side of the world, in Australia and New Zealand. She has become a by-word for every conversation on artistry in gardening, a cue name for every producer of radio and television programmes; only Gertrude Jekyll, The Movie, is awaited.

All this is due to her many virtues, but not least to her humanity. To everyone who consults her she imparts her experience, her judgement, her knowledge, and leaves the firm, though unspoken, intention that now she has started us off, it is up to us to follow through and develop our own ideas and talents. Her essential humanity pervades all, from the particular to the universal, from the propagating of bunch primroses after blooming ('the plants then seem willing to divide, some almost falling apart in one's hands'[30]) to her intrinsic care for nature on this planet. She was, in her deepest conscience, truly Green, and believed in living a sensible life in her own small world as her best contribution. In every gardener, and in more and more of every one of us, this is the nub of Greenness — concern for our plot, our surroundings, our countryside and then our planet. Gertrude Jekyll believed profoundly in the plot of

England on which her own size eight gardening boots stood, and she was acutely aware that the depth of her belief should be demonstrated and broadcast for the benefit of others. She is our truly eminent gardener because she taught us that the quality of life on this small planet begins at home.

Endword

THERE is a final question that is often asked about Gertrude Jekyll, and it reverberates through this book, landing with a dull thud at my feet as I finish writing: 'If Miss Jekyll is so important, then why isn't her garden preserved and in the care of the National Trust?'

The great flaw in gardening as an expressionist art that this book expounds is, of course, that gardeners die, and that the garden that has matured with them must die also. I am fascinated, intrigued and concerned about the art of garden conservation, because I believe it is a good thing, but I fear that we are treating the garden as though it were a finite object, like a building, a painting or a marquetry commode. In the forty years since the National Trust acquired Hidcote Manor garden for the purpose of preserving it, Britain has undoubtedly triumphed in the techniques and systems of the conservation business. In bestowing eternal life on works of art, including buildings, the craft skills of restoration and repair and the marketing skills of management in the public sphere have flourished as new and worthwhile industries. But gardens *are* different: a garden is more than its design laid out on paper and its collection of plants in a list. A garden is an experience, a moving picture, or a series of pictures through which one moves, and as Sir Frederick Gibberd said, 'if you step into the picture it dissolves, and other pictures appear'.[1] This changes according to the mood of the weather, the season or the time of day. And it changes constantly with time and with the daily prinking, pruning and care from its maker that is the essence of expressionist gardening. So when the gardener dies, how can it stay the same?

It is obvious that the essential element in the conservation of gardens is that the vanished owner or garden-maker must be replaced by an equally accomplished and entirely sympathetic mind. There are two options, then: the garden is strictly maintained within the limits of knowledge of a given moment in its creation, or the new 'owner' is allowed to develop and the garden to grow into something newly creative. Only the most exceptional, well-documented and 'great' gardens can be conserved in the former way, and if the applause indicator of the world could be heard it would suggest that of English twentieth-century gardens, Vita Sackville-West's Sissinghurst Castle and Miss Jekyll's Munstead Wood would fall into this category. Garden conservation, properly done, can be for only a very few gardens.

Most of the gardens I have talked about in this book are, or would be, best in the care of an understanding mind, under which they can grow. The key is in that word 'understanding', and the very best reason for trying to find out what made our garden-makers 'tick' is to further that understanding, which is what I have tried to do with these 'eminent gardeners'. It is, after all, very much a matter of practising the kind of humility, respect and informed devotion that has gone into the re-awakening of Charleston farm-house, described on pages 10–12. Conservation will teach us nothing if it merely replicates showy flowers or an arid style. The conservation of a garden requires the re-making of the atmosphere of its day, a restoration of the sense of place, which makes it comfortable enough for the ghosts to return.

Notes

Introduction

1. See Jane Brown, *Gardens of a Golden Afternoon. The Story of a Partnership: Edwin Lutyens and Gertrude Jekyll*, Viking, London, 1982.

2. See Jane Brown, *Vita's Other World*, Viking, London, 1985.

3. See Jane Brown, *Lanning Roper and His Gardens*, Weidenfeld & Nicolson, 1987.

4. Victoria Glendinning, *Vita: The Life of Vita Sackville-West*, Weidenfeld & Nicolson, London, 1983.

5. V. Sackville-West, 'Hidcote Manor Garden', *Journal of the Royal Horticultural Society*, Vol. LXXIV, Part 11, November 1949.

6. See note 3 above.

7. David Watkin, *Basil Champneys and the Building of Newnham College*, published by Newnham College, Cambridge, 1990.

8. Barbara Bodichon (1827–91), formerly Barbara Leigh-Smith, was a close friend of Gertrude Jekyll's. She is the subject of a biography by Hester Burton (*Barbara Bodichon 1827–91*, John Murray, London, 1949) but has been seemingly neglected in the literature of the women's movement, except for Dale Spender's *Women of Ideas* (Routledge, London, 1982).

9. Lady Constance Lytton became Edwin Lutyens's sister-in-law.

10. The Hon. Emily Lawless is less well known than Barbara Bodichon and Constance Lytton, but she was a woman of advanced ideas, with a deep love of nature; she kept a nature diary. Miss Jekyll planned a woodland garden with her, for her house at Shere in Surrey.

11. See note 2 above.

12. Nigel Nicolson, *Portrait of a Marriage*, Weidenfeld & Nicolson, London, 1973. Filmed during 1989 for BBC TV screening in 1990.

13. See note 4 above.

14. Quoted from Harold Acton's review of Victoria Glendinning's *Vita* in *Books and Bookmen*, September 1983.

15. William Morris, 'A Garden by the Sea'.

16. D. H. Lawrence, *Women in Love*, Chapter 8, quoted in Margaret Drabble, *A Writer's Britain*, Thames & Hudson, London, 1979, p. 143.

17. Letter from D. H. Lawrence to Lady Ottoline Morrell, 1 December 1915, quoted ibid.

18. ibid.

19. Noel Carrington, *Carrington: Paintings, Drawings and Decorations*, Thames & Hudson, London, 1978, p. 31.

20. For details of the house and garden restoration of Charleston farmhouse see Quentin Bell, Angelica Garnett, Henrietta Garnett and Richard Shone, *Charleston: Past and Present*, Hogarth Press, London, 1987.

21. W. Dallimore, *Poisonous Plants: Deadly, Dangerous and Suspect*, with an introduction and illustrations by John Nash, Etchells & Macdonald, London, 1927.

22. H. E. Bates, *Flowers and Faces*, with illustrations by John Nash, Golden Cockerel Press, London, 1935.

23. Patrick Synge, *Plants with Personality*, illustrated by John Nash, 1938.

24. Robert Gathorne-Hardy, *The Native Garden*, Thomas Nelson, London, 1961, and *The Tranquil Gardener*, Thomas Nelson, London, 1958, both illustrated by John Nash.

25. Ronald Blythe, 'A Garden of My Own', *Observer*, 4 August 1985.

26. Sir Cedric Morris, four contributions on iris species and their cultivation in *The Iris Year Book*, 1943 (pp. 43–5), 1948 (pp. 39–40), 1956 (pp. 140–42) and 1962 (pp. 135–7).

27. From Beth Chatto, 'Sir Cedric Morris, Artist-Gardener', in *Hortus*, 1, Spring 1987, p. 14.

28. Ursula Vaughan Williams, *A Life of Ralph Vaughan Williams*, Oxford University Press, 1964, p. 237.

29. Quoted by Ursula Vaughan Williams, op. cit., p. 321, from *Thyrsis: In Memoriam A. H. Clough* by Matthew Arnold. See text, pp. 83–91, for Arthur Hugh Clough's daughter, Blanche Athena Clough's, interest in gardens.

30. Ursula Vaughan Williams, op. cit., p. 321.

31. Susana Gil Passo (Lady Walton), *Behind the Façade*, Oxford University Press, 1988.

32. Sir Frederick Gibberd, 'The Design of a Garden', in *The Garden* (the journal of the Royal Horticultural Society), April 1979.

33. Wilfred Blunt, *Of Flowers and a Village*, Hamish Hamilton, London, 1963, p. 75.

34. For a more detailed description of the ornaments in West Green Manor's garden, see Clive Aslet, *Quinlan Terry*, Viking, London, 1988.

Chapter 1: Frances Wolseley

1. Augustus Hare's *Memorials of a Quiet Life* was, Lady Wolseley felt, 'sweet-smelling and elevating, after a little "Season"' (letter, 9 June 1891, from *The Letters of Lord and Lady Wolseley 1870–1911*, ed. Sir George Arthur, Heinemann, London, n.d.). The *Memorials* were a great favourite of the time; they made Thomas Carlyle cry, and the Queen of Sweden admitted them 'her greatest comfort'. There were three ponderous volumes of country gossip about mid-Victorian life in rural southern England, published 1872–6.

2. See note 1 above for *The Letters of Lord and Lady Wolseley*; see also Joseph H. Lehman, *All Sir Garnet: A Life of Field Marshal Lord Wolseley*, Cape, London, 1964.

3. *Letters*, op. cit., pp. 290–91.

4. ibid., p. 351.

5. ibid., p. 382.

6. Mary Watts's fascinating ideas for her village industry intrigued her friends and fellow artists; see Wilfrid Blunt, *England's Michelangelo*, Hamish Hamilton, London, 1975, p. 231.

7. The prospectus of the Glynde College for Lady Gardeners, Ragged Lands, Glynde, is dated 1914 and was issued by the Principal and Sole Manager, Miss Else More F.R.H.S. I have a photocopy of this, kindly supplied by Dr Andrew Sclater; also an article on the 'School of Lady Gardeners at Ragged Lands, Glynde' by Mary Campion (one of the patrons) from *The Country Home* (undated). I understand that both are from the archive of Mr Andrew Lusted, who lives in Glynde.

8. The term 'suffragette' first appeared in the *Daily Mail* on 10 January 1906.

9. Letter from Lady Wolseley to Lord Wolseley, 22 February 1903, in *Letters*, op. cit.

10. Anna Bateson (1863–1928) was the daughter of the Master of St John's College, Cambridge, and took a Natural Science Tripos at Newnham College. She was assistant to Sir Francis Darwin until she became an apprentice market gardener, opening her own business at New Milton in 1892. She became completely involved in local politics, including the New Forest Suffragette Society.

11. Frances Wolseley, *Gardens: Their Form and Design*, Edward Arnold, London, 1919, p. 10.

12. ibid., p. 11.

13. ibid.

14. ibid., p. 149.

15. ibid., p. 60.

16. ibid., p. 28.

17. ibid., pp. 242–3.

18. Rosemary Alexander and Anthony du Gard Pasley, *The English Gardening*

School: A Complete Course in Garden Planning and Design, Michael Joseph, London, 1987.

19. Frances Wolseley, *Some of the Smaller Manor Houses of Sussex*, Medici Society, London, 1925.

20. 'King Edward VII Sanatorium', *Country Life*, Vol XXVI, 20 November 1909, p. 701.

Chapter 2: The Henry James Americans

1. Stanley Olson, 'On the Question of Sargent's Nationality', in *John Singer Sargent*, catalogue of an exhibition at the Whitney Museum of American Art, New York, 1986, p. 13.

2. Evan Charteris, *Life of John S. Sargent*, Heinemann, London, 1927, pp. 75–6.

3. The painting of the picture is fully described in Evan Charteris, op. cit., and in Richard Ormond, 'Carnation Lily, Lily Rose', in *Sargent at Broadway: The Impressionist Years*, Universe/Coe Kerr Gallery, New York, and John Murray, London, 1986.

4. Henry James, 'Our Artists in England', *Harper's Magazine*, New York, 1889.

5. Abbey is well documented in two volumes by E. V. Lucas, *Edwin Austin Abbey RA: Record of his Life and Work*, Methuen, London, and Scribner's, New York, 1921. Wilfrid Blunt, in *England's Michelangelo*, Hamish Hamilton, London, 1975, records that George Frederic Watts wanted to marry Mary Gertrude Mead.

6. Mary Anderson de Navarro wrote of her Broadway years in *A Few More Memories*, Hutchinson, London, 1936.

7. Henry James, 'In Warwickshire', in *English Hours*, Oxford University Press edn, 1982, p. 113.

8. Edward Prioleau Warren (1856–1937), architect, known for his extensive work on Oxford and Cambridge colleges and English domestic revival buildings, notably at Bedales School (1907). He and his wife Margaret were friends of James and helped him considerably with Lamb House. See H. Montgomery Hyde, *Henry James at Home*, Methuen, London, 1969, p. 70.

9. H. Montgomery Hyde, op. cit., p. 83.

10. ibid., p. 91.

11. Beatrix Cadwalader Jones (1872–1959), who was the daughter of James's great friend Mary 'Minnie' Jones, became a distinguished landscape gardener and designer; she designed campus layouts for Princeton, Yale and the University of Chicago, and the garden of Dumbarton Oaks in Washington DC.

12. See Mavis Batey, *Oxford Gardens*, Oxford, 1982, p. 190.

13. Wilfrid Blunt, *The Art of Botanical Illustration*, Collins New Naturalist Series, London, 1950, plate 43.

14. The story of Parsons and *The Genus Rosa* is related by Bryan N. Brooke in

A Garden of Roses, commentary by G. S. Thomas, Pavilion/Michael Joseph/Royal Horticultural Society, London, 1987.

15. Alan Crawford, 'New Life for an Artist's Village', in *Country Life*, 24 January 1980.

16. See note 4 above.

17. Henry James, 'In Warwickshire', op. cit.

18. Mary Anderson de Navarro, op. cit.

19. ibid.

20. Charles Platt, *Italian Gardens*, Harper & Row, New York, 1894.

21. See Ethne Clarke's *Hidcote: The Making of the Garden*, Michael Joseph, London, 1989, which has been published since I wrote this chapter.

22. V. Sackville-West, 'Hidcote Manor Garden', *Journal of the Royal Horticultural Society*, Vol. LXXIV, Part 11, November 1949.

23. ibid.

24. ibid.

Chapter 3: Norah Lindsay

1. Philip Tilden, *True Remembrances: The Memoirs of an Architect*, Country Life, London, 1954, p. 34.

2. Diana Cooper (formerly Manners), *The Rainbow Comes and Goes*, Hart-Davis, London, 1958.

3. James Lees-Milne, *Ancestral Voices*, Chatto & Windus, London, 1975, p. 152.

4. See John Cornforth, *The Inspiration of the Past*, Viking, London, 1985, p. 29, quoting Christopher Hussey, *Country Life*, 1931.

5. Geoffrey Taylor, *The Victorian Flower Garden*, Skeffington, London, 1952, p. 88.

6. Norah Lindsay, 'The Garden of the Manor House, Sutton Courtenay', *Country Life*, May 1931.

7. I am grateful to the National Trust, and in particular to John Maddison, for letting me see the Blickling Hall visitors' book which is kept in the house.

8. Alice Fullerton, *To Persia for Flowers*, Oxford University Press, 1938.

9. ibid., p. 67.

10. Nancy Lindsay to V. Sackville-West, undated letter in the Sissinghurst Castle papers.

11. V. Sackville-West, 'Hidcote Manor Garden', *Journal of the Royal Horticultural Society*, Vol. LXXIV, Part 11, November 1949.

12. ibid.

13. *House and Garden*, Vol. 3, No. 4, April 1948.

14. John Cornforth, op. cit., p. 157.

15. Peter Shepheard, *Modern Gardens*, Architectural Press, London, 1953, pp. 66–7.

16. Graham Stuart Thomas, *The Old Shrub Roses*, Phoenix House, London, 1955.

Chapter 4: Academic Gardeners

1. Jane Brown, *The Everywhere Landscape*, Wildwood House, London, 1982.

2. The following is the result of my research for *Newnham College: The Making of the Gardens*, published by Newnham College, Cambridge, 1989.

3. For Anne Jemima Clough and her relationship with her brother, see David Williams, *Too Quick Despairer: The Life of Arthur Hugh Clough*, Hart-Davis, London, 1969, p. 155.

4. Hester Burton, *Barbara Bodichon 1827–91*, John Murray, London, 1949, p. 178.

5. *A Memoir of Anne Jemima Clough by B. A. Clough*, Edward Arnold, London, 1897, p. 201.

6. ibid., p. 203.

7. Hester Burton, op. cit., p. 178.

8. Ethel Sidgwick, *Mrs Henry Sidgwick: A Memoir*, Sidgwick & Jackson, London, 1938, p. 20.

9. David Watkin, *Basil Champneys and the Building of Newnham College*, published by Newnham College, Cambridge, 1990.

10. Mark Girouard, *Sweetness and Light: The Architecture of the Queen Anne Movement 1860–1900*, Yale University Press, 1977.

11. David Watkin, op. cit.

12. Gwen Raverat, *Period Piece*, Faber, London, 1952, p. 45.

13. ibid., p. 126.

14. Chapter XXII of Gertrude Jekyll's *Home and Garden*, Longmans Green, London, 1900, is devoted to 'Things Worth Doing'.

15. In the R.I.B.A. library there is a copy of *Portuguese Architecture*, Constable, London, 1908, and the further information on Walter C. Watson that he lived in Northfield, Balerno, Midlothian, and died in the early 1940s.

16. See Mavis Batey, *Oxford Gardens*, Oxford, 1982.

17. See also John Raven, *A Botanist's Garden*, Collins, London, 1971.

18. Mavis Batey, op. cit., p. 185ff.

19. ibid., p. 160.

20. ibid., p. 199.

21. ibid., p. 201.

Chapter 5: The Lords Fairhaven

1. See Justin Kaplan, *Mr Clemens and Mark Twain*, Cape, London, 1967, pp. 321–2.

2. The H. H. Rogers house at Southampton, Long Island was designed by Walker and Gillette and the garden was by Olmsted Brothers; see John Taylor Boyd Jr,

'The Country House of H. H. Rogers Esq.', *Architectural Review*, Vol XXXIX, No. 1, January 1916, pp. 1–23.

3. Justin Kaplan, op. cit., p. 321.

4. ibid., p. 385.

5. Letter to the author from Lorraine Gilligan, Coe Hall, at Planting Fields Arboretum, 1 February 1988.

6. The plan of Anglesey Abbey is based on that in the National Trust guide to the gardens, 1984.

7. Geoffrey Jellicoe, *Italian Gardens of the Renaissance*, Alec Tiranti, London, 1925.

8. By Lanning Roper, in 'Landscape Design', *Journal of the Royal Horticultural Society*, lecture given on 24 September 1968.

9. Edith Wharton, *Italian Villas and Their Gardens*, The Bodley Head, London, 1904.

10. Michael Jaffe, introduction to David Scrase, *Flowers of Three Centuries: One Hundred Drawings and Watercolours from the Broughton Collection*, International Exhibitions Foundation, Washington, DC, 1983–4.

11. Lord Fairhaven's garden at South Walsham is open regularly from April to the end of September: for details write to the Fairhaven Garden Trust, South Walsham, Norfolk (tel: South Walsham 060 549).

Chapter 6: Christopher Tunnard

1. V. Sackville-West, *The Garden*, Michael Joseph, London, 1946.

2. Christopher Tunnard, *Gardens in the Modern Landscape*, Architectural Press, London, 1938.

3. Le Corbusier, *Towards a New Architecture*, trans. Frederick Etchells, Architectural Press, London, 1927; 1978 edn, p. 164.

4. See Jane Brown, *The Art and Architecture of English Gardens*, Weidenfeld & Nicolson, London, pp. 188–9, for the Behrens drawings.

5. Peter Shepheard, *Modern Gardens*, Architectural Press, London, 1953, p. 106.

6. ibid., pp. 26–33.

7. Christopher Tunnard, op. cit., p. 6.

8. ibid., pp. 9–10.

9. ibid., pp. 21–3.

10. ibid., p. 49.

11. ibid., p. 54 (quoting John Claudius Loudon).

12. ibid., p. 109.

13. Raymond Mortimer, *The New Interior Design*, 1929, introduction.

14. Jane Brown, op. cit., pp. 192–3.

15. Peter Shepheard, op. cit., pp. 80–81.

16. Christopher Tunnard, op. cit., p. 178.

17. Norman Newton, *Design on the Land*, Belknap Press of the Harvard University Press, Cambridge, Mass., 1971.

18. Christopher Tunnard, *City of Man*, Scribner's, New York, 1953.

19. Christopher Tunnard, *American Skyline*, with Henry Hope Reed, Houghton Mifflin, Boston, 1955.

20. Christopher Tunnard, *Man-made America*, with Boris Pushkarov, Yale University Press, 1963.

21. Robert Arvill, *Man and Environment*, Penguin, Harmondsworth, 1973, p. 322.

22. Christopher Tunnard, *The World with a View*, Yale University Press, 1978.

23. ibid., p. 184.

24. ibid.

25. ibid.

26. ibid., p. 185.

Chapter 7: Gertrude Jekyll – At Home and Abroad

1. My first article about Edwin Lutyens and Gertrude Jekyll appeared in *Landscape Design*, May 1977, p. 8.

2. Quoted from George Leslie in Jane Brown, *Gardens of a Golden Afternoon*, Viking, London, 1982, p. 23.

3. A bibliography of Gertrude Jekyll's published works will be found in *Gertrude Jekyll: Artist, Gardener, Craftswoman*, ed. Michael Tooley, Michaelmas Books, Witton-le-Wear, 1984. The bibliography is compiled by Margaret Hastings and Michael Tooley.

4. Gertrude Jekyll, *Home and Garden*, Longmans Green, London, 1900, p. 14.

5. ibid., p. 191.

6. ibid., p. 22.

7. ibid., p. 24.

8. Lawrence Weaver, *The Houses and Gardens of E. L. Lutyens*, Country Life, London, 1913, p. 19.

9. Gertrude Jekyll, op. cit., p. 34.

10. ibid., pp. 168–72.

11. ibid., p. 24.

12. ibid., p. 30.

13. ibid., pp. 25–6.

14. The planting of the garden at King Edward VII Sanatorium is described in *Country Life*, Vol. XXVI, 20 November 1909, p. 701, and on pp. 37–9 here.

15. The planting plans for Deanery Garden are published in Gertrude Jekyll and Lawrence Weaver, *Gardens for Small Country Houses*, Newnes/Country Life, London, 1912, p. 20.

16. The gardener who restores Miss Jekyll's planting as she planned it, then adjusts as the plants dictate, as Miss Jekyll intended, finds this out. The best example is the restoration of the garden of the Manor House, Upton Grey in Hampshire by Mrs John Wallinger, who has thus learned her gardening 'with Miss Jekyll holding her hand'. The Manor House is open for the National Gardens Scheme.

17. Mary Lutyens, *Edwin Lutyens, A Memoir*, John Murray, London, 1980, p. 261.

18. I was fortunate enough to meet Mr Frank Young, Miss Jekyll's last surviving gardener, and take him back to Munstead Wood. His memories of the garden are recorded in 'Memories of Munstead Wood', *The Garden* (the journal of the Royal Horticultural Society), April 1987, pp. 162–3.

19. Mary Lutyens, op. cit., p. 27.

20. Betty Massingham, *Miss Jekyll: Portrait of a Great Gardener*, Country Life, London, 1966, p. 165.

21. Michael M. Laurie, *The Reef Point Collection at the University of California*, in the Eighth Dumbarton Oaks Colloquium on the History of Landscape Architecture, Dumbarton Oaks, 1982, p. 12.

22. ibid., pp. 14–16, for how Mrs Farrand bequeathed her archives to the College of Environmental Design at Berkeley.

23. ibid., p. 11.

24. Some of the photographs from Miss Jekyll's collection have been published in *A Vision of Garden and Wood*, with commentary and essays by Judith Tankard and Michael van Valkenburgh, John Murray, London, and Sagapress, New York, 1989.

25. ibid., p. 5.

26. Gavin Stamp, *The Rise and Fall and Rise Again of Sir Edwin Lutyens*, Architectural Review, November 1981.

27. See the catalogue of the Lutyens Exhibition, edited by Margaret Richardson and Colin Amery, Arts Council, London, 1981.

28. *Miss Gertrude Jekyll 1843–1932, Gardener*, my catalogue for the Architectural Association, London, 1981.

29. See my foreword to Judith Tankard and Michael von Valkenburgh, op. cit.

30. Gertrude Jekyll, *Wood and Garden*, Longmans Green, London, 1899, p. 296.

Endword

1. Frederick Gibberd, in 'The Design of a Garden', *The Garden* (the journal of the Royal Horticultural Society), April 1979, p. 135.

Bibliography

ARTHUR, SIR GEORGE (ED.): *The Letters of Lord and Lady Wolseley 1870–1911*, Heinemann, London, n.d.

BATES, H. E.: *Flowers and Faces* (with illustrations by John Nash), Golden Cockerel Press, London, 1935.

BATEY, MAVIS: *Oxford Gardens*, Oxford, 1982.

BELL, QUENTIN ET AL.: *Charleston: Past and Present*, Hogarth Press, London, 1987.

BLUNT, WILFRID: *England's Michelangelo*, Hamish Hamilton, London, 1975.

BROWN, JANE: *Lanning Roper and His Gardens*, Weidenfeld, London, 1987.

BROWN, JANE: *Gardens of a Golden Afternoon. The Story of a Partnership: Edwin Lutyens and Gertrude Jekyll*, Viking, London, 1982.

BROWN, JANE: *Newnham College: The Making of the Gardens*, Newnham College, Cambridge, 1988.

BROWN, JANE: *Vita's Other World: a gardening biography of Vita Sackville-West*, Viking, London, 1985.

CHARTERIS, EVAN: *Life of J. S. Sargent*, Heinemann, London, 1927.

CORNFORTH, JOHN: *The Inspiration of the Past*, Viking, London, 1985.

CROWE, SYLVIA: *Garden Design*, Country Life, London, 1958.

DALLIMORE, W.: *Poisonous Plants: Deadly, Dangerous and Suspect* (with an introduction and illustrations by John Nash), Etchells & Macdonald, London, 1927.

ELLIOTT, BRENT: *Victorian Gardens*, Batsford, London, 1986.

GATHORNE-HARDY, ROBERT: *The Tranquil Gardener* (with illustrations by John Nash), Thomas Nelson, London, 1958.

GATHORNE-HARDY, ROBERT: *The Native Garden* (with illustrations by John Nash), Thomas Nelson, London, 1961.

GIROUARD, MARK: *Sweetness and Light: The Architecture of the Queen Anne Movement 1860–1900*, Yale University Press, London, 1977.

HOBHOUSE, PENELOPE: *Gertrude Jekyll on Gardening*, Collins/National Trust, London, 1983.

HYDE, H. MONTGOMERY: *Henry James at Home*, Methuen, London, 1969.

JEKYLL, G., AND WEAVER, L.: *Gardens for Small Country Houses*, Country Life, London, 1912.

JEKYLL, GERTRUDE: *Home and Garden*, Longmans, Green, London, 1900.

KAPLAN, JUSTIN: *Mr Clemens and Mark Twain*, Jonathan Cape, London, 1967.

LEARY, LEWIS (ED.): *Mark Twain's Correspondence with Henry H. Rogers 1893–1909*, University of California Press, Berkeley, 1969.

LEHMANN, J. H.: *All Sir Garnet: A Life of Field Marshal Lord Wolseley*, Jonathan Cape, London, 1964.

LUCAS, E. V.: *Edwin Austin Abbey RA: A Record of His Life and Work*, 2 vols., Methuen, London, and Scribner's, New York, 1921.

MACLEOD, DAWN: *Down to Earth Women*, Blackwood, Edinburgh, 1982.

MASSINGHAM, BETTY: *Miss Jekyll, Portrait of a Great Gardener*, Country Life, London, 1966.

MORPHET, RICHARD: *Cedric Morris*, Tate Gallery, London, 1984.

NAVARRO, MARY ANDERSON DE: *A Few More Memories*, Hutchinson, London, 1936.

ORMOND, RICHARD: *Sargent at Broadway: The Impressionist Years*, Universe/Coe Kerr Gallery, New York, and John Murray, London, 1986.

OTTEWILL, DAVID: *The Edwardian Garden*, Yale University Press, New Haven and London, 1989.

RAVEN, JOHN: *A Botanist's Garden*, Collins, London, 1971.

RAVERAT, GWEN: *Period Piece*, Faber & Faber, London, 1952.

ROPER, LANNING: *The Gardens of Anglesey Abbey*, Faber & Faber, London, 1965.

ROTHENSTEIN, SIR JOHN: *John Nash*, Macdonald, London, 1983.

SHEPHEARD, PETER: *Modern Gardens*, Architectural Press, London, 1953.

SIDGWICK, ETHEL: *Mrs Henry Sidgwick: A Memoir*, Sidgwick & Jackson, London, 1938.

SYNGE, PATRICK: *Plants with Personality* (with illustrations by John Nash), Lindsay Drummond, London, 1938.

TANKARD, JUDITH, AND VAN VALKENBURGH, MICHAEL (EDS.): *Gertrude Jekyll: A Vision of Garden and Wood*, John Murray, London, and Sagapress, New York, 1989.

TAYLOR, GEOFFREY: *The Victorian Flower Garden*, Skeffington, London, 1952.

TOOLEY, MICHAEL (ED.): *Gertrude Jekyll: Artist, Gardener, Craftswoman*, Michaelmas Books, Witton-le-Wear, Northumberland, 1984.

TUNNARD, CHRISTOPHER: *Gardens in the Modern Landscape*, Architectural Press, London, 1938.

TUNNARD, CHRISTOPHER: *A World with a View*, Yale University Press, New Haven, 1978.

TUNNARD, CHRISTOPHER: *The City of Man*, Scribner's, New York, 1953.

WOLSELEY, FRANCES: *Gardening for Women*, Cassell, London, 1908.

WOLSELEY, FRANCES: *Women and the Land*, Chatto & Windus, London, 1916.

WOLSELEY, FRANCES: *In a College Garden*, John Murray, London, 1916.

WOLSELEY, FRANCES: *Gardens: Their Form and Design*, Edward Arnold, London, 1919.

WOLSELEY, FRANCES: *Some of the Smaller Manor Houses of Sussex*, Medici Society, London, 1925.

Index

ABBEY, Edwin Austin, 42–4, 46, 47, 51
Abbey Chase, Chertsey, Surrey, 118
Abbotswood, Stow-on-the-Wold, Gloucester-
  shire, 51–2, 118
Aberconway, Henry, 1st Baron, 16
Aberconway, Laura, Lady, 16
Acton, Sir Harold, 8
Adams, Frank, 56
Adams, H. Percy, 37, pl. 2
Addison, Joseph, 123
Agar, Barbara (Barbie), 70
Alexander, Rosemary
  English Gardening School, 36
Allwood, Montague, 29
Alma-Tadema, Sir Lawrence, 43
America see United States of America
Amery, Colin, 157
Anderson, Mary see Navarro, Mary
  Anderson de
Anglesey Abbey, Cambridgeshire
  furnishings, 99–100
  garden, 96, 101–9, 114, pl. 16, pl. 17. pl. 19
    Italian influence, 101
    Lanning Roper on, 5
    restoration of, 98
Architectural Association
  Jekyll Exhibition (1981–2), 158–9
Architectural Review, 105, 117, 123, 130
Arnander, Primrose, 7
Arts and Crafts Movement, 6, 26–7, 28, 46, 50,
  51, 55, 81, 85, 86, 91
Arts Council, 157
Ashridge Park, Hertfordshire, 22, 95
Association for Promoting the Higher Education
  of Women in Cambridge, 79
Astor, Francis David, 75
Astor, Nancy, Viscountess, 60, 68
Astor, William Waldorf, 1st Viscount, 40, 52
Astor family, 68, 70

Austin, Alfred, 22

BACKHOUSE (James) of York, 83, pl. 22
Bakeham House, Englefield Green, Berkshire,
  109
Baker, Herbert, 68, 69
Balfour, Arthur James, 1st Earl of, 80, 84
Balfour, Blanche, 79, 80
Balfour, Eleanor Mildred see Sidgwick, Eleanor
  Mildred
Balfour, Lady Evelyn, 18
Balfour, Gerald, 2nd Earl of, 84, 85
Barnard family, 41–2
Barrie, Sir James, 43, pl. 5
Bateman, Charles, 45, 47, 49, 50
Bates, H. E.
  Flowers and Faces, 13
Bateson, Anna (market gardener), 31, pl. 22
Bateson, Mrs William, pl. 22
Batey, Mavis
  Oxford Gardens, 46, 93
Bawden, Edward, 117
Beaton, Sir Cecil, 70
Beechwood, Lavington, Sussex, 70
Behrens, Peter, 119
Bell, Clive, 11
Bell, Vanessa, 10–12
Bentley Wood, Halland, East Sussex, 126–7,
  pl. 23
Benton End, Colchester, Essex, 14–15
Berenson, Bernard, 40
Berkeley, Rose, 18, 50, 55
Berkeley see California, University of
Berners, 8th Baron, 69
Betteshanger Manor, Kent, 51
Bidder, Dr Henry Jardine, 93
Blackman, Professor Geoffrey, 93–4
Blenheim Palace, Oxfordshire, 124

Blickling Hall, Norfolk, 4, 57, 60, 69–70, 81, 82
Bliss, Mildred, 156
Blomfield, Reginald, 118
  The Formal Garden in England, 35, 46
Bloomsbury Set, 9, 11–12
Blumenthal, Jacques, 22
Blunt, Wilfrid Scawen, 17, 46, 62
Blythe, Ronald, 13, 15
Boden's Ride, Ascot, Berkshire, 118
Bodichon, Barbara, 7, 79, 80, 145, 146
Bodley, G. F., 23
Bodnant, North Wales, 16
Bottengoms, Essex, 13–14
Bourke family, 62
Bourke, N. M. M. *see* Lindsay, Norah Mary
  Madeleine
Brabazon, Hercules B., 145, 154
Braddell, Darcy, 118
Bramley Park, Guildford, Surrey, 8, 139
British Association of Garden Architects, 36,
  119
Broadway, Hereford and Worcester, 41–8, 50,
  58, pl. 5, pl. 6
Broughton, Urban Hanlon, 95
Broughton family *see* Fairhaven
Broughton Collection, Fitzwilliam Museum, 92,
  110, 112, 113
Brown, Lancelot 'Capability', 124
Brownlow, Maud, Lady, 22
Builder, The, 82
Burley, Hampshire, 85–6
Burne-Jones, Sir Edward, 23, 85, 140

CADWALADER Jones, Beatrix, 45
California, University of at Berkeley, 154, 156
Cambridge, Massachusetts, 133
Campion, Alice, 31
Campion, Mary, 30
Cane, Percy, 118
Caneel-Claes, Jean, 122–3
Cant, Frank, 29
Carnegie, Andrew, 97, 113
Carrington, Dora, 10
Carrington, Noel, 10
Carrington, Peter, 6th Baron, 18
Champneys, Basil, 6, 78, 81–2, 84, 87
Charleston farmhouse, Sussex, 10–12, 162
  Charleston Trust, 12
Charoux, Siegfried, 75

Charteris, Ivo, 53
Chartwell, Westerham, Kent, 5, 18
Chatto, Beth, 15
Chermayeff, Serge, 117, 126, 135, pl. 23
Chipping Campden, Gloucestershire, 49, 50
Choate, William, 55
Churchill, Sir Winston, 17
Clare College, Cambridge, 92
Clark, Kenneth (later Lord Clark), 68
Clayton, Savile, 48
Clemens, Livy, 97
Cliveden, Buckinghamshire, 68
Clough, Anne Jemima, 78–9, 81–4, 87, 91,
  pl. 20
Clough, Arthur, 83, 85–6
Clough, Arthur Hugh, 78, 83
Clough, Blanche Athena, 78, 83–4, 85–6, 87–8,
  91, pl. 21
Coates, Wells, 117
Codrington, John, 91
Coe, William Robertson *and* Mary (Mai), 98
Cole, Henry, 140
Colefax, Sibyl, Lady, 60, 61, 68, 74
Colvin, Brenda, 75, 153
Coneyhurst, Ewhurst, Surrey, 85
Connell, Amyas, 117
conservation of gardens, 161–2
Contemporary Review, 32
Cooper, Colonel Reginald, 63
Cornforth, John, 74
Correvon (Swiss plantsman), 129
Country Life, 38, 61, 64, 118, 141, 154, pl. 11,
  pl. 12
Craft Cottage, Paston, Norfolk, 118
Crawford, Alan, 47
Crowe, Dame Sylvia, 92, 153
Cullen, Gordon, 129
Culpepers, Ardingly, Sussex, 36
Cunard, Emerald, Lady, 68

DALLIMORE, W.
  Poisonous Plants: Deadly and Suspect, 13
Daniel, Dr, 46
Danny, Hurstpierpoint, Sussex, 30, 31
Darwin family, 84–5, 88, 90
Davies, Emily, 79, 80
Dawber, Guy, 47, 50
Dawson, Geoffrey, 70
Deane, Humphry, 118

176

Deanery Garden, Sonning, Berkshire, 66, 150–52

Debbage family, 111–12, 113

Decorative Arts Exposition (1925), 121

Dillistone, George, 119

Docwra's Manor, Shepreth, Cambridgeshire, 92

Douglas, Miss (of Shedfield Grange), 31

Downing College, Cambridge, 92

Duncombe, Lady Ulrica, 23

Durbins, Guildford, Surrey, 11

EARLE family, 18, 23, 26, 28

Edinburgh, Botanic Gardens, 31

Edward VII *see* King Edward VII Hospital; Wales, Edward, Prince of

Elliott, Clarence, 13, 55, 56, 58

Emmanuel College, Cambridge, 91

Ewart, Mary Ann, 85, 86

FAIRHAVEN, Ailwyn Harry Broughton, 3rd Baron, 109, 111

Fairhaven, Cara Leland, Lady, 95–7, 98–9, 106, 109

Fairhaven, Henry, 2nd Baron, 95, 96, 109–11, 112

Fairhaven, Huttleston Broughton, 1st Baron, 5, 95, 99–101, 107, 109, 114, pl. 15

Fairhaven, Massachusetts, 96–7

Fairhaven Garden Trust, 111

Faithfull, Miss (of Studley College), 31

Falkner, Harold, 154

Farmington, Connecticut, 133

Farrand, Beatrix, 55, 58, 155, 156

Farrand, Max, 155

Faringdon, Oxfordshire, 60, 69

Fellowes, Diana (Lady Fairhaven), 109

Fenwick, Mark, 51–2, 55, 118

Finzi, Gerald *and* Joy, 15

Firbank, Ronald
The Flower Beneath the Foot, 9

Fish, Margery, 18

Fishers' Hill, Woking, 85, 91

Fitzwilliam Museum, Cambridge, 92, 109, 110, 112, 113

Forrest, George,

Forster, E. M., 12

Fowler, John, 7, 70, 74

Fry, Maxwell, 118

Fry, Roger, 11

Fullerton, Alice, 70

Garden, The, 141

Gardeners, Worshipful Company of, 32

Gardening Illustrated, 141

Garnett, David, 10

Garsington Manor, Oxfordshire, 9, 69

Gathorne-Hardy, Robert, 13

George, Ernest, 16

Gibberd, Sir Frederick, 16–17, 161

Gifford, Abbie Palmer (later Regas), 96

Gill, Eric, 90

Girton College, Cambridge, 79

Gladstone, Helen, 85, pl. 21

Glebe House, Woodbury, Connecticut, 159

Glendinning, Victoria
Vita: The Life of Vita Sackville-West, 2, 8

Glennie, Ian, 152

Glenveagh Castle, Donegal, 5

Glynde College for Lady Gardeners, 27–33, 36, 39, pl. 1, pl. 2

Glynde District Federation of Growers, 33

Glynde Place, Sussex, 24

Godmersham Park, Kent, 60, 61, 70

Godwin, Philip, 133

Goodhart-Rendel, H. S., 74

Gordon, General Charles, 20–21

Gosse, Sir Edmund, 22, 42

Gough, Piers, 158

Grant, Duncan, 10–12

Graves, Michael, 157

Gravetye Manor, Sussex, 26, 29

Grey, Colonel Hoare, 58

Griggs, Frederick Landseer, 50

Gropius, Walter, 117–18, 135

Guevrekian, Gabriel, 121

Guildford, Surrey, 153–4

HAM Spray House, Wiltshire, 10

Hambling, Maggi, 15

Hare, Augustus
Memorials of a Quiet Life, 22

Harland, Peter, 15

Harper's Magazine, 42, 47

Hastings, de Cronin, 117

Havergal, Beatrice, 18, 153

Hayward, Captain Simpson, 49–50, 51, 55

Hayward Gallery, South Bank, London, 157–8

Hepworth, Barbara, 117

Heseltine, Michael *and* Anne, 18
Hestercombe, Somerset, 66, 118
Hever Castle, Kent, 52
Hicks, David, 7
Hidcote Manor, Gloucestershire
  its garden, 50–56, pl. 8, pl. 9, pl. 10
    Italian influence, 52–5
  influence of, 2–3, 58–9
  and Nancy Lindsay, 4–5, 74, 75, 76
  National Trust, acquired by, 57, 74, 161
  and Norah Lindsay, 3–4, 61, 72–5
  purchase of, 49
  V. Sackville-West on, 2, 3, 50, 56–7, 72–3
Hill, Oliver, 120, 154
Hobhouse, Penelope, 159
Hodgkin, Eliot, 17
Holden, Charles, 37, pl. 2
Holford, Sir George, 56
Hornby family, 17
Horner, Edward, 53
House and Garden, 73, 74
Hudnut, Joseph, 133, 134
Hudson, Edward, 150
Hussey, Christopher, 61, 118, 154
  Life of Lutyens, 157
Hyères, château, 121–2

Icomb Place, Gloucestershire, 51
Ilford Manor, Wiltshire, 16, 52
Ingram, Cherry Collingwood, 56
Innes, John, 29
Institute of Landscape Architects, 36, 119, 132
  Basic Plant List, 130
Iris Year Book, 14

Jagger, Charles Sargent, 118
James, Henry, 5, 22, 40, 42, 45, 47, 51
  The Awkward Age, 45
James, Robert, 17, 51, 54
James, Walter (Lord Northbourne), 51
Jaffe, Professor Michael, 110
Jekyll, Agnes, Lady, 152
Jekyll, Francis, 152
  Memoirs, 125, 152, 154–5
Jekyll, Gertrude, 139–60, pl. 25, pl. 26 (*see also*
    Munstead Wood)
  appearance, 141
  artistic talents, 2, 140

biography of, 152, 154
birth and early years, 1, 139–40
criticism of, 125
diaries and letters, 154
drawings, 154, 156–7
and feminism, 7–8
garden designs, 44, 66, 86, 87, 119, 120,
  pl. 2, pl. 27
and Glynde College, 28, pl. 2
Home and Garden, 86, 87, 147
and King Edward VII Hospital, 28, pl. 2,
  pl. 27
last years and death, 152
and Lutyens, 26, 85, 88–9, 141–2, 152, 158
and Newnham College, 6, 88, 90
nursery business, 139
philosophy of, 149, 159–60
photography, 141, 156, 159
reading, 146–7
takes up gardening, 140–41
Wood and Garden, 26
writing, 141, 159
Jekyll, Sir Hubert, 152
Jekyll family, 23
Jellicoe, Geoffrey, 74, 117, 132
  Italian Gardens of the Renaissance, 106
Johnson, President Lyndon, 136
Johnson, Philip, 157
Johnston, Elliott, 48
Johnston, G. C. *see* Winthrop, Gertrude
    Cleveland
Johnston, Major Lawrence, 17 (*see also* Hidcote
    Manor)
  character, 2
  death, 57
  early years, 48–9
  as garden planner, 50–54, 73, pl. 10
    American influence, 52–3, 55
    Italian influence, 52
  plant-hunting expeditions, 56
  retires to France, 4, 55, 71, 73, 74
  war experiences, 53
Joldwynds, Holmbury Hill, Surrey, 120

Kelmscott Manor, Gloucestershire, 9, 42
Kemp, Edward, 35
Kempe, Charles Eamer, 23–6
Kerr, Philip *see* Lothian, Marquis of
Keynes, John Maynard, 12

King Edward VII Hospital, Midhurst, 37–9, 150, pl. 1, pl. 2, pl. 27
Kingdon-Ward, Frank, 94
King's College, Cambridge, 92
Knole, Sevenoaks, Kent, 30–31
Kuhlenthal (Nash), Christine, 13

Ladew, Harvey, 58–9
Lakeland Nurseries, 118
Lamb House, Rye, Sussex, 45
Lancaster, Nancy, 70
Land's End, Garby, Leicestershire, 131
Lane Fox, Robin, 94
Laurie, Michael, 155
Lawless, Emily, 7–8
Lawrence, D. H., 9–10
Leach, Bernard, 117, 129
Le Corbusier, M. (Jeanneret), 116, 117, 119, 120, 125
Lees-Milne, Alvilde, 53
Lees-Milne, George, 50
Lees-Milne, James, 61
Leslie, George, 140
Lett-Haines, Arthur, 14
Liederkerke, Belgium, 122
Lincoln, Massachusetts, 133
Lindfield, Haywards Heath, Sussex, 24–5
Lindsay, Lt.-Col. Harry Edith, 62–3
Lindsay, Nancy
  early years, 63, 68
  at Hidcote Manor, 4, 75–6
  plant-hunting trip, 4, 71
  plantswoman, 70–72
Lindsay, Norah Mary Madeleine, 18, pl. 11 (see also Manor House, Sutton Courtenay)
  assessment of, 60
  at Blickling Hall, 69–70
  commissions, 70
  gardening philosophy, 64, 67, 74
  at Hidcote Manor, 3–4, 61, 72–4, 76, pl. 10
  Manor House garden, 60, 61, 74–5, pl. 11, pl. 12, pl. 13, pl. 14
  marriage, 62–3
  'Norah Lindsay Garden', 76
  at Port Lympne, 68–9
  socialite, 60
Lindsay, Violet, 62
Little Paddocks, Sunningdale, Berkshire, 118
Lloyd, Christopher, 159

Long Barn, Sevenoaks, Kent, 8
Loos, Adolf, 126
Lothian, Philip Kerr, 11th Marquess of, 69, 70
Luggershill, Broadway, Hereford and Worcester, 45
Lutyens, Sir Edwin (see also Munstead Wood)
  as architect, 81, 95, 118, 144–5
  criticism of, 6
  in Delhi, 68, 118
  early life, 16, 23
  Exhibition (1981–2), 157–8
  garden designs, 52, 66, 118
  and Jekyll, 85, 87, 88–9, 141–2, 144, 152
  light, use of, 144–5
  revival of interest in, 157
Lutyens, Elisabeth, 152
Lutyens, Lady Emily, 154
Lutyens, Mary, 152, 157
Lygon Arms, Broadway, 47
Lyminge, Robert, 82
Lytton, Lady Constance, 7
Lytton family, 26

McAlpine, Alistair, Baron, 18
McGrath, Raymond, 127–8, pl. 24
McIlhenny, Henry, P., 5
McLaren, Harry and Laura see Aberconway, 1st Baron
Magna Carta meadow, Runnymede, 95
Mallet-Stevens, Robert, 121
Mander, Samuel Theodore, 46
Manners, Lady Diana, 60
Manor House, Sutton Courtenay, Oxfordshire, pl. 11, pl. 12, pl. 13, pl. 14
  and David Astor, 74–5
  gardens described, 60–68, 73
  'jungle of beauty', 4
Marlborough, Henrietta, Duchess of, 36–7
Marsh, George Perkins, 135
Massachusetts Horticultural Society, 156
Massetts Place, Sussex, 36
Massingham, Betty, 156–7
Mawson, Thomas, 116, 118
Mead, Mary Gertrude (Abbey), 43–4
Mead, William Rutherford, 43–4, 55
Melchett Court, Romsey, Kent, 118
Mellerstein, Berwickshire, 118
Mendelsohn, Erich, 117, 135

Merrist Wood Agricultural College, 158
Merton Hall, Cambridge, 79, 81
Mill House, Tidmarsh, Berkshire, 10
Milles, Carl, 118, 127
Millet family, 41, 42, 43
Milner, Henry
 The Art and Practice of Landscape Gardening,
  35, 83
Modern Movement, 6, 116–21, 125–6, 130
Moghul Garden, Delhi, 118
Monet, Claude, 6, 12
Monkton, Maryland, 58–9
Moore, Henry, 117, 127, 130, pl. 23
More, Elsa, 30, 32, 36
Morgan, John Pierpont, 55
Morgan Hall, Fairford, Gloucestershire, 51
Morrell, Lady Ottoline, 9, 69
Morris, Sir Cedric, 14
Morris, Jane, 42, 84
Morris, William, 9, 23, 42, 50, 84
Mortimer, Raymond
 New Interior Design, 12
Mottisfont Abbey, Hampshire, 70
Muir-Mackenzie, Susan, 45
Mumford, Lewis, 135
Munstead Wood, Surrey (*see also* Jekyll,
  Gertrude)
 garden, 26, 39, 149, pl. 25
  conservation of, 162
 house described, 141–8
 Jekyll's death, effect of, 152–3
 and Lutyens, 85, 158
 nursery business, 139
 sale of contents, 7, 142, 153
Museum of Modern Art, New York, 133

Nash, John, 12–13
Nash, Paul, 117
National Trust
 Anglesey Abbey, 99, 108, 109
 Gardens Committee, 2, 3
 Hidcote Manor, 2, 3, 5, 57, 161
 Sissinghurst Castle, 9
Navarro, Antonio, 44, pl. 6
Navarro, Mary Anderson de, 44–5, 47, 49–51,
  53, 55, 58, pl. 5, pl. 6
New Ways, Northampton, 119
Newnham College, Cambridge, 23, 77–91,
  pl. 21

 buildings, 81–3, 87
 foundation of, 79, 80, pl. 20
 gardens, 6, 83–91, 94, pl. 22
Newport, Rhode Island, 132–3
Newton, Ernest, 81
Newton, Norman K.
 Design on the Land, 135
Nicholson, Ben, 117
Nicholson, Kit, 117
Nicolson, Sir Harold, 2, 8, 9, 58
Nicolson, Nigel
 Portrait of a Marriage, 8
Nineteenth Century, 32
Noailles, Charles, Vicomte de, 121

O'Keeffe, Georgia, 14
Olmsted, Frederick Law, 135
Olsen, Stanley, 40

Page, Russell, 16
Painshill, 124
Palmer, Samuel, 12
Park Close, Windsor, Berkshire, 98
Parsons, Alfred, 42, 43, 44–7, 49, 50–51, 54,
  pl. 6, pl. 7, pl. 8
Partridge, Bernard, pl. 5
Pasley, Anthony du Gard, 153
 English Gardening School, 36
Passingham, Betty, 156–7
 Miss Jekyll: Portrait of a Great Gardener, 154
Penshurst Place, Kent, 124
Perrin, Hester, 31
Peto, Harold, 16, 52
Phillimore, Claude, 74
Phipps, Paul, 70
Piper, John, 117
Planting Fields, Long Island, New York, 98, 99,
  pl. 18
Platt, Charles, 54, 58
 Italian Gardens, 54–5
Port Lympne, Kent, 68–9
Portmeirion, North Wales, 16, 118
Post-Modernism, 157
Potters' Art Guild, 26
Powell, Alfred, 86
Pugin, Augustus W. N., 124
Pulhams (nurserymen), 29
Pusey House, Faringdon, Berkshire, 17

Pushkarov, Boris, 135
Pym, Sir Francis, 18

RAGGED Lands *see* Glynde College
Ranger's House, Greenwich Park, 22, 24
Raven, Faith, 92
Raven, John, 92, 110
Raverat, Gwen
  Period Piece, 84
Reading University, 31
Reed, Henry Hope, 135
Reef Point, Bar Harbor, Maine, 155, 156
Reiss, Phyllis, 18
Rice, Clarence, 97
Richards, J. M., 117
Richardson, Professor Sir Albert, 100
Ridley Hall, Cambridge, 81
Robinson, William, 26, 35, 42, 82
  The Wild Garden, 42
Rogers, Annie, 92–3
Rogers, Henry Huttleston, 96–8, 99, 106, 113
Rohde, Eleanour Sinclair, 18
Roper, Lanning, 18
  Gardens of Anglesey Abbey, 5
Roper, Laura Wood, 135
Rossetti, Dante Gabriel, 140
Royal Botanic Society, 31
Royal Horticultural Society, 3, 109, 118
  Journal, 56–7, 72
Ruskin, John, 124, 140
Russell, Mrs Gilbert, 70
Russell, Gordon, 132

SACKVILLE-WEST, Vita (Lady Nicolson), 1, 2, 11, 18, 109
  and Hidcote Manor, 2, 3, 50, 56–7, 72–3
  at Knole, 30–31
  and Nancy Lindsay, 72
  and Norah Lindsay, 2–3, 70
  personal life, 8–9
  and Sissinghurst Castle, 2, 8, 57, 61, 115
St Ann's Hill, Chertsey, Surrey, 127–9, 132, pl. 24
St Germain-en-Laye, France, 120–21
St Hugh's College, Oxford, 93
St John's College, Oxford, 93–4
St Nicholas, Richmond, North Yorkshire, 17, 51, 54, 58
Sargent, Andrew Robeson, 98

Sargent, John Singer, 5, 40–41, 47
  Carnation Lily, Lily Rose, 41–2, 43, 46, 47, pl. 4
Sargent, Mary Newbold Singer, 40
Sassoon, Sir Philip, 68, 69
Satterthwaite, Ann, 136
Savill, Sir Eric, 109
Savill (Alfred) & Sons, 153
Scalands, Sussex, 146
Scrase, David, 110
Sedding, John Dando, 86
Selwyn College, Cambridge, 81
Serre de la Madrone, La, France, 55, 71
Shedfield Grange, Hampshire, 31
Shepheard, Sir Peter
  Modern Gardens, 75, 121
Sidgwick, Eleanor Mildred (Nora), 79–82, 84–5, 87, 88–91, pl. 21
Sidgwick, Professor Henry, 78, 79, 80–81, 82, 84, 86, 93
Sidney, Colonel Henry, 53
Sissinghurst Castle, Kent
  garden, 2, 9, 57, 61, 108, 115
  conservation of, 162
Six Hills Nursery, Stevenage, Hertfordshire, 13
Soby, James Thrall, 133
Solomon, Simeon, 140
Soukup, Willi, 117, 128, 130
South Walsham Hall, Norfolk, 110–13
Spectator, 123
Spencer, Edward John, 8th Earl, 114
Spetchley Park, Gloucestershire, 50
Spry, Constance, 70
Stamp, Gavin, 157
Stefanidis, John, 7
Stein, Gertrude, 40
Stephen, Katharine, 85, pl. 21
Stowe School, Buckinghamshire, 77, 118, 124, 134
Strachey, Lytton, 10
  Eminent Victorians, 1, 20
Studley College, 29, 37
suffragettes, 8, 30
Surrey Archaeological Society, 153–4
Swanley, Kent, 153
Synge, Patrick
  Plants with Personality, 13

TANKARD, Judith
  Vision of Garden and Wood, 159

Taut, Bruno, 119
Tennyson, Hallam, 2nd Baron, 22
Thatcham Fruit and Flower School, 31
Thatcher, Margaret, 18
Thomas, Graham Stuart
  Old Shrub Roses, 76
Tilden, Philip, 4, 76
  True Remembrances, 60
Tipping, H. Avray, 38, 118, 119
Tree, Nancy, 74
Trefusis, Violet, 8
Tritton family, 61, 70
Tunnard, Christopher, 115–38
  American Skyline, 135
  Anglesey Abbey, 105
  City of Man, 135
  early life, 116
  in Europe, 120–23
  garden designer, 126–9, 131–2, pl. 23, pl. 24
  Gardens in the Modern Landscape, 6, 116, 123,
    131, 133
  Japanese influence, 129
  on Jekyll, 125
  landscape planning, 129–31
  Man-made America: Chaos or Control?, 135–6
  and Modernism, 6–7, 116–20
  planting design, 133–8
  on received ideas, 124–5
  World with a View . . ., 136–7
Twain, Mark (Samuel Langhorne Clemens), 97,
  114

United Nations
  environment secretariat, 138
United States of America
  influence on garden design, 5, 40–59
  East Coast gardens, 55, 58–9, 132–3, 159

Van der Rohe, Mies, 119
van Valkenburgh, Michael
  Vision of Garden and Wood, 159
Vaughan Williams, Ralph, 15, 70
Vaughan Williams, Ursula, 15
Vera, André and Paul, 120, 121
Victoria, Queen, 20
Vita's Other World (Brown), 8

Wadsworth, Edward, 117
Wales, Edward, Prince of, 21–2

Wallace, Lily Acheson, 12
Walter, Dr Max, 92
Walton, Susana (Gil Passo), Lady, 15–16
Walton, Sir William, 15–16
Wantage, Lord, 63
Wargrave, Berkshire, 140
Warley Place, Essex, 46–7
Warren, Edward Prioleau, 45
Warwick, Daisy, Countess of, 18, 29, 31, 37
Waterbury, Gertrude Cleveland see Winthrop,
  G. C.
Waterhouse, Alfred, 89
Waterperry, Buckinghamshire, 153
Watkins, David, 6
Watson, Walter Crum, 89–90
Watts, George Frederick, 26, 44, 140
Watts, Mary, 26, 28
Weaver, Lawrence
  Houses and Gardens by E. L. Lutyens, 144–5
Webb, Philip, 85
West Green Manor, Hartley Wintney, Hamp-
  shire, 18
West Wood House, Bagley Wood, Oxfordshire,
  93–4
Westonbirt, Gloucestershire, 56
Wharton, Edith, 40, 45, 52, 54, 108
Whistler, Rex, 4, 70
White Gates, Dorking, Surrey, 15
Whitney, John ('Jock') Hay, 5
Whittinghame, East Lothian, 80
Wightwick Manor, Wolverhampton, 45–6
Wilkinson, Ellen, 31
William-Ellis, Clough, 118
Willmer, Nevill, 92
Willmott, Ellen, 18, 28
  The Genus Rosa, 46–7
Willmott, Rose see Berkeley, Rose
Wills, Trenwith, 74
Winthrop, Charles, 48
Winthrop, Gertrude Cleveland, 48–9, 51, 56, 71,
  pl. 9
Wolseley, Frances Garnet, Viscountess, 18, 20–
  39, pl. 3
  arts and crafts, 24–5
  assessment of, 36–7
  early years, 1, 2, 21–3
  garden designs, 34–6
  Gardening for Women, 30, 31
  Gardens, Their Form and Design, 1, 34–6
  Glynde College, 1, 26–32, pl. 1, pl. 2

Wolseley, Frances Garnet, Viscountess—*cont.*
  In a College Garden, 33, pl. 3
  Some of the Smaller Manor Houses of Sussex,
    36
  travels, 33–4
  wartime work, 32–3
  Women and the Land, 32
Wolseley, Louisa, Viscountess, 21–6, 30, 31, 36
Wolseley, Garnet Joseph, Viscount, 20–21, 22,
    24, 26, 32
women gardeners, 18
Wood Croft, Bagley Wood, Oxfordshire, 94
Woodhouse Copse, Holmbury Hill, Surrey, 120
Woodlands, Cobham, Surrey, 26
Woolf, Virginia, 9, 11
Worcester College, Oxford, 46
Wright, Frank Lloyd, 120, 122–3
Wyatville, Sir Jeffrey, 22

7/95-8